THE GIRL WITH SILVER EYES

The Complete

THE BLACK MASK

Cases of the Continental Op

Volume 2: 1924–25

DASHIELL HAMMETT

introduction by Bob Byrne

BLACK MASK

2024

Table of Contents

Introduction

THE FIRST VOLUME in this series, *The Complete Black Mask Cases of the Continental Op, Volume 1: Zigzags of Treachery*, ended with "The House in Turk Street." That was the tenth Op story, and as I wrote in the introduction to that volume:

> For me, it's in "The House in Turk Street" (which was adapted for the 2002 Samuel L. Jackson movie, *No Good Deed)* where we really see the classic Hammett for the first time. The characters, the pace, the tension, the plot elements: he was moving from learning, to improving, to the verge of mastering.

Hammett had been honing his craft, and "The House on Turk Street" really saw things come together. While that was the first Hammett story to appear under Phil Cody's editorship, it was surely accepted by George Sutton.

Next up two months later in June of 1924 was "The Girl with the Silver Eyes." It was a sequel to "The House in Turk Street," and twice the length. Together, they are about as long as the first four Op stories combined. Hammett was moving towards the long form that would result in four serialized novels: at least three of which are regarded among his best works.

"The Girl with the Silver Eyes" appeared in the same issue as Carroll John Daly's "The Red Peril." Compare the two stories. Daly (who I talked about in the previous volume) was still writing the same one-dimensional character, with the same ultra-violent action. Hammett had continued to use his real-world Pinkerton experiences while honing his writing skills, and his work was notably improved from the first Op tale.

It is rightly considered one of his best stories. Burke Pangburn (client), Jeanne Delano (silver-eyed girl), and Porky Grout (criminal informant) are all well-drawn characters, with depth. Delano takes the femme fatale seen in "The House in Turk Street" a level further, and Hammett doesn't just tell us that men cannot resist her—he shows it in dramatic fashion. In dealing with her, the Op faces his greatest emotional test so far.

I said in Volume 1: "Hammett used his experience as a Pinkerton to write more realistic detective fiction. As Raymond Chandler wrote of him: 'He made some of it up; all writers do; but it had a basis in fact; it was made up out of real things.'"

Porky Grout is a snitch. Today's cop shows would call him a CI (criminal informant). He's a stool pigeon in Hammett's slang. He's been mentioned before, but we meet him for the first time and get the full view:

> I don't know a single thing that could be said in his favor. He was a coward. He was a liar. He was a thief, and a hophead. He was a traitor to his kind and, if not watched, to his employer....
>
> Detecting is a hard business, and you use whatever tools come to hand. This Porky was an effective tool if handled right, which meant keeping your hand on his throat all the time and checking up every piece of information he brought in.

It's more practical advice from Hammett, via the Op. I find Porky, and how he interacts with the Op—and how that reflects another relationship—one of the most interesting aspects of this volume.

An odd thing happened before "Women, Politics, and Murder," saw print in September of 1924. I mentioned last volume that Harry North was George Sutton's, and then Phil Cody's, right-hand man. He was also 'the bad guy' with the writers. Cody rejected two of Hammett's stories, with North sending a letter (and returning the stories) to Hammett. Cody was establishing his authority and took to passively-aggressively shaming Hammett. The August issue included Cody talking about rejecting these two stories, and all of Hammett's response, under the heading *Our Own Short Story Course.* In the intro, Cody says:

> We recently were obliged to reject two of Mr. Hammett's detective stories... But in our opinion, the stories were not up to the standard of Mr. Hammett's own work—so they had to go back.

Sarcasm can certainly be detected in Hammett's response. Cody would publish him less frequently than Sutton did, and he was rejecting stories. This August feature did not evince a happy editor-writer relationship. Of one of the rejected stories, Hammett wrote:

> I don't think I shall send "Women, Politics, and Murder" back to you—not in time for the July issue anyways. The trouble is that this sleuth of mine has degenerated into a meal-ticket. I liked him at first and used to enjoy putting him through his tricks; but recently I have fallen into the habit of bringing him out and running him around whenever the landlord, or the butcher, or the grocer, shows signs of nervousness.

He says he could possibly patch it up to get by with the story, but doesn't think it's worth the trouble.

Cody said that Hammett's letter could be a primary course in short story writing. I think he totally missed Hammett's sarcasm. You tell me if this isn't a bit of snark: "I want to thank both you (North) and Mr. Cody for jolting me into wakefulness. There's no telling how much good this will do me. And you me sure that whenever you get a story from me hereafter, frequently, I hope, it will be one that I enjoyed writing."

The Cody/North-Hammett relationship was not a healthy one, as evidenced by this incident, and in less than two years, with Cody still as editor, Hammett would quit *Black Mask*. Interestingly enough, Cody and Hammett both were largely correct about the story. It's not a particularly good one. And it's clearly a regression from "The House in Turk Street," and "The Girl With the Silver Eyes."

A frantic Mrs. Gilmore has hired the Continental Detective Agency to discover who murdered her husband, Bernard. He had been involved in politics, and recently had an affair with a Carla Kenbrook. The widow suspects that the police may not want anything unseemly to come out, and aren't investigating as hard as they should be.

Bernard had had a shady reputation as a guy who had gone from construction grunt to business owner to politician. Scandals had surfaced, but none had stuck to him. Hammett shows what a master wordsmith he is by describing him as "a roughneck with a manicure." That, in only four sparse words, is absolutely perfect to give us our picture of the man.

As for Cara: "It wasn't a beautiful face, although It should have been. Everything was there—perfect features; smooth, white skin; big, almost enormous, brown eyes, but the eyes were dead-dull, and the face was empty of expression as a china door-knob, and what I said didn't change it."

This is one hard sister.

"Women, Politics, & Murder" all takes place in the space of one day. And, frankly, it's not that great a story. The characters aren't compelling, the crime isn't that absorbing, and the denouement is rather weak. This is one of the least-read Op stories for me. I can understand why Cody wasn't thrilled with it. I find the whole *Our Own Short Story Course* matter more interesting than the actual story itself.

But it's still the Op. And watching him work is always interesting. He finds himself in a tight spot, working against lies, and against a powerful figure. Hammett gives the Op the upper hand, then paints him into a corner. I leave it to you to decide if the resolution was satisfactory.

Hammett's lung problems worsened in 1924 and he was writing to pay the mounting bills. Cody didn't want to saturate the magazine with his stories, and only printed him every other issue, at most. Hammett was extremely displeased that the editor was limiting his income. As was the case for most Pulp writers, Hammett was not making a great deal of money at a penny or two a word (Stephen King's "Get rid of your adverbs" advice did *not* apply to the Pulps!). And he wasn't nearly as prolific as contemporaries Erle Stanley Gardner, and Raoul Whitfield. He needed the income from *Black Mask*. Tensions would continue to rise.

All but two of the Op stories appeared in *Black Mask*. The second appeared in *True Detective*, the same month in which *Black Mask* had "The Golden Horseshoe." Two stories in a month meant twice as much income to the cash-strapped Hammett. And Cody wouldn't print a new Op story until March—four months away.

Vance Richmond, the client in "Zigzags of Treachery" and "One Hour," gets the Op another case. Reading the opening, it feels like he's hiring the Op directly, not the Continental Detective Agency. But that could just be my take. And while I noticed it, frankly, it doesn't matter, so let's move on.

Norman Ashcraft was a clean-cut Britisher whose wife inherited a lot of money. She was rather possessive, and accused him of paying too much attention to another woman. He was already sensitive about their financial disparity and he packed up and left. She repented within a week, but he had fled England.

Eventually, they ended up exchanging letters while he was in San Francisco, telling her to quit searching for him, and to just leave him alone. Then he revealed that he was a drug addict; he wouldn't return until he cleaned himself up. She sent him money regularly "to help." She packs up and moves to San Francisco: he says he's getting better, and then relapsing, while she continues to pay him monthly, care of General Delivery. Finally, she wants some answers one way or another, and goes to Richmond, who hires the Op to find Ashcraft—under whatever name he is likely using. That's the chapter one setup.

Once again, Hammett uses his Pinkerton knowledge—this time, regarding postal inspectors—and has the Op stake out General Delivery. And when someone who is not Ashcroft picks up the monthly letter, he bumps into the man to get a look at the address. It doesn't go smoothly and he knocks the man down: its obvious what the Op is up to. Knowing Ashcroft will certainly be warned somebody is after him, Hammett pretends to have a gun and forces the letter carrier to the man's apartment. Now pretending to be the law, he gets some info, then has him put on ice (turns out the man, Ryan, had an out-of-state warrant on him). And off to Tijuana and The Golden Horseshoe, goes the Op.

The Op finds Ashcroft (now going under the name Bohannon (we'll stick with Ashcraft), gets drunk a lot, gathers some info, and returns to San Francisco… to find the client dead, along with two servants—all with their throats slit.

The Op makes things happen in this one. He doesn't just follow clues and ferret out the villain. As he says:

> One way of finding what's at the bottom of either a cup of coffee or a situation is to keep stirring it up until whatever is on the bottom comes to the surface. I had been playing that system thus far on this affair.

He suspects who the killer is, then uses some stooges to spook him, causing him to run and hide. The Op confronts Ashcraft and his girlfriend and when the muscle-in-hiding shows up, the stirring is done—with bodies left on the floor and a car chase across the desert.

One weakness for me: the entire final chapter up to the very last part, is the villain revealing everything he did. He's already been captured, so it's not like the super villain telling all to the spy hanging over the shark tank with a candle burning the rope: but it's a long confession and of course, leads to his downfall. I was kind of tired by the end of it, and the end of the story.

The Op has his own sense of justice at the end of the story, and the reader is left believing that the bad guy is absolutely getting his just desserts: but not for the reason we thought.

Just before things blow up, the Op voluntarily gives up his gun and tells the bad guy he wants to take him back to San Francisco in handcuffs, but he's got plenty of time to do so. Can you imagine Race Williams offering up his gun so he can talk a guy into capture? Whenever that might work out? And the Op doesn't kill anybody in this one, toning down the violence which had been escalating in his stories.

"Who Killed Bob Teal" was less than half as long as "The Golden Horseshoe." It wasn't even as long as "Women, Politics, and Murder." What it was, was the other story rejected by Cody and North as revealed in *Our Own Short Story Course*. In his reply, Hammett had referred to it as "The Question's One Answer." *That* would have been a terrible title. *True Detective* magazine presented fictional stories as if they were real. So, the Pulp's name was a bit of a stretch. The title page for "Who Killed Bob Teal?" identified it as "by Dashiell Hammett of the Continental Detective Agency." That isn't exactly the truth now, is it?

Teal was a young operative at the Continental, having previously appeared in "Slippery Fingers" and "Zigzags of Treachery." While he was described as "a youngster who will be a world-beater some day," it's safe to guess from the title that there would be no fourth appearance.

This is another compressed story, which takes place in less than a day. It's definitely far more like "Women, Politics, and Murder," than it is the sprawling "The Golden Horseshoe." The Op wears out some shoe leather in this one. In the intro to volume one, I talked about how Hammett had the Op doing the mundane tasks involved in solving a case. It's not all guns blazing, as with Daly's Race Williams. Here, he chases clues by talking to people until something breaks, and then he turns the tables on the unsuspecting bad guy.

Almost the last quarter of the story is a long monologue by the Op, explaining everything to the clueless cop. There are constraints in a short story, of course. But for me, the long-winded explanation at the end is always a flaw, unless it's done in a way that keeps you engaged. I find that Rex Stout often avoids the pitfalls in the gatherings that Inspector Cramer calls Wolfe's "charades" at story end.

I had to stop and re-read parts as the Op droned on, explaining who did what and why. It's simply a weak ending. But the story itself isn't without merit. In fact, if you reflect on it when you're finished, you'll realize that Hammett drew on this in writing *The Maltese Falcon*. I don't wanna give any spoilers, but when you stop and look for them, you will absolutely see the similarities. This isn't a bad little story, but Hammett took elements of it and made it better, by 'borrowing' from it for his tour de force novel.

I like this story better than I do "Women, Politics, and Murder," though I'm guessing neither makes anyone's Top Ten list. Hammett sent it off to *True Detective*—likely with little or no revision—after telling Cody that he didn't think it was worth the trouble of "patching up." And by submitting it to a different magazine, it strengthens my feeling that he was insincere is his response to Cody's rejection in *Our Short Story Course*.

"Mike or Alec or Rufus" appeared in January of 1925, and it was even shorter than "Who Killed Bob Teal." Hammett had reached his high point (so far) with "The House in Turk Street," and "The Girl with the Silver Eyes." It seems that a combination of his health issues, financial difficulties, and dislike of Cody, had retarded his progress. He was writing shorter, lower quality stories. I will still read lesser stories by Hammett, Frederick Nebel, and Raoul Whitfield. But it can be obvious to me when the writer is on his game, and when it's just a story to get published. And Hammett not near his best is still a talented guy. But his ongoing growth was stalled, as his feelings towards Cody grew more negative.

I have to say, "Mike or Alec or Rufus" (briefly) has quite an attention-getting opener:

> I don't know if Joseph Coplin was tall or short. All of him I ever got a look at was his round head—naked scalp and wrinkled face, both of them the color and texture of Mila paper—propped op on white pillows in a big four-poster bed. The rest of him was buried under a thick pile of bedding.

First time I was reading it, I thought the head was not attached to the body. Then I got to that final sentence, and realized it wasn't a detached head on the pillow. But for a second, I thought this one was off to one crazy start.

A robber forced his way into the Coplin apartment, stole some jewelry, shot Joseph in the leg, and locked him, his wife, daughter, and the maid, in a closet. The insurance company hired the Continental agency, and the Op was assigned to the case.

The story takes place in a couple of hours, and entirely within the Conlin's apartment building. Bill Garren, a detective on the police's Pawn Shop Detail, shows up and works hand-in-hand with the Op. This story feels like it could be turned into a play, with only a few rooms needed for the sets.

Garren shows up with an obvious (and obviously wrong) suspect, and is annoyed when he clearly strikes out. It's the Op who just keep asking questions and trying to fit pieces together. He sets aside the puzzle pieces that don't fit, and tries to join other ones together. No guns blazing and bad dialogue like, "He made his bed and I laid him out in it—full of holes."

The robber couldn't flee the building, but couldn't be found in it, either. It's as if Hammett wanted to tinker with the conventional locked-room mystery and turn it into a hard-boiled locked-building mystery, with no gun play or violence. It's an interesting idea, and I think he pretty much pulls it off.

The robber had inside knowledge, which made the Op suspect the family. Garren's suspect was the son of a neighbor. It's like the ensemble of an Agatha Christie country house murder. But the Op just keeps looking for information and discarding what doesn't work.

This story contains another example of Hammett sharing his real-world experience, through the Op:

> An identification of the sort the janitor was giving isn't worth a damn one way or the other. Even positive and immediate identifications aren't always the goods. A lot of people who don't know any better—and some who do, or should—have given circumstantial evidence a bad name. It is misleading sometimes. But for genuine, undiluted, pre-war untrustworthiness, it can't come within gunshot of human testimony.
>
> Take any man you like—unless he is the one in a hundred thou-

sand with a mind trained to keep things straight—and not always even then—get him excited, show him something, give him a few hours to think it over and talk it over, and then ask him about it. It's dollars to marks that you'll heave a hard time finding any connection between what he saw and what he says he saw. Like this McBirney—another hour, and he be ready to gamble is life on Jack Wagner's being the robber.

That's Hammett praising the value of circumstantial evidence, over eye-witness testimony. Even in this, his shortest story (about the same length as "Bodies Piled Up"), Hammett can still provide insights from his Pinkerton days, lending an authenticity and sense of grounding to his stories.

The finale is stronger than in the prior story. There is some conversation—it's not a monologue. And the villain is revealed over the course of the speech. It's not an after-the-fact explanation. This is a much more satisfactory way to close out the story. Including a final paragraph in which he reveals where the stolen jewels were found.

This is a slight story, but a pleasant read. More of a "hmm, I wonder"-type of story, than something you get absorbed in. And there's zero action. It really does feel like more of a small play.

The final story in this volume is "The Whosis Kid," and it's longer than the previous two stories combined. Hammett was back on an every-other-month schedule with Cody, and it appeared in the March, 1925 issue.

After a couple relatively minor efforts (some might even say lackluster), Hammett returned to the longer, action-packed form that marked his best work. It's definitely the best story in this volume. And, as with "Who Killed Bob Teal," the reader can find ideas and elements which Hammett would draw on for *The Maltese Falcon*. Raymond Chandler referred to cannibalizing his short stories, for his novels. Hammett certainly didn't go to that extreme, but you can see that he definitely remembered some things from a few of his short stories when he wrote *The Maltese Falcon*.

The story starts with the Op having a flashback to almost eight years prior, when he worked out of the Boston office. We get about as much of his past life as we ever do, in this opening. The Op happens to run into Lew Maher (who may be another Continental operative). We learn that a week or two later, the Op joined the Army until the war ended, after which he went to the agency's Chicago office. A few years later, he transferred to San Francisco, which is where he was when the stories started.

Maher points out a passing gunman, the Whosis Kid. Hammett was so good at adding little touches to his stories. Things that aren't vital, but which add depth. Maher says:

> "I'm going to clamp (catch) him some day, though—and that's a promise."
>
> Lew never kept his promise. A prowler killed him in an Audobon Road residence a month later.

Something about this makes me stop and take a breath. Lew Maher existed solely to point out The Whosis Kid to the Op, eight years in the past. That's it: Only reason we ever hear of him. But somehow, with that little comment about Maher being killed in the line of duty a month later, he has a memorable presence in the series. He's never mentioned again, but when we come across this story again, or hear of The Whosis kid, we remember that guy who pointed him out to the Op, and how he died not long after.

It's not a big thing. It's not even important. But it's Hammett reminding us that, Damn, he's good.

Boxing was a *huge* sport on the West Coast in the thirties and forties. Going to the fights was a regular thing. The Op had been working hard and goes to the fights at Dreamland Rink, which was a San Francisco institution for seventy years. He had noticed, back in Boston, that The Whosis Kid had irregularly-shaped ears. And he notices those ears again, a few rows ahead of him, as he watches the action in the ring. It tickles a memory, but it's not until he sees the Kid's face that he makes the identification.

He figures, "once a criminal, always a criminal," and decides to follow him. He tells the office boss (The Old Man) about the Kid, and learns that the Kid is suspected in a jewelry robbery back East, and the Boston branch authorizes San Francisco (and the Op) to check him out.

The Op is tailing the Kid when somebody shoots at the gunman during a drive-by. The Op gets busy: following the car; then switching to a man who gets out of the car; connecting with a house dick and monitoring calls at the switchboard; seeing an intentional car wreck and attempted kidnapping; and ending up with a femme fatale, with a gun, in the car with him as they flee the scene.

The most recent stories had been rather sedate. This was full-blown Op action. There's a cast of characters and more mistrust than a bootlegger at a Prohibition meeting. There is no honor among thieves, and the Op finds himself in an apartment with all the players, some jewels missing, and a lot of guns. If, like me, your favorite hardboiled novel—and movie—is *The Maltese Falcon*, you might be seeing a few similarities at this point.

Maurious is a weaker Caspar Gutman. Imagine The Whosis Kid as Wilmer-tough, but a third party—not just a gunman. Ines is the classic femme fatale playing her own game. She even picked up a sort-of Floyd Thursby along the way, though it's a different relationship. There's a guy nicknamed Big Chin who serves as Maurious' heavy, in lieu of Gutman's Wilmer.

Unlike Race Williams, the Op uses his brains, not guns, to manipulate the situation. But he's a man of action who isn't afraid to shoot, and when things blow up, lead and blood follow. This one doesn't get resolved with the delivery of a wrapped-up statue.

The action ends in the next-to-last chapter, and Hammett gives us an O. Henry twist which I find entirely satisfying. It's perfect. There's a short final bit with the Op narrating the details of the whole thing, but it's not too long, and it's not too confusing. As far as these "Op Wrap-Ups" go, I thought it was one of the better ones. And it followed crazy action, which makes it more palatable. Kind of like a five-minute cool down after a half-hour jog.

This book starts and finishes with top-drawer Hammett: "The Girl with the Silver Eyes," and "The Whosis Kid." Due, I think in large part to his unhappiness with Cody; and also the health and financial difficulties in his real life, the stuff in-between could have been better. It's still Hammett, and it's absolutely still worth reading. But the momentum that had built through "The Girl with the Silver Eyes," definitely decreases.

However, "The Whosis Kid" is a welcome return to form. And as we know, the terrific serial novels were soon to come.

Frederick Nebel, who Joseph "Cap" Shaw would tag to replace Hammett when the latter quit *Black Mask* for good, was still a year away from his first story in the magazine. Erle Stanley Gardner was in his third year at *Black Mask*, but the first Ed Jenkins story had only appeared two months before, in January. "Average" Hammett was still the best hardboiled stuff being printed in the magazine: unless you were partial to Carroll John Daly's style.

Hammett wasn't always at his best, but he was still always just about the best. He continued to write with a lean prose style, and incorporating his experiences as a Pinkerton brought a realism not found elsewhere. Pulpsters were cranking out stories to make a living on miserly wages. But Hammett was doing it with a professional style in a field he was continuing to shape.

New Op stories would appear in *Black Mask* in May, September, November, and December. So, it was Cody's every-other-month schedule, until a December "bonus." Then, there wouldn't be one until March of 1926, and he would quit *Black Mask*.

Hammett had now written fifteen Op stories for *Black Mask* (with a sixteenth appearing in *True Detective*). In merely a year and-a-half, he had co-created (with Daly) a new type of mystery story, evolved both, the form, and as a writer, and was redefining the mystery story in America. The novels were still ahead, but Hammett's impact in only eighteen months was colossal.

The Cody-Hammett relationship would deteriorate, and

as you'll read in the volume three intro, Hammett would quit *Black Mask,* and the Pulps altogether. It would take Joseph 'Cap' Shaw's editorship to lure Hammett back to the *Mask.*

—Bob Byrne

The Girl With the Silver Eyes

Mr. Hammett has written some lively and unusual tales about his realistic detective from the Continental Detective Agency, whose name has never been disclosed; but for action, shrewd detective-work, sheer interest, and surprise, his latest, herewith, surpasses them all.

1

A BELL JANGLED me into wakefulness. I rolled to the edge of my bed and reached for the telephone. The neat voice of the Old Man—the Continental Detective Agency's San Francisco manager—came to my ears:

"Sorry to disturb you, but you'll have to go up to the Glenton Apartments on Leavenworth Street. A man named Burke Pangburn, who lives there, phoned me a few minutes ago asking to have someone sent up to see him at once. He seemed rather excited. Will you take care of it? See what he wants."

I said I would and, yawning, stretching and cursing Pangburn—whoever he was—got my fat body out of pajamas and into street clothes.

The man who had disturbed my Sunday morning sleep—I found when I reached the Glenton—was a slim, white-faced person of about twenty-five, with big brown eyes that were red-rimmed just now from either sleeplessness or crying, or both. His long brown hair was rumpled when he opened the door to admit me; and he wore a mauve dressing-robe spotted with big jade parrots over wine-colored silk pajamas.

The room into which he led me resembled an auctioneer's establishment just before the sale—or maybe one of these alley tea-rooms. Fat blue vases, crooked red vases, lanky yellow vases, vases of various shapes and colors; marble statuettes, ebony statuettes, statuettes of any material; lanterns, lamps and candlesticks; draperies, hangings and rugs of all sorts; odds and ends of furniture that were all somehow queerly designed;

peculiar pictures hung here and there in unexpected places. A hard room to feel comfortable in.

"My fiancée," he began immediately in a high-pitched voice that was within a notch of hysteria, "has disappeared! Something has happened to her! Foul play of some horrible sort! I want you to find her—to save her from this terrible thing that…."

I followed him this far and then gave it up. A jumble of words came out of his mouth—"spirited away… mysterious something… lured into a trap"—but they were too disconnected for me to make anything out of them. So I stopped trying to understand him, and waited for him to babble himself empty of words.

I have heard ordinarily reasonable men, under stress of excitement, run on even more crazily than this wild-eyed youth; but his dress—the parroted robe and gay pajamas—and his surroundings—this deliriously furnished room—gave him too theatrical a setting; made his words sound utterly unreal.

He himself, when normal, should have been a rather nice-looking lad: his features were well spaced and, though his mouth and chin were a little uncertain, his broad forehead was good. But standing there listening to the occasional melodramatic phrase that I could pick out of the jumbled noises he was throwing at me, I thought that instead of parrots on his robe he should have had cuckoos.

Presently he ran out of language and was holding his long, thin hands out to me in an appealing gesture, saying,

"Will you?" over and over. "Will you? Will you?"

I nodded soothingly, and noticed that tears were on his thin cheeks.

"Suppose we begin at the beginning," I suggested, sitting

down carefully on a carved bench affair that didn't look any too strong.

"Yes! Yes!" He was standing, legs apart, in front of me, running his fingers through his hair. "The beginning. I had a letter from her every day until—"

"That's not the beginning," I objected. "Who is she? What is she?"

"She's Jeanne Delano!" he exclaimed in surprise at my ignorance. "And she is my fiancée. And now she is gone, and I know that—"

The phrases "victim of foul play," "into a trap" and so on began to flow hysterically out again.

Finally I got him quieted down and, sandwiched in between occasional emotional outbursts, got a story out of him that amounted to this:

This Burke Pangburn was a poet. About two months before, he had received a note from a Jeanne Delano—forwarded from his publishers—praising his latest book of rhymes. Jeanne Delano happened to live in San Francisco, too, though she hadn't known that he did. He had answered her note, and had received another. After a little of this they met. If she really was as beautiful as he claimed, then he wasn't to be blamed for falling in love with her. But whether or not she was really beautiful, he thought she was, and he had fallen hard.

This Delano girl had been living in San Francisco for only a little while, and when the poet met her she was living alone in an Ashbury Avenue apartment. He did not know where she came from or anything about her former life. He suspected— from certain indefinite suggestions and peculiarities of conduct which he couldn't put in words—that there was a cloud of some sort hanging over the girl; that neither her past nor her present were free from difficulties. But he hadn't the least idea what those difficulties might be. He hadn't cared. He knew absolutely nothing about her, except that she was beautiful, and he loved her, and she had promised to marry him.

Then, on the third of the month—exactly twenty-one days before this Sunday morning—the girl had suddenly left San Francisco. He had received a note from her, by messenger.

This note, which he showed me after I had insisted point blank on seeing it, read:

Burkelove:

Have just received a wire, and must go East on next train. Tried to get you on the phone, but couldn't. Will write you as soon as I know what my address will be. If anything. (These two words were erased and could be read only with great difficulty.) *Love me until I'm back with you forever.*

Your Jeanne.

Nine days later he had received another letter from her, from Baltimore, Maryland. This one, which I had a still harder time getting a look at, read:

Dearest Poet:

It seems like two years since I have seen you, and I have a fear that it's going to be between one and two months before I see you again.

I can't tell you now, beloved, about what brought me here. There are things that can't be written. But as soon as I'm back with you, I shall tell you the whole wretched story.

If anything should happen—I mean to me—you'll go on loving me

forever, won't you, beloved? But that's foolish. Nothing is going to
happen. I'm just off the train, and tired from traveling.

Tomorrow I shall write you a long, long letter to make up for this.

My address here is 215 N. Stricker St. Please, Mister, at least one
letter a day! Your own

Jeanne.

For nine days he had had a letter from her each day—with
two on Monday to make up for the none on Sunday—and
then her letters had stopped. And the daily letters he had sent
to the address she gave—215 N. Stricker Street—had begun
to come back to him, marked "Not known."

He had sent a telegram, and the telegraph company had
informed him that its Baltimore office had been unable to find
a Jeanne Delano at the North Stricker Street address.

For three days he had waited, expecting hourly to hear from
the girl, and no word had come. Then he had bought a ticket
for Baltimore.

"But," he wound up, "I was afraid to go. I know she's in some
sort of trouble—I can feel that—but I'm a silly poet. I can't
deal with mysteries. Either I would find nothing at all or, if by
luck I did stumble on the right track, the probabilities are that
I would only muddle things; add fresh complications, perhaps
endanger her life still further. I can't go blundering at it in that
fashion, without knowing whether I am helping or harming
her. It's a task for an expert in that sort of thing. So I thought
of your agency. You'll be careful, won't you? It may be—I don't
know—that she won't want assistance. It may be that you can
help her without her knowing anything about it. You are accustomed to that sort of thing; you can do it, can't you?"

2

I TURNED THE job over and over in my mind before answering him. The two great bugaboos of a reputable detective agency are the persons who bring in a crooked plan or a piece of divorce work all dressed up in the garb of a legitimate operation, and the irresponsible person who is laboring under wild and fanciful delusions—who wants a dream run out.

This poet—sitting opposite me now twining his long, white fingers nervously together—was, I thought, sincere; but I wasn't so sure of his sanity.

"Mr. Pangburn," I said after a while, "I'd like to handle this thing for you, but I'm not sure that I can. The Continental is rather strict, and, while I believe this thing is on the level, still I am only a hired man and have to go by the rules. Now if you could give us the endorsement of some firm or person of standing—a reputable lawyer, for instance, or any legally responsible party—we'd be glad to go ahead with the work. Otherwise, I am afraid—"

"But I know she's in danger!" he broke out. "I know that— And I can't be advertising her plight—airing her affairs—to everyone."

"I'm sorry, but I can't touch it unless you can give me some such endorsement." I stood up. "But you can find plenty of detective agencies that aren't so particular."

His mouth worked like a small boy's, and he caught his lower lip between his teeth. For a moment I thought he was going to burst into tears. But instead he said slowly:

"I dare say you are right. Suppose I refer you to my brother-in-law, Roy Axford. Will his word be sufficient?"

"Yes."

Roy Axford—R.F. Axford—was a mining man who had a finger in at least half of the big business enterprises of the Pacific Coast; and his word on anything was commonly considered good enough for anybody.

"If you can get in touch with him now," I said, "and arrange for me to see him today, I can get started without much delay."

Pangburn crossed the room and dug a telephone out from among a heap of his ornaments. Within a minute or two he was talking to someone whom he called "Rita."

"Is Roy home?... Will he be home this afternoon?... No, you can give him a message for me, though.... Tell him I'm sending a gentleman up to see him this afternoon on a personal matter—personal with me—and that I'll be very grateful if he'll do what I want.... Yes.... You'll find out, Rita.... It isn't a thing to talk about over the phone.... Yes, thanks!"

He pushed the telephone back into its hiding place and turned to me.

"He'll be at home until two o'clock. Tell him what I told you and if he seems doubtful, have him call me up. You'll have to tell him the whole thing; he doesn't know anything at all about Miss Delano."

"All right. Before I go, I want a description of her."

"She's beautiful!" he exclaimed. "The most beautiful woman in the world!"

That would look nice on a reward circular.

"That isn't exactly what I want," I told him. "How old is she?"

"Twenty-two."

"Height?"

"About five feet eight inches, or possibly nine."

"Slender, medium or plump?"

"She's inclined toward slenderness, but she—"

There was a note of enthusiasm in his voice that made me fear he was about to make a speech, so I cut him off with another question.

"What color hair?"

"Brown—so dark that it's almost black—and it's soft and thick and—"

"Yes, yes. Long or bobbed?"

"Long and thick and—"

"What color eyes?"

"You've seen shadows on polished silver when—"

I wrote down *grey eyes* and hurried on with the interrogation.

"Complexion?"

"Perfect!"

"Uh-huh. But is it light, or dark, or florid, or sallow, or what?"

"Fair."

"Face oval, or square, or long and thin, or what shape?"

"Oval."

"What shaped nose? Large, small, turned-up—"

"Small and regular!" There was a touch of indignation in his voice.

"How did she dress? Fashionably? And did she favor bright or quiet colors?"

"Beaut—" And then as I opened my mouth to head him off he came down to earth with:

"Very quietly—usually dark blues and browns."

"What jewelry did she wear?"

"I've never seen her wear any."

"Any scars, or moles?" The horrified look on his white face urged me on to give him a full shot. "Or warts, or deformities that you know?"

He was speechless, but he managed to shake his head.

"Have you a photograph of her?"

"Yes, I'll show you."

He bounded to his feet, wound his way through the room's excessive furnishings and out through a curtained doorway. Immediately he was back with a large photograph in a carved ivory frame. It was one of these artistic photographs—a thing of shadows and hazy outlines—not much good for identification purposes. She was beautiful—right enough—but that meant nothing; that's the purpose of an artistic photograph.

"This the only one you have?"

"Yes."

"I'll have to borrow it, but I'll get it back to you as soon as I have my copies made."

"No! No!" he protested against having his ladylove's face given to a lot of gumshoes. "That would be terrible!"

I finally got it, but it cost me more words than I like to waste on an incidental.

"I want to borrow a couple of her letters, or something in her writing, too," I said.

"For what?"

"To have photostatic copies made. Handwriting specimens come in handy—give you something to go over hotel registers with. Then, even if going under fictitious names, people now and then write notes and make memorandums."

We had another battle, out of which I came with three envelopes and two meaningless sheets of paper, all bearing the girl's angular writing.

"She have much money?" I asked, when the disputed photograph and handwriting specimens were safely tucked away in my pocket.

"I don't know. It's not the sort of thing that one would pry into. She wasn't poor; that is, she didn't have to practice any petty economies; but I haven't the faintest idea either as to the amount of her income or its source. She had an account at the Golden Gate Trust Company, but naturally I don't know anything about its size."

"Many friends here?"

"That's another thing I don't know. I think she knew a few people here, but I don't know who they were. You see, when we were together we never talked about anything but ourselves. You know what I mean: there was nothing we were interested in but each other. We were simply—"

"Can't you even make a guess at where she came from, who she was?"

"No. Those things didn't matter to me. She was Jeanne Delano, and that was enough for me."

"Did you and she ever have any financial interests in common? I mean, was there ever any transaction in money or other valuables in which both of you were interested?"

What I meant, of course, was had she got into him for a loan, or had she sold him something, or got money out of him in any other way.

He jumped to his feet, and his face went fog-grey. Then he sat down again—slumped down—and blushed scarlet.

"Pardon me," he said thickly. "You didn't know her, and of

course you must look at the thing from all angles. No, there was nothing like that. I'm afraid you are going to waste time if you are going to work on the theory that she was an adventuress. There was nothing like that! She was a girl with something terrible hanging over her; something that called her to Baltimore suddenly; something that has taken her away from me. Money? What could money have to do with it? I love her!"

3

R.F. AXFORD RECEIVED me in an office-like room in his Russian Hill residence: a big blond man, whose forty-eight or -nine years had not blurred the outlines of an athlete's body. A big, full-blooded man with the manner of one whose self-confidence is complete and not altogether unjustified.

"What's our Burke been up to now?" he asked amusedly when I told him who I was. His voice was a pleasant vibrant bass.

I didn't give him all the details.

"He was engaged to marry a Jeanne Delano, who went East about three weeks ago and then suddenly disappeared. He knows very little about her; thinks something has happened to her; and wants her found."

"Again?" His shrewd blue eyes twinkled. "And to a Jeanne this time! She's the fifth within a year, to my knowledge, and no doubt I missed one or two who were current while I was in Hawaii. But where do I come in?"

"I asked him for responsible endorsement. I think he's all right, but he isn't, in the strictest sense, a responsible person. He referred me to you."

"You're right about his not being, in the strictest sense, a responsible person." The big man screwed up his eyes and mouth in thought for a moment. Then: "Do you think that something has really happened to the girl? Or is Burke imagining things?"

"I don't know. I thought it was a dream at first. But in a

couple of her letters there are hints that something was wrong."

"You might go ahead and find her then," Axford said. "I don't suppose any harm will come from letting him have his Jeanne back. It will at least give him something to think about for a while."

"I have your word for it then, Mr. Axford, that there will be no scandal or anything of the sort connected with the affair?"

"Assuredly! Burke is all right, you know. It's simply that he is spoiled. He has been in rather delicate health all his life; and then he has an income that suffices to keep him modestly, with a little over to bring out books of verse and buy doo-daws for his rooms. He takes himself a little too solemnly—is too much the poet—but he's sound at bottom."

"I'll go ahead with it, then," I said, getting up. "By the way, the girl has an account at the Golden Gate Trust Company, and I'd like to find out as much about it as possible, especially where her money came from. Clement, the cashier, is a model of caution when it comes to giving out information about depositors. If you could put in a word for me it would make my way smoother."

"Be glad to."

He wrote a couple of lines across the back of a card and gave it to me; and, promising to call on him if I needed further assistance, I left.

4

I TELEPHONED PANGBURN that his brother-in-law had given the job his approval. I sent a wire to the agency's Baltimore branch, giving what information I had. Then I went up to Ashbury Avenue, to the apartment house in which the girl had lived.

The manager—an immense Mrs. Clute in rustling black—knew little, if any, more about the girl than Pangburn. The girl had lived there for two and a half months; she had had occasional callers, but Pangburn was the only one that the manager could describe to me. The girl had given up the apartment on the third of the month, saying that she had been called East, and she had asked the manager to hold her mail until she sent her new address. Ten days later Mrs. Clute had received a card from the girl instructing her to forward her mail to 215 N. Stricker Street, Baltimore, Maryland. There had been no mail to forward.

The single thing of importance that I learned at the apartment house was that the girl's two trunks had been taken away by a green transfer truck. Green was the color used by one of the city's largest transfer companies.

I went then to the office of this transfer company, and found a friendly clerk on duty. (A detective, if he is wise, takes pains to make and keep as many friends as possible among transfer company, express company and railroad employees.) I left the office with a memorandum of the transfer company's check numbers and the Ferry baggage-room to which the two trunks had been taken.

At the Ferry Building, with this information, it didn't take me many minutes to learn that the trunks had been checked to Baltimore. I sent another wire to the Baltimore branch, giving the railroad check numbers.

Sunday was well into night by this time, so I knocked off and went home.

5

HALF AN HOUR before the Golden Gate Trust Company opened for business the next morning I was inside, talking to Clement, the cashier. All the traditional caution and conservatism of bankers rolled together wouldn't be one-two-three to the amount usually displayed by this plump, white-haired old man. But one look at Axford's card, with *"Please give the bearer all possible assistance"* inked across the back of it, made Clement even eager to help me.

"You have, or have had, an account here in the name of Jeanne Delano," I said. "I'd like to know as much as possible about it: to whom she drew checks, and to what amounts; but especially all you can tell me about where her money came from."

He stabbed one of the pearl buttons on his desk with a pink finger, and a lad with polished yellow hair oozed silently into the room. The cashier scribbled with a pencil on a piece of paper and gave it to the noiseless youth, who disappeared. Presently he was back, laying a handful of papers on the cashier's desk.

Clement looked through the papers and then up at me.

"Miss Delano was introduced here by Mr. Burke Pangburn on the sixth of last month, and opened an account with eight hundred and fifty dollars in cash. She made the following deposits after that: four hundred dollars on the tenth; two hundred and fifty on the twenty-first; three hundred on the twenty-sixth; two hundred on the thirtieth; and twenty thousand dollars on the second of this month. All of these deposits except the last were made with cash. The last one was a check—which I have here."

He handed it to me: a Golden Gate Trust Company check.

PAY TO THE ORDER OF JEANNE DELANO,
TWENTY THOUSAND DOLLARS.
(SIGNED) BURKE PANGBURN.

It was dated the second of the month.

"Burke Pangburn!" I exclaimed, a little stupidly. "Was it usual for him to draw checks to that amount?"

"I think not. But we shall see."

He stabbed the pearl button again, ran his pencil across another slip of paper, and the youth with the polished yellow hair made a noiseless entrance, exit, entrance, and exit.

The cashier looked through the fresh batch of papers that had been brought to him.

"On the first of the month, Mr. Pangburn deposited twenty thousand dollars—a check against Mr. Axford's account here."

"Now how about Miss Delano's withdrawals?" I asked.

He picked up the papers that had to do with her account again.

"Her statement and canceled checks for last month haven't been delivered to her yet. Everything is here. A check for eighty-five dollars to the order of H.K. Clute on the fifteenth of last month; one 'to cash' for three hundred dollars on the twentieth, and another of the same kind for one hundred dollars on the twenty-fifth. Both of these checks were apparently cashed here by her. On the third of this month she closed out her account, with a check to her own order for twenty-one thousand, five hundred and fifteen dollars."

"And that check?"

"Was cashed here by her."

I lighted a cigarette, and let these figures drift around in my head. None of them—except those that were fixed to Pangburn's and Axford's signatures—seemed to be of any value to me. The Clute check—the only one the girl had drawn in anyone else's favor—had almost certainly been for rent.

"This is the way of it," I summed up aloud. "On the first of the month, Pangburn deposited Axford's check for twenty thousand dollars. The next day he gave a check to that amount to Miss Delano, which she deposited. On the following day she closed her account, taking between twenty-one and twenty-two thousand dollars in currency."

"Exactly," the cashier said.

6

BEFORE GOING UP to the Glenton Apartments to find
out why Pangburn hadn't come clean with me about the twenty
thousand dollars, I dropped in at the agency, to see if any word
had come from Baltimore. One of the clerks had just finished
decoding a telegram.

It read:

> Baggage arrived Mt. Royal Station on eighth. Taken away
> same day. Unable to trace. 215 North Stricker Street is Baltimore
> Orphan Asylum. Girl not known there. Continuing our efforts
> to find her.

The Old Man came in from luncheon as I was leaving. I went
back into his office with him for a couple of minutes.

"Did you see Pangburn?" he asked.

"Yes. I'm working on his job now—but I think it's a bust."

"What is it?"

"Pangburn is R.F. Axford's brother-in-law. He met a girl a
couple of months ago, and fell for her. She sizes up as a worker.
He doesn't know anything about her. The first of the month
he got twenty thousand dollars from his brother-in-law and
passed it over to the girl. She blew, telling him she had been
called to Baltimore, and giving him a phoney address that turns
out to be an orphan asylum. She sent her trunks to Baltimore,
and sent him some letters from there—but a friend could have
taken care of the baggage and could have remailed her letters

for her. Of course, she would have needed a ticket to check the trunks on, but in a twenty-thousand-dollar game that would be a small expense. Pangburn held out on me; he didn't tell me a word about the money. Ashamed of being easy pickings, I reckon. I'm going to the bat with him on it now."

The Old Man smiled his mild smile that might mean anything, and I left.

7

TEN MINUTES OF ringing Pangburn's bell brought no answer. The elevator boy told me he thought Pangburn hadn't been in all night. I put a note in his box and went down to the railroad company's offices, where I arranged to be notified if an unused Baltimore-San Francisco ticket was turned in for redemption.

That done, I went up to the *Chronicle* office and searched the files for weather conditions during the past month, making a memorandum of four dates upon which it had rained steadily day and night. I carried my memorandum to the offices of the three largest taxicab companies.

That was a trick that had worked well for me before. The girl's apartment was some distance from the street car line, and I was counting upon her having gone out—or having had a caller—on one of those rainy dates. In either case, it was very likely that she—or her caller—had left in a taxi in preference to walking through the rain to the car line. The taxicab companies' daily records would show any calls from her address, and the fares' destinations.

The ideal trick, of course, would have been to have the records searched for the full extent of the girl's occupancy of the apartment; but no taxicab company would stand for having that amount of work thrust upon them, unless it was a matter of life and death. It was difficult enough for me to persuade them to turn clerks loose on the four days I had selected.

I called up Pangburn again after I left the last taxicab office, but he was not at home. I called up Axford's residence, thinking that the poet might have spent the night there, but was told that he had not.

Late that afternoon I got my copies of the girl's photograph and handwriting, and put one of each in the mail for Baltimore. Then I went around to the three taxicab companies' offices and got my reports. Two of them had nothing for me. The third's records showed two calls from the girl's apartment.

On one rainy afternoon a taxi had been called, and one passenger had been taken to the Glenton Apartments. That passenger, obviously, was either the girl or Pangburn. At half-past twelve one night another call had come in, and this passenger had been taken to the Marquis Hotel.

The driver who had answered this second call remembered it indistinctly when I questioned him, but he thought that his fare had been a man. I let the matter rest there for the time; the Marquis isn't a large hotel as San Francisco hotels go, but it is too large to make canvassing its guests for the one I wanted practicable.

I spent the evening trying to reach Pangburn, with no success. At eleven o'clock I called up Axford, and asked him if he had any idea where I might find his brother-in-law.

"Haven't seen him for several days," the millionaire said. "He was supposed to come up for dinner last night, but didn't. My wife tried to reach him by phone a couple times today, but couldn't."

8

THE NEXT MORNING I called Pangburn's apartment before I got out of bed, and got no answer. Then I telephoned Axford and made an appointment for ten o'clock at his office.

"I don't know what he's up to now," Axford said good-naturedly when I told him that Pangburn had apparently been away from his apartment since Sunday, "and I suppose there's small chance of guessing. Our Burke is nothing if not erratic. How are you progressing with your search for the damsel in distress?"

"Far enough to convince me that she isn't in a whole lot of distress. She got twenty thousand dollars from your brother-in-law the day before she vanished."

"Twenty thousand dollars from Burke? She must be a wonderful girl! But wherever did he get that much money?"

"From you."

Axford's muscular body straightened in his chair.

"From me?"

"Yes—your check."

"He did not."

There was nothing argumentative in his voice; it simply stated a fact.

"You didn't give him a check for twenty thousand dollars on the first of the month?"

"No."

"Then," I suggested, "perhaps we'd better take a run over to the Golden Gate Trust Company."

Ten minutes later we were in Clement's office.

"I'd like to see my cancelled checks," Axford told the cashier.

The youth with the polished yellow hair brought them in presently—a thick wad of them—and Axford ran rapidly through them until he found the one he wanted. He studied that one for a long while, and when he looked up at me he shook his head slowly but with finality.

"I've never seen it before."

Clement mopped his head with a white handkerchief, and tried to pretend that he wasn't burning up with curiosity and fears that his bank had been gypped.

The millionaire turned the check over and looked at the endorsement.

"Deposited by Burke," he said in the voice of one who talks while he thinks of something entirely different, "on the first."

"Could we talk to the teller who took in the twenty-thou-sand-dollar check that Miss Delano deposited?" I asked Clement.

He pressed one of his desk's pearl buttons with a fumbling pink finger, and in a minute or two a little sallow man with a hairless head came in.

"Do you remember taking a check for twenty thousand from Miss Jeanne Delano a few weeks ago?" I asked him.

"Yes, sir! Yes, sir! Perfectly."

"Just what do you remember about it?"

"Well, sir, Miss Delano came to my window with Mr. Burke Pangburn. It was his check. I thought it was a large check for him to be drawing, but the bookkeepers said he had enough money in his account to cover it. They stood there—Miss Delano and Mr. Pangburn—talking and laughing while I entered the deposit in her book, and then they left, and that was all."

"This check," Axford said slowly, after the teller had gone back to his cage, "is a forgery. But I shall make it good, of course. That ends the matter, Mr. Clement, and there must be no more to-do about it."

"Certainly, Mr. Axford. Certainly."

Clement was all enormously relieved smiles and head-noddings, with this twenty-thousand-dollar load lifted from his bank's shoulders.

Axford and I left the bank then and got into his coupé, in which we had come from his office. But he did not immediately start the engine. He sat for a while staring at the traffic of Montgomery Street with unseeing eyes.

"I want you to find Burke," he said presently, and there was no emotion of any sort in his bass voice. "I want you to find him without risking the least whisper of scandal. If my wife knew of all this— She mustn't know. She thinks her brother is a choice morsel. I want you to find him for me. The girl doesn't matter any more, but I suppose that where you find one you will find the other. I'm not interested in the money, and I don't want you to make any special attempt to recover that; it could hardly be done, I'm afraid, without publicity. I want you to find Burke before he does something else."

"If you want to avoid the wrong kind of publicity," I said, "your best bet is to spread the right kind first. Let's advertise him as missing, fill the papers up with his pictures and so forth. They'll play him up strong. He's your brother-in-law and he's a poet. We can say that he has been ill—you told me that he had been in delicate health all his life—and that we fear he has dropped dead somewhere or is suffering under some mental derangement. There will be no necessity of mentioning the girl or the money, and our explanation may keep people—especially your wife—from guessing the truth when the fact that he is missing leaks out. It's bound to leak out somehow."

He didn't like my idea at first, but I finally won him over.

We went up to Pangburn's apartment then, easily securing admittance on Axford's explanation that we had an engagement with him and would wait there for him. I went through the rooms inch by inch, prying into each hole and hollow and crack; reading everything that was written anywhere, even down to his manuscripts; and I found nothing that threw any light on his disappearance.

I helped myself to his photographs—pocketing five of the dozen or more that were there. Axford did not think that any of the poet's bags or trunks were missing from the pack-room. I did not find his Golden Gate Trust Company deposit book.

I spent the rest of the day loading the newspapers up with what we wished them to have; and they gave my ex-client one grand spread: first-page stuff with photographs and all possible trimmings. Anyone in San Francisco who didn't know that Burke Pangburn—brother-in-law of R.F. Axford and author of Sandpatches and Other Verse—was missing, either couldn't read or wouldn't.

9

THIS ADVERTISING BROUGHT results. By the following morning, reports were rolling in from all directions, from dozens of people who had seen the missing poet in dozens of places. A few of these reports looked promising—or at least possible—but the majority were ridiculous on their faces.

I came back to the agency from running out one that had—until run out—looked good, to find a note on my desk asking me to call up Axford.

"Can you come down, to my office now?" he asked when I got him on the wire.

There was a lad of twenty-one or -two with Axford when I was ushered into his office: a narrow-chested, dandified lad of the sporting clerk type.

"This is Mr. Fall, one of my employees," Axford told me. "He says he saw Burke Sunday night."

"Where?" I asked Fall.

"Going into a roadhouse near Halfmoon Bay."

"Sure it was him?"

"Absolutely! I've seen him come in here to Mr. Axford's office to know him. It was him all right."

"How'd you come to see him?"

"I was coming up from further down the shore with some friends, and we stopped in at the roadhouse to get something to eat. As we were leaving, a car drove up and Mr. Pangburn and a girl or woman—I didn't notice her particularly—got out and went inside. I didn't think anything of it until I saw in the paper last night that he hadn't been seen since Sunday. So then I thought to myself that—"

"What roadhouse was this?" I cut in, not being interested in his mental processes.

"The White Shack."

"About what time?"

"Somewhere between eleven-thirty and midnight, I guess."

"He see you?"

"No. I was already in our car when he drove up. I don't think he'd know me anyway."

"What did the woman look like?"

"I don't know. I didn't see her face, and I can't remember how she was dressed or even if she was short or tall."

That was all Fall could tell me.

We shooed him out of the office, and I used Axford's telephone to call up "Wop" Healey's dive in North Beach and leave word that when "Porky" Grout came in he was to call up "Jack." That was a standing arrangement by which I got word to Porky whenever I wanted to see him, without giving anybody a chance to tumble to the connection between us.

"Know the White Shack?" I asked Axford, when I was through phoning.

"I know where it is, but I don't know anything about it."

"Well, it's a tough hole. Run by 'Tin-Star' Joplin, an ex-yegg who invested his winnings in the place when Prohibition made the roadhouse game good. He makes more money now than he ever heard of in his piking safe-ripping days. Retailing liquor is a sideline with him; his real profit comes from acting as a relay station for the booze that comes through Halfmoon Bay for points beyond; and the dope is that half the booze put ashore by the Pacific rum fleet is put ashore in Halfmoon Bay.

"The White Shack is a tough hole, and it's no place for your brother-in-law to be hanging around. I can't go down there myself without stirring things up; Joplin and I are old friends. But I've got a man I can put in there for a few nights. Pangburn may be a regular visitor, or he may even be staying there. He wouldn't be the first one Joplin had ever let hide-out there. I'll put this man of mine in the place for a week, anyway, and see what he can find."

"It's all in your hands," Axford said. "Find Burke without scandal—that's all I ask."

10

FROM AXFORD'S OFFICE I went straight to my rooms, left the outer door unlocked, and sat down to wait for Porky Grout. I had waited an hour and a half when he pushed the door open and came in.

"'Lo! How's tricks?"

He swaggered to a chair, leaned back in it, put his feet on the table and reached for a pack of cigarettes that lay there.

That was Porky Grout. A pasty-faced man in his thirties, neither large nor small, always dressed flashily—even if sometimes dirtily—and trying to hide an enormous cowardice behind a swaggering carriage, a blustering habit of speech, and an exaggerated pretense of self-assurance.

But I had known him for three years; so now I crossed the room and pushed his feet roughly off the table, almost sending him over backward.

"What's the idea?" He came to his feet, crouching and snarling. "Where do you get that stuff? Do you want a smack in the—"

I took a step toward him. He sprang away, across the room.

"Aw, I didn't mean nothin'. I was only kiddin'!"

"Shut up and sit down," I advised him.

I had known this Porky Grout for three years, and had been using him for nearly that long, and I didn't know a single thing that could be said in his favor. He was a coward. He was a liar. He was a thief, and a hophead. He was a traitor to his kind and, if not watched, to his employers. A nice bird to deal with! But detecting is a hard business, and you use whatever tools come to hand. This Porky was an effective tool if handled right, which meant keeping your hand on his throat all the time and checking up every piece of information he brought in.

His cowardice was—for my purpose—his greatest asset. It was notorious throughout the criminal Coast; and though nobody—crook or not—could possibly think him a man to be trusted, nevertheless he was not actually distrusted. Most of his fellows thought him too much the coward to be dangerous; they thought he would be afraid to betray them; afraid of the summary vengeance that crookdom visits upon the squealer. But they didn't take into account Porky's gift for convincing himself that he was a lion-hearted fellow, when no danger was near. So he went freely where he desired and where I sent him, and brought me otherwise unobtainable bits of information upon matters in which I was interested.

For nearly three years I had used him with considerable success, paying him well, and keeping him under my heel. *Informant* was the polite word that designated him in my reports; the underworld has even less lovely names than the common *stool-pigeon* to denote his kind.

"I have a job for you," I told him, now that he was seated again, with his feet on the floor.

His loose mouth twitched up at the left corner, pushing that eye into a knowing squint.

"I thought so."

He always says something like that.

"I want you to go down to Halfmoon Bay and stick around Tin-Star Joplin's joint for a few nights. Here are two photos"— sliding one of Pangburn and one of the girl across the table. "Their names and descriptions are written on the backs. I want to know if either of them shows up down there, what they're doing, and where they're hanging out. It may be that Tin-Star is covering them up."

Porky was looking knowingly from one picture to the other.

"I think I know this guy," he said out of the corner of his mouth that twitches.

That's another thing about Porky. You can't mention a name or give a description that won't bring that same remark, even though you make them up.

"Here's some money." I slid some bills across the table. "If you're down there more than a couple of nights, I'll get some more to you. Keep in touch with me, either over this phone or the under-cover one at the office. And—remember this—lay off the stuff! If I come down there and find you all snowed up, I promise that I'll tip Joplin off to you."

He had finished counting the money by now—there wasn't a whole lot to count—and he threw it contemptuously back on the table.

"Save that for newspapers," he sneered. "How am I goin' to get anywheres if I can't spend no money in the joint?"

"That's plenty for a couple of days' expenses; you'll probably knock back half of it. If you stay longer than a couple of days, I'll get more to you. And you get your pay when the job is done, and not before."

He shook his head and got up.

"I'm tired of pikin' along with you. You can turn your own jobs. I'm through!"

"If you don't get down to Halfmoon Bay tonight, you *are* through," I assured him, letting him get out of the threat whatever he liked.

After a little while, of course, he took the money and left. The dispute over expense money was simply a preliminary that went with every job I sent him out on.

11

AFTER PORKY HAD cleared out, I leaned back in my chair and burned half a dozen Fatimas over the job. The girl had gone first with the twenty thousand dollars, and then the poet had gone; and both had gone, whether permanently or not, to the White Shack. On its face, the job was an obvious affair. The girl had given Pangburn the *work* to the extent of having him forge a check against his brother-in-law's account; and then, after various moves whose value I couldn't determine at the time, they had gone into hiding together.

There were two loose ends to be taken care of. One of them— the finding of the confederate who had mailed the letters to Pangburn and who had taken care of the girl's baggage—was in the Baltimore branch's hands. The other was: Who had ridden in the taxicab that I had traced from the girl's apartment to the Marquis Hotel?

That might not have any bearing upon the job, or it might. Suppose I could find a connection between the Marquis Hotel and the White Shack. That would make a completed chain of some sort. I searched the back of the telephone directory and found the roadhouse number. Then I went up to the Marquis Hotel.

The girl on duty at the hotel switchboard, when I got there, was one with whom I had done business before.

"Who's been calling Halfmoon Bay numbers?" I asked her.

"My God!" She leaned back in her chair and ran a pink hand gently over the front of her rigidly waved red hair. "I got enough to do without remembering every call that goes through. This ain't a boarding-house. We have more'n one call a week."

"You don't have many Halfmoon Bay calls," I insisted, leaning an elbow on the counter and letting a folded five-spot peep out between the fingers of one hand. "You ought to remember any you've had lately."

"I'll see," she sighed, as if willing to do her best on a hopeless task.

She ran through her tickets.

"Here's one—from room 522, a couple weeks ago."

"What number was called?"

"Halfmoon Bay 51."

That was the roadhouse number. I passed over the five-spot.

"Is 522 a permanent guest?"

"Yes. Mr. Kilcourse. He's been here three or four months."

"What is he?"

"I don't know. A perfect gentleman, if you ask me."

"That's nice. What does he look like?"

"Tall and elegant."

"Be yourself," I pleaded. "What does he look like?"

"He's a young man, but his hair is turning gray. He's dark and handsome. Looks like a movie actor."

"Bull Montana?" I asked, as I moved off toward the desk.

The key to 522 was in its place in the rack. I sat down where I could keep an eye on it. Perhaps an hour later a clerk took it out and gave it to a man who did look somewhat like an actor. He was a man of thirty or so, with dark skin, and dark hair that showed grey around the ears. He stood a good six feet of fashionably dressed slenderness.

Carrying the key, he disappeared into an elevator.

I called up the agency then and asked the Old Man to send Dick Foley over. Ten minutes later Dick arrived. He's a little shrimp of a Canadian—there isn't a hundred and ten pounds of him—who is the smoothest shadow I've ever seen, and I've seen most of them.

"I have a bird in here I want tailed," I told Dick. "His name is Kilcourse and he's in room 522. Stick around outside, and I'll give you the spot on him."

I went back to the lobby and waited some more.

At eight o'clock Kilcourse came down and left the hotel. I went after him for half a block—far enough to turn him over to Dick—and then went home, so that I would be within reach of a telephone if Porky Grout tried to get in touch with me. No call came from him that night.

12

WHEN I ARRIVED at the agency the next morning, Dick was waiting for me.

"What luck?" I asked.

"Damndest!" The little Canadian talks like a telegram when his peace of mind is disturbed, and just now he was decidedly peevish. "Took me two blocks. Shook me. Only taxi in sight."

"Think he made you?"

"No. Wise head. Playing safe."

"Try him again, then. Better have a car handy, in case he tries the same trick again."

My telephone jingled as Dick was going out. It was Porky Grout, talking over the agency's unlisted line.

"Turn up anything?" I asked.

"Plenty," he bragged.

"Good! Are you in town?"

"Yes."

"I'll meet you in my rooms in twenty minutes," I said.

The pasty-faced informant was fairly bloated with pride in himself when he came through the door I had left unlocked for him. His swagger was almost a cake-walk; and the side of his mouth that twitches was twisted into a knowing leer that would have fit a Solomon.

"I knocked it over for you, kid," he boasted. "Nothin' to it—for me! I went down there and talked to ever'body that knowed anything, seen ever'thing there was to see, and put the X-ray on the whole dump. I made a—"

"Uh-huh," I interrupted. "Congratulations and so forth. But just what did you turn up?"

"Now le'me tell you." He raised a dirty hand in a traffic-cop sort of gesture, and blew a stream of cigarette smoke at the ceiling. "Don't crowd me. I'll give you all the dope."

"Sure," I said. "I know. You're great, and I'm lucky to have you to knock off my jobs for me, and all that! But is Pangburn down there?"

"I'm gettin' around to that. I went down there and—"

"Did you see Pangburn?"

"As I was sayin', I went down there and—"

"Porky," I said, "I don't give a damn what you did! Did you see Pangburn?"

"Yes. I seen him."

"Fine! Now what did you see?"

"He's camping down there with Tin-Star. Him and the broad that you give me a picture of are both there. She's been there a month. I didn't see her, but one of the waiters told me about her. I seen Pangburn myself. They don't show themselves much—stick back in Tin-Star's part of the joint—where he lives—most of the time. Pangburn's been there since Sunday. I went down there and—"

"Learn who the girl is? Or anything about what they're up to?"

"No. I went down there and—"

"All right! *Went down there* again tonight. Call me up as soon as you know positively Pangburn is there—that he hasn't gone out. Don't make any mistakes. I don't want to come down there and scare them up on a false alarm. Use the agency's under-cover line, and just tell whoever answers that you won't be in town until late. That'll mean that Pangburn is there; and it'll let you call up from Joplin's without giving the play away."

"I got to have more dough," he said, as he got up. "It costs—"

"I'll file your application," I promised. "Now beat it, and let me hear from you tonight, the minute you're sure Pangburn is there."

Then I went up to Axford's office.

"I think I have a line on him," I told the millionaire. "I hope to have him where you can talk to him tonight. My man says he was at the White Shack last night, and is probably living there. If he's there tonight, I'll take you down, if you want."

"Why can't we go now?"

"No. The place is too dead in the daytime for my man to hang around without making himself conspicuous, and I don't want to take any chances on either you or me showing ourselves there until we're sure we're coming face to face with Pangburn."

"What do you want me to do then?"

"Have a fast car ready tonight, and be ready to start as soon as I get word to you."

"Righto. I'll be at home after five-thirty. Phone me as soon as you're ready to go, and I'll pick you up."

13

AT NINE-THIRTY THAT evening I was sitting beside Axford on the front seat of a powerfully engined foreign car, and we were roaring down a road that led to Halfmoon Bay. Porky's telephone call had come.

Neither of us talked much during that ride, and the imported monster under us made it a rather short ride. Axford sat comfortable and relaxed at the wheel, but I noticed for the first time that he had a rather heavy jaw.

The White Shack is a large building, square-built, of imitation stone. It is set away back from the road, and is approached by two curving driveways, which, together, make a semi-circle whose diameter is the public road. The center of this semi-circle is occupied by sheds under which Joplin's patrons stow their cars, and here and there around the sheds are flower-beds and clumps of shrubbery.

We were still going at a fair clip when we turned into one end of this semi-circular driveway, and—

Axford slammed on his brakes, and the big machine threw us into the wind-shield as it jolted into an abrupt stop—barely in time to avoid smashing into a cluster of people who had suddenly loomed up before us.

In the glow from our headlights faces stood sharply out; white, horrified faces, furtive faces, faces that were callously curious. Below the faces, white arms and shoulders showed, and bright gowns and jewelry, against the duller background of masculine clothing.

This was the first impression I got, and then, by the time I had removed my face from the windshield, I realized that this cluster of people had a core, a thing about which it centered. I stood up, trying to look over the crowd's heads, but I could see nothing.

Jumping down to the driveway, I pushed through the crowd.

Face down on the white gravel a man sprawled—a thin man in dark clothes—and just above his collar, where the head and neck join, was a hole. I knelt to peer into his face.

Then I pushed through the crowd again, back to where Axford was just getting out of the car, the engine of which was still running.

"Pangburn is dead—shot!"

14

METHODICALLY, AXFORD TOOK off his gloves, folded them and put them in a pocket. Then he nodded his understanding of what I had told him, and walked toward where the crowd stood around the dead poet. I looked after him until he had vanished in the throng. Then I went winding through the outskirts of the crowd, hunting for Porky Grout.

I found him standing on the porch, leaning against a pillar. I passed where he could see me, and went on around to the side of the roadhouse that afforded most shadow.

In the shadows Porky joined me. The night wasn't cool, but his teeth were chattering.

"Who got him?" I demanded.

"I don't know," he whined, and that was the first thing of which I had ever known him to confess complete ignorance. "I was inside, keepin' an eye on the others."

"What others?"

"Tin-Star, and some guy I never seen before, and the broad. I didn't think the kid was going out. He didn't have no hat."

"What do you know about it?"

"A little while after I phoned you, the girl and Pangburn came out from Joplin's part of the joint and sat down at a table around on the other side of the porch, where it's fairly dark. They eat for a while and then this other guy comes over and sits down with 'em. I don't know his name, but I think I've saw him around town. He's a tall guy, all rung up in fancy rags."

That would be Kilcourse.

"They talk for a while and then Joplin joins 'em. They sit around the table laughin' and talkin' for maybe a quarter of a hour. Then Pangburn gets up and goes indoors. I got a table that I can watch 'em from, and the place is crowded, and I'm afraid I'll lose my table if I leave it, so I don't follow the kid. He ain't got no hat; I figure he ain't goin' nowhere. But he must of gone through the house and out front, because pretty soon there's a noise that I thought was a auto backfire, and then the sound of a car gettin' away quick. And then some guy squawks that there's a dead man outside. Ever'body runs out here, and it's Pangburn."

"You dead sure that Joplin, Kilcourse and the girl were all at the table when Pangburn was killed?"

"Absolutely," Porky said, "if this dark guy's name is Kilcourse."

"Where are they now?"

"Back in Joplin's hang-out. They went up there as soon as they seen Pangburn had been croaked."

I had no illusions about Porky. I knew he was capable of selling me out and furnishing the poet's murderer with an alibi. But there was this about it: if Joplin, Kilcourse or the girl had fixed him, and had fixed my informant, then it was hopeless for me to try to prove that they weren't on the rear porch when the shot was fired. Joplin had a crowd of hangers-on who would swear to anything he told them without batting an eye. There would be a dozen supposed witnesses to their presence on the rear porch.

Thus the only thing for me to do was to take it for granted that Porky was coming clean with me.

"Have you seen Dick Foley?" I asked, since Dick had been shadowing Kilcourse.

"No."

"Hunt around and see if you can find him. Tell him I've gone up to talk to Joplin, and tell him to come on up. Then you can stick around where I can get hold of you if I want you."

I went in through a French window, crossed an empty dance-floor and went up the stairs that lead to Tin-Star Joplin's living quarters in the rear second story. I knew the way, having been up there before. Joplin and I were old friends.

I was going up now to give him and his friends a shake-down on the off-chance that some good might come of it, though I knew that I had nothing on any of them. I could have tied something on the girl, of course, but not without advertising the fact that the dead poet had forged his brother-in-law's signature to a check. And that was no go.

"Come in," a heavy, familiar voice called when I rapped on Joplin's living-room door.

I pushed the door open and went in.

Tin-Star Joplin was standing in the middle of the floor: a big-bodied ex-yegg with inordinately thick shoulders and an expressionless horse face. Beyond him Kilcourse sat dangling one leg from the corner of a table, alertness hiding behind an amused half-smile on his handsome dark face. On the other side of a room a girl whom I knew for Jeanne Delano sat on the arm of a big leather chair. And the poet hadn't exaggerated when he told me she was beautiful.

"You!" Joplin grunted disgustedly as soon as he recognized me. "What the hell do you want?"

"What've you got?"

My mind wasn't on this sort of repartee, however; I was studying the girl. There was something vaguely familiar about her—but I couldn't place her. Perhaps I hadn't seen her before; perhaps much looking at the picture Pangburn had given me was responsible for my feeling of recognition. Pictures will do that.

Meanwhile, Joplin had said:

"Time to waste is one thing I ain't got."

And I had said:

"If you'd saved up all the time different judges have given you, you'd have plenty."

I had seen the girl somewhere before. She was a slender girl in a glistening blue gown that exhibited a generous spread of front, back and arms that were worth showing. She had a mass of dark brown hair above an oval face of the color that pink ought to be. Her eyes were wide-set and of a grey shade that wasn't altogether unlike the shadows on polished silver that the poet had compared them to.

I studied the girl, and she looked back at me with level eyes, and still I couldn't place her. Kilcourse still sat dangling a leg from the table corner.

Joplin grew impatient.

"Will you stop gandering at the girl, and tell me what you want of me?" he growled.

The girl smiled then, a mocking smile that bared the edges of razor-sharp little animal teeth. And with the smile I knew her!

Her hair and skin had fooled me. The last time I had seen her—the only time I had seen her before—her face had been marble-white, and her hair had been short and the color of fire. She and an older woman and three men and I had played hide-and-seek one evening in a house in Turk Street over a matter of the murder of a bank messenger and the theft of a hundred thousand dollars' worth of Liberty Bonds. Through her intriguing three of her accomplices had died that evening, and the fourth—the Chinese—had eventually gone to the gallows at Folsom prison. Her name had been Elvira then, and since her escape from the house that night we had been fruitlessly hunting her from border to border, and beyond.

Recognition must have shown in my eyes in spite of the effort I made to keep them blank, for, swift as a snake, she had left the arm of the chair and was coming forward, her eyes more steel than silver.

I put my gun in sight.

Joplin took a half-step toward me.

"What's the idea?" he barked.

Kilcourse slid off the table, and one of his thin dark hands hovered over his necktie.

"This is the idea," I told them. "I want the girl for a murder a couple months back, and maybe—I'm not sure—for tonight's. Anyway, I'm—"

The snapping of a light-switch behind me, and the room went black.

I moved, not caring where I went so long as I got away from where I had been when the lights went out.

My back touched a wall and I stopped, crouching low.

"Quick, kid!" A hoarse whisper that came from where I thought the door should be.

But both of the room's doors, I thought, were closed, and could hardly be opened without showing gray rectangles. People moved in the blackness, but none got between me and the lighter square of windows.

Something clicked softly in front of me—too thin a click for the cocking of a gun—but it could have been the opening of a spring-knife, and I remembered that Tin-Star Joplin had a fondness for that weapon.

"Let's go! Let's go!" A harsh whisper that cut through the dark like a blow.

Sounds of motion, muffled, indistinguishable... one sound not far away....

Abruptly a strong hand clamped one of my shoulders, a hard-muscled body strained against me. I stabbed out with my gun, and heard a grunt.

The hand moved up my shoulder toward my throat.

I snapped up a knee, and heard another grunt.

A burning point ran down my side.

I stabbed again with my gun—pulled it back until the muzzle was clear of the soft obstacle that had stopped it, and squeezed the trigger.

The crash of the shot. Joplin's voice in my ear—a curiously matter-of-fact voice:

"God damn! That got me."

15

I SPUN AWAY from him then, toward where I saw the dim yellow of an open door. I had heard no sounds of departure. I had been too busy. But I knew that Joplin had tied into me while the others made their get-away.

Nobody was in sight as I jumped, slid, tumbled down the steps—any number at a time. A waiter got in my path as I plunged toward the dance-floor. I don't know whether his interference was intentional or not. I didn't ask. I slammed the flat of my gun in his face and went on. Once I jumped a leg that came out to trip me; and at the outer door I had to smear another face.

Then I was out in the semi-circular driveway, from one end of which a red tail-light was turning east into the county road.

While I sprinted for Axford's car I noticed that Pangburn's body had been removed. A few people still stood around the spot where he had lain, and they gaped at me now with open mouths.

The car was as Axford had left it, with idling engine. I swung it through a flower-bed and pointed it east on the public road. Five minutes later I picked up the red point of a tail-light again.

The car under me had more power than I would ever need, more than I would have known how to handle. I don't know how fast the one ahead was going, but I closed in as if it had been standing still.

A mile and a half, or perhaps two—

Suddenly a man was in the road ahead—a little beyond the

reach of my lights. The lights caught him, and I saw that it was Porky Grout!

Porky Grout standing facing me in the middle of the road, the dull metal of an automatic in each hand.

The guns in his hands seemed to glow dimly red and then go dark in the glare of my headlights—glow and then go dark, like two bulbs in an automatic electric sign.

The windshield fell apart around me.

Porky Grout—the informant whose name was a synonym for cowardice the full length of the Pacific Coast—stood in the center of the road shooting at a metal comet that rushed down upon him....

I didn't see the end.

I confess frankly that I shut my eyes when his set white face showed close over my radiator. The metal monster under me trembled—not very much—and the road ahead was empty except for the fleeing red light. My windshield was gone. The wind tore at my uncovered hair and brought tears to my squinted-up eyes.

Presently I found that I was talking to myself, saying, "That was Porky. That was Porky." It was an amazing fact. It was no surprise that he had double-crossed me. That was to be expected. And for him to have crept up the stairs behind me and turned off the lights wasn't astonishing. But for him to have stood straight up and died—

An orange streak from the car ahead cut off my wonderment. The bullet didn't come near me—it isn't easy to shoot accurately from one moving car into another—but at the pace I was going it wouldn't be long before I was close enough for good shooting.

I turned on the searchlight above the dashboard. It didn't quite reach the car ahead, but it enabled me to see that the girl was driving, while Kilcourse sat screwed around beside her, facing me. The car was a yellow roadster.

I eased up a little. In a duel with Kilcourse here I would have been at a disadvantage, since I would have had to drive as well as shoot. My best play seemed to be to hold my distance until we reached a town, as we inevitably must. It wasn't midnight yet. There would be people on the streets of any town, and policemen. Then I could close in with a better chance of coming off on top.

A few miles of this and my prey tumbled to my plan. The yellow roadster slowed down, wavered, and came to rest with its length across the road. Kilcourse and the girl were out immediately and crouching in the road on the far side of their barricade.

I was tempted to dive pell-mell into them, but it was a weak temptation, and when its short life had passed I put on the brakes and stopped. Then I fiddled with my searchlight until it bore full upon the roadster.

A flash came from somewhere near the roadster's wheels, and the searchlight shook violently, but the glass wasn't touched. It would be their first target, of course, and....

Crouching in my car, waiting for the bullet that would smash the lense, I took off my shoes and overcoat.

The third bullet ruined the light.

I switched off the other lights, jumped to the road, and when I stopped running I was squatting down against the near side of the yellow roadster. As easy and safe a trick as can be imagined.

The girl and Kilcourse had been looking into the glare of a powerful light. When that light suddenly died, and the weaker ones around it went, too, they were left in pitch unseeing blackness, which must last for the minute or longer that their eyes would need to readjust themselves to the gray-black of the night. My stockinged feet had made no sound on the macadam road, and now there was only a roadster between us; and I knew it and they didn't.

From near the radiator Kilcourse spoke softly:

"I'm going to try to knock him off from the ditch. Take a shot at him now and then to keep him busy."

"I can't see him," the girl protested.

"Your eyes'll be all right in a second. Take a shot at the car anyway."

I moved toward the radiator as the girl's pistol barked at the empty touring car.

Kilcourse, on hands and knees, was working his way toward the ditch that ran along the south side of the road. I gathered my legs under me, intent upon a spring and a blow with my gun upon the back of his head. I didn't want to kill him, but I wanted to put him out of the way quick. I'd have the girl to take care of, and she was at least as dangerous as he.

As I tensed for the spring, Kilcourse, guided perhaps by some instinct of the hunted, turned his head and saw me—saw a threatening shadow.

Instead of jumping I fired.

I didn't look to see whether I had hit him or not. At that range there was little likelihood of missing. I bent double and slipped back to the rear of the roadster, keeping on my side of it.

Then I waited.

The girl did what I would perhaps have done in her place. She didn't shoot or move toward the place the shot had come from. She thought I had forestalled Kilcourse in using the ditch and that my next play would be to circle around behind her. To offset this, she moved around the rear of the roadster, so that she could ambush me from the side nearest Axford's car.

Thus it was that she came creeping around the corner and poked her delicately chiseled nose plunk into the muzzle of the gun that I held ready for her.

She gave a little scream.

Women aren't always reasonable: they are prone to disregard trifles like guns held upon them. So I grabbed her gun hand, which was fortunate for me. As my hand closed around the weapon, she pulled the trigger, catching a chunk of my forefinger between hammer and frame. I twisted the gun out of her hand; released my finger.

But she wasn't done yet.

With me standing there holding a gun not four inches from her body, she turned and bolted off toward where a clump of trees made a jet-black blot to the north.

When I recovered from my surprise at this amateurish procedure, I stuck both her gun and mine in my pockets, and set out after her, tearing the soles of my feet at every step.

She was trying to get over a wire fence when I caught her.

16

"STOP PLAYING, WILL you?" I said crossly, as I set the fingers of my left hand around her wrist and started to lead her back to the roadster. "This is a serious business. Don't be so childish!"

"You are hurting my arm."

I knew I wasn't hurting her arm, and I knew this girl for the direct cause of four, or perhaps five, deaths; yet I loosened my grip on her wrist until it wasn't much more than a friendly clasp. She went back willingly enough to the roadster, where, still holding her wrist, I switched on the lights.

Kilcourse lay just beneath the headlight's glare, huddled on his face, with one knee drawn up under him.

I put the girl squarely in the line of light.

"Now stand there," I said, "and behave. The first break you make, I'm going to shoot a leg out from under you," and I meant it.

I found Kilcourse's gun, pocketed it, and knelt beside him.

He was dead, with a bullet-hole above his collar-bone.

"Is he—" her mouth trembled.

"Yes."

She looked down at him, and shivered a little.

"Poor Fag," she whispered.

I've gone on record as saying that this girl was beautiful, and, standing there in the dazzling white of the headlights, she was more than that. She was a thing to start crazy thoughts even in the head of an unimaginative middle-aged thief-catcher. She was—

Anyhow, I suppose that is why I scowled at her and said:

"Yes, poor Fag, and poor Hook, and poor Tai, and poor kind of a Los Angeles bank messenger, and poor Burke," calling the roll, so far as I knew it, of men who had died loving her.

She didn't flare up. Her big grey eyes lifted, and she looked at me with a gaze that I couldn't fathom, and her lovely oval face under the mass of brown hair—which I knew was phoney—was sad.

"I suppose you do think—" she began.

But I had had enough of this; I was uncomfortable along the spine.

"Come on," I said. "We'll leave Kilcourse and the roadster here for the present."

She said nothing, but went with me to Axford's big machine, and sat in silence while I laced my shoes. I found a robe on the back seat and gave it to her.

"Better wrap this around your shoulders. The windshield is gone. It'll be cool."

She followed my suggestion without a word, but when I had edged our vehicle around the rear of the roadster, and had straightened out in the road again, going east, she laid a hand on my arm.

"Aren't we going back to the White Shack?"

"No. Redwood City—the county jail."

A mile perhaps, during which, without looking at her, I knew she was studying my rather lumpy profile. Then her hand was on my forearm again and she was leaning toward me so that her breath was warm against my cheek.

"Will you stop for a minute? There's something—some things I want to tell you."

I brought the car to a halt in a cleared space of hard soil off to one side of the road, and screwed myself a little around in the seat to face her more directly.

"Before you start," I told her, "I want you to understand that we stay here for just so long as you talk about the Pangburn affair. When you get off on any other line—then we finish our trip to Redwood City."

"Aren't you even interested in the Los Angeles affair?"

"No. That's closed. You and Hook Riordan and Tai Choon Tau and the Quarres were equally responsible for the messenger's death, even if Hook did the actual killing. Hook and the Quarres passed out the night we had our party in Turk Street. Tai was hanged last month. Now I've got you. We had enough evidence to swing the Chinese, and we've even more against you. That is done—finished—completed. If you want to tell me anything about Pangburn's death, I'll listen. Otherwise—"

I reached for the self-starter.

A pressure of her fingers on my arm stopped me.

"I do want to tell you about it," she said earnestly. "I want you to know the truth about it. You'll take me to Redwood City, I know. Don't think that I expect—that I have any foolish hopes. But I'd like you to know the truth about this thing. I don't know why I should care especially what you think, but—"

Her voice dwindled off to nothing.

17

THEN SHE BEGAN to talk very rapidly—as people talk when they fear interruptions before their stories are told—and she sat leaning slightly forward, so that her beautiful oval face was very close to mine.

"After I ran out of the Turk Street house that night—while you were struggling with Tai—my intention was to get away from San Francisco. I had a couple of thousand dollars, enough to carry me any place. Then I thought that going away would be what you people would expect me to do, and that the safest thing for me to do would be to stay right here. It isn't hard for a woman to change her appearance. I had bobbed red hair, white skin, and wore gay clothes. I simply dyed my hair, bought these transformations to make it look long, put color on my face, and bought some dark clothes. Then I took an apartment on Ashbury Avenue under the name of Jeanne Delano, and I was an altogether different person.

"But, while I knew I was perfectly safe from recognition anywhere, I felt more comfortable staying indoors for a while, and, to pass the time, I read a good deal. That's how I happened to run across Burke's book. Do you read poetry?"

I shook my head. An automobile going toward Halfmoon Bay came into sight just then—the first one we'd seen since we left the White Shack. She waited until it had passed before she went on, still talking rapidly.

"Burke wasn't a genius, of course, but there was something about some of his things that—something that got inside me.

I wrote him a little note, telling him how much I had enjoyed these things, and sent it to his publishers. A few days later I had a note from Burke, and I learned that he lived in San Francisco. I hadn't known that.

"We exchanged several notes, and then he asked if he could call, and we met. I don't know whether I was in love with him or not, even at first. I did like him, and, between the ardor of his love for me and the flattery of having a fairly well-known poet for a suitor, I really thought that I loved him. I promised to marry him.

"I hadn't told him anything about myself, though now I know that it wouldn't have made any difference to him. But I was afraid to tell him the truth, and I wouldn't lie to him, so I told him nothing.

"Then Fag Kilcourse saw me one day on the street, and knew me in spite of my new hair, complexion and clothes. Fag hadn't much brains, but he had eyes that could see through anything. I don't blame Fag. He acted according to his code. He came up to my apartment, having followed me home; and I told him that I was going to marry Burke and be a respectable house-wife. That was dumb of me. Fag was square. If I had told him that I was ribbing Burke up for a trimming, Fag would have let me alone, would have kept his hands off. But when I told him that I was through with the graft, had 'gone queer,' that made me his meat. You know how crooks are: everyone in the world is either a fellow crook or a prospective victim. So if I was no longer a crook, then Fag considered me fair game.

"He learned about Burke's family connections, and then he put it up to me—twenty thousand dollars, or he'd turn me up. He knew about the Los Angeles job, and he knew how badly

I was wanted. I was up against it then. I knew I couldn't hide from Fag or run away from him. I told Burke I had to have twenty thousand dollars. I didn't think he had that much, but I thought he could get it. Three days later he gave me a check for it. I didn't know at the time how he had raised it, but it wouldn't have mattered if I had known. I had to have it.

"But that night he told me where he got the money; that he had forged his brother-in-law's signature. He told me because, after thinking it over, he was afraid that when the forgery was discovered I would be caught with him and considered equally guilty. I'm rotten in spots, but I wasn't rotten enough to let him put himself in the pen for me, without knowing what it was all about. I told him the whole story. He didn't bat an eye. He insisted that the money be paid Kilcourse, so that I would be safe, and began to plan for my further safety.

"Burke was confident that his brother-in-law wouldn't send him over for forgery, but, to be on the safe side, he insisted that I move and change my name again and lay low until we knew how Axford was going to take it. But that night, after he had gone, I made some plans of my own. I did like Burke—I liked him too much to let him be the goat without trying to save him, and I didn't have a great deal of faith in Axford's kindness. This was the second of the month. Barring accidents, Axford wouldn't discover the forgery until he got his cancelled checks early the following month. That gave me practically a month to work in.

"The next day I drew all my money out of the bank, and sent Burke a letter, saying that I had been called to Baltimore, and I laid a clear trail to Baltimore, with baggage and letters and all, which a pal there took care of for me. Then I went down to

Joplin's and got him to put me up. I let Fag know I was there, and when he came down I told him I expected to have the money for him in a day or two.

"He came down nearly every day after that, and I stalled him from day to day, and each time it got easier. But my time was getting short. Pretty soon Burke's letters would be coming back from the phoney address I had given him, and I wanted to be on hand to keep him from doing anything foolish. And I didn't want to get in touch with him until I could give him the twenty thousand, so he could square the forgery before Axford learned of it from his cancelled checks.

"Fag was getting easier and easier to handle, but I still didn't have him where I wanted him. He wasn't willing to give up the twenty thousand dollars—which I was, of course, holding all this time—unless I'd promise to stick with him for good. And I still thought I was in love with Burke, and I didn't want to tie myself up with Fag, even for a little while.

"Then Burke saw me on the street one Sunday night. I was careless, and drove into the city in Joplin's roadster—the one back there. And, as luck would have it, Burke saw me. I told him the truth, the whole truth. And he told me that he had just hired a private detective to find me. He was like a child in some ways: it hadn't occurred to him that the sleuth would dig up anything about the money. But I knew the forged check would be found in a day or two at the most. I knew it!

"When I told Burke that he went to pieces. All his faith in his brother-in-law's forgiveness went. I couldn't leave him the way he was. He'd have babbled the whole thing to the first person he met. So I brought him back to Joplin's with me. My idea was to hold him there for a few days, until we could see how things were going. If nothing appeared in the papers about the check, then we could take it for granted that Axford had hushed the matter up, and Burke could go home and try to square himself. On the other hand, if the papers got the whole story, then Burke would have to look for a permanent hiding-place, and so would I.

"Tuesday evening's and Wednesday morning's papers were full of the news of his disappearance, but nothing was said about the check. That looked good, but we waited another day for good measure. Fag Kilcourse was in on the game by this time, of course, and I had had to pass over the twenty thousand dollars, but I still had hopes of getting it—or most of it—back, so I continued to string him along. I had a hard time keeping him off Burke, though, because he had begun to think he had some sort of right to me, and jealousy made him wicked. But I got Tin-Star to throw a scare into him, and I thought Burke was safe.

"Tonight one of Tin-Star's men came up and told us that a man named Porky Grout, who had been hanging around the place for a couple of nights, had made a couple of cracks that might mean he was interested in us. Grout was pointed out to me, and I took a chance on showing myself in the public part of the place, and sat at a table close to his. He was plain rat— as I guess you know—and in less than five minutes I had him at my table, and half an hour later I knew that he had tipped you off that Burke and I were in the White Shack. He didn't tell me all this right out, but he told me more than enough for me to guess the rest.

"I went up and told the others. Fag was for killing both Grout and Burke right away. But I talked him out of it. That wouldn't help us any, and I had Grout where he would jump in the ocean for me. I thought I had Fag convinced, but— We finally decided that Burke and I would take the roadster and leave, and that when you got here Porky Grout was to pretend he was hopped up, and point out a man and a woman—any who happened to be handy—as the ones he had taken for us. I stopped to get a cloak and gloves, and Burke went on out to the car alone—and Fag shot him. I didn't know he was going to! I wouldn't have let him! Please believe that! I wasn't as much in love with Burke as I had thought, but please believe that after all he had done for me I wouldn't have let them hurt him!

"After that it was a case of stick with the others whether I liked it or not, and I stuck. We ribbed Grout to tell you that all three of us were on the back porch when Burke was killed, and we had any number of others primed with the same story. Then you came up and recognized me. Just my luck that it had to be you—the only detective in San Francisco who knew me!

"You know the rest: how Porky Grout came up behind you and turned off the lights, and Joplin held you while we ran for the car; and then, when you closed in on us, Grout offered to stand you off while we got clear, and now...."

18

HER VOICE DIED, and she shivered a little. The robe I had given her had fallen away from her white shoulders. Whether or not it was because she was so close against my shoulder, I shivered, too. And my fingers, fumbling in my pocket for a cigarette, brought it out twisted and mashed.

"That's all there is to the part you promised to listen to," she said softly, her face turned half away. "I wanted you to know. You're a hard man, but somehow I—"

I cleared my throat, and the hand that held the mangled cigarette was suddenly steady.

"Now don't be crude, sister," I said. "Your work has been too smooth so far to be spoiled by rough stuff now."

She laughed—a brief laugh that was bitter and reckless and just a little weary, and she thrust her face still closer to mine, and the grey eyes were soft and placid.

"Little fat detective whose name I don't know"—her voice had a tired huskiness in it, and a tired mockery—"you think I am playing a part, don't you? You think I am playing for liberty. Perhaps I am. I certainly would take it if it were offered me. But— Men have thought me beautiful, and I have played with them. Women are like that. Men have loved me and, doing what I liked with them, I have found men contemptible. And then comes this little fat detective whose name I don't know, and he acts as if I were a hag—an old squaw. Can I help then being piqued into some sort of feeling for him? Women are like that. Am I so homely that any man has a right to look at me without even interest? Am I ugly?"

I shook my head.

"You're quite pretty," I said, struggling to keep my voice as casual as the words.

"You beast!" she spat, and then her smile grew gentle again. "And yet it is because of that attitude that I sit here and turn myself inside out for you. If you were to take me in your arms and hold me close to the chest that I am already leaning against, and if you were to tell me that there is no jail ahead for me just now, I would be glad, of course. But, though for a while you might hold me, you would then be only one of the men with which I am familiar: men who love and are used and are succeeded by other men. But because you do none of these things, because you are a wooden block of a man, I find myself wanting you. Would I tell you this, little fat detective, if I were playing a game?"

I grunted noncommittally, and forcibly restrained my tongue from running out to moisten my dry lips.

"I'm going to this jail tonight if you are the same hard man who has goaded me into whining love into his uncaring ears, but before that, can't I have one whole-hearted assurance that you think me a little more than 'quite pretty'? Or at least a hint that if I were not a prisoner your pulse might beat a little faster when I touch you? I'm going to this jail for a long while—perhaps to the gallows. Can't I take my vanity there not quite in tatters to keep me company? Can't you do some slight thing to keep me from the afterthought of having bleated all this out to a man who was simply bored?"

Her lids had come down half over the silver-grey eyes; her head had tilted back so far that a little pulse showed throbbing in her white throat; her lips were motionless over slightly parted teeth, as the last word had left them. My fingers went deep into the soft white flesh of her shoulders. Her head went further back, her eyes closed, one hand came up to my shoulder.

"You're beautiful as all hell!" I shouted crazily into her face, and flung her against the door.

It seemed an hour that I fumbled with starter and gears before I had the car back in the road and thundering toward the San Mateo County jail. The girl had straightened herself up in the seat again, and sat huddled within the robe I had given her. I squinted straight ahead into the wind that tore at my hair and face, and the absence of the windshield took my thoughts back to Porky Grout.

Porky Grout, whose yellowness was notorious from Seattle to San Diego, standing rigidly in the path of a charging metal monster, with an inadequate pistol in each hand. She had done that to Porky Grout—this woman beside me! She had done that to Porky Grout, and he hadn't even been human! A slimy reptile whose highest thought had been a skinful of dope had gone grimly to death that she might get away—she—this woman whose shoulders I had gripped, whose mouth had been close under mine!

I let the car out another notch, holding the road somehow.

We went through a town: a scurrying of pedestrians for safety, surprised faces staring at us, street lights glistening on the moisture the wind had whipped from my eyes. I passed blindly by the road I wanted, circled back to it, and we were out in the country again.

19

AT THE FOOT of a long, shallow hill I applied the brakes and we snapped to motionlessness.

I thrust my face close to the girl's.

"Furthermore, you are a liar!" I knew I was shouting foolishly, but I was powerless to lower my voice. "Pangburn never put Axford's name on that check. He never knew anything about it. You got in with him because you knew his brother-in-law was a millionaire. You pumped him, finding out everything he knew about his brother-in-law's account at the Golden Gate Trust. You stole Pangburn's bank book—it wasn't in his room when I searched it—and deposited the forged Axford check to his credit, knowing that under those circumstances the check wouldn't be questioned. The next day you took Pangburn into the bank, saying you were going to make a deposit. You took him in because with him standing beside you the check to which his signature had been forged wouldn't be questioned. You knew that, being a gentleman, he'd take pains not to see what you were depositing.

"Then you framed the Baltimore trip. He told the truth to me—the truth so far as he knew it. Then you met him Sunday night—maybe accidentally, maybe not. Anyway, you took him down to Joplin's, giving him some wild yarn that he would swallow and that would persuade him to stay there for a few days. That wasn't hard, since he didn't know anything about either of the twenty-thousand-dollar checks. You and your pal Kilcourse knew that if Pangburn disappeared nobody would ever know that he hadn't forged the Axford check, and nobody would ever suspect that the second check was phoney. You'd have killed him quietly, but when Porky tipped you off that I was on my way down you had to move quick—so you shot him down. That's the truth of it!" I yelled.

All this while she had watched me with wide grey eyes that were calm and tender, but now they clouded a little and a pucker of pain drew her brows together.

I yanked my head away and got the car in motion.

Just before we swept into Redwood City one of her hands came up to my forearm, rested there for a second, patted the arm twice, and withdrew.

I didn't look at her, nor, I think, did she look at me, while she was being booked. She gave her name as Jeanne Delano, and refused to make any statement until she had seen an attorney. It all took a very few minutes.

As she was being led away, she stopped and asked if she might speak privately with me.

We went together to a far corner of the room.

She put her mouth close to my ear so that her breath was warm again on my cheek, as it had been in the car, and whispered the vilest epithet of which the English language is capable.

Then she walked out to her cell.

Women, Politics & Murder

Mr. Hammett's San Francisco detective is on the job again, working on a mystery the solution of which is so simple that you'll be ashamed of yourself for not figuring it out. And take our word for it, you won't come within a thousand miles of the explanation—yet this is the most realistic and probable story in the issue.

1

A PLUMP MAID with bold green eyes and a loose, full-lipped mouth led me up two flights of steps and into an elaborately furnished boudoir, where a woman in black sat at a window. She was a thin woman of a little more than thirty; this murdered man's widow, and her face was white and haggard.

"You are from the Continental Detective Agency?" she asked before I was two steps inside the room.

"Yes."

"I want you to find my husband's murderer." Her voice was shrill, and her dark eyes had wild lights in them. "The police have done nothing. Four days, and they have done nothing. They say it was a robber, but they haven't found him. They haven't found anything!"

"But, Mrs. Gilmore," I began, not exactly tickled to death with this explosion, "you must—"

"I know! I know!" she broke in. "But they have done nothing, I tell you—nothing. I don't believe they've made the slightest effort. I don't believe they want to find h-him!"

"Him?" I asked, because she had started to say *her*. "You think it was a man?"

She bit her lip and looked away from me, out of the window to where San Francisco Bay, the distance making toys of its boats, was blue under the early afternoon sun.

"I don't know," she said hesitantly; "it might have—"

Her face spun toward me—a twitching face—and it seemed

impossible that anyone could talk so fast, hurl words out so rapidly one after the other.

"I'll tell you. You can judge for yourself. Bernard wasn't faithful to me. There was a woman who calls herself Cara Kenbrook. She wasn't the first. But I learned about her last month. We quarreled. Bernard promised to give her up. Maybe he didn't. But if he did, I wouldn't put it past her—A woman like that would do anything—anything. And down in my heart I really believe she did it!"

"And you think the police don't want to arrest her?"

"I didn't mean exactly that. I'm all unstrung, and likely to say anything. Bernard was mixed up in politics, you know; and if the police found, or thought, that politics had anything to do with his death, they might—I don't know just what I mean. I'm a nervous, broken woman, and full of crazy notions." She stretched a thin hand out to me. "Straighten this tangle out for me! Find the person who killed Bernard!"

I nodded with empty assurance, still not any too pleased with my client.

"Do you know this Kenbrook woman?" I asked.

"I've seen her on the street, and that's enough to know what sort of person she is!"

"Did you tell the police about her?"

"No-o." She looked out of the window again, and then, as I waited, she added, defensively:

"The police detectives who came to see me acted as if they thought I might have killed Bernard. I was afraid to tell them that I had cause for jealousy. Maybe I shouldn't have kept quiet about that woman, but I didn't think she had done it until afterward, when the police failed to find the murderer. Then I began to think she had done it; but I couldn't make myself go to the police and tell them that I had withheld information. I knew what they'd think. So I—You can twist it around so it'll look as if I hadn't known about the woman, can't you?"

"Possibly. Now as I understand it, your husband was shot on Pine Street, between Leavenworth and Jones, at about three o'clock Tuesday morning. That right?"

"Yes."

"Where was he going?"

"Coming home, I suppose; but I don't know where he had been. Nobody knows. The police haven't found out, if they have tried. He told me Monday evening that he had a business engagement. He was a building contractor, you know. He went out at about half-past eleven, saying he would probably be gone four or five hours."

"Wasn't that an unusual hour to be keeping a business engagement?"

"Not for Bernard. He often had men come to the house at midnight."

"Can you make any guess at all where he was going that night?"

She shook her head with emphasis.

"No. I knew nothing at all about his business affairs, and even the men in his office don't seem to know where he went that night."

That wasn't unlikely. Most of the B.F. Gilmore Construction Company's work had been on city and state contracts, and it isn't altogether unheard-of for secret conferences to go with that kind of work. Your politician-contractor doesn't always move in the open.

"How about enemies?" I asked.

"I don't know anybody that hated him enough to kill him."

"Where does this Kenbrook woman live, do you know?"

"Yes—in the Garford Apartments on Bush Street."

"Nothing you've forgotten to tell *me*, is there?" I asked, stressing the me a little.

"No, I've told you everything I know—every single thing."

2

WALKING OVER TO California Street, I shook down my memory for what I had heard here and there of Bernard Gilmore. I could remember a few things—the opposition papers had been in the habit of exposing him every election year—but none of them got me anywhere. I had known him by sight: a boisterous, red-faced man who had hammered his way up from hod-carrier to the ownership of a half-a-million-dollar business and a pretty place in local politics. "A roughneck with a manicure," somebody had called him; a man with a lot of enemies and more friends; a big, good-natured, hard-hitting rowdy.

Odds and ends of a dozen graft scandals in which he had been mixed up, without anybody ever really getting anything on him, flitted through my head as I rode downtown on the too-small outside seat of a cable-car. Then there had been some talk of a bootlegging syndicate of which he was supposed to be the head....

I left the car at Kearny Street and walked over to the Hall of Justice. In the detectives' assembly-room I found O'Gar, the detective-sergeant in charge of the Homicide Detail: a squat man of fifty who goes in for wide-brimmed hats of the movie-sheriff sort, but whose little blue eyes and bullet head aren't handicapped by the trick headgear.

"I want some dope on the Gilmore killing," I told him.

"So do I," he came back. "But if you'll come along I'll tell you what little I know while I'm eating. I ain't had lunch yet."

Safe from eavesdroppers in the clatter of a Sutter Street lunchroom, the detective-sergeant leaned over his clam chowder and told me what he knew about the murder, which wasn't much.

"One of the boys, Kelly, was walking his beat early Tuesday morning, coming down the Jones Street hill from California Street to Pine. It was about three o'clock—no fog or nothing—a clear night. Kelly's within maybe twenty feet of Pine Street when he hears a shot. He whisks around the corner, and there's a man dying on the north sidewalk of Pine Street, halfway between Jones and Leavenworth. Nobody else is in sight. Kelly runs up to the man and finds it's Gilmore. Gilmore dies before he can say a word. The doctors say he was knocked down and then shot; because there's a bruise on his forehead, and the bullet slanted upward in his chest. See what I mean? He was lying on his back when the bullet hit him, with his feet pointing toward the gun it came from. It was a .38."

"Any money on him?"

O'Gar fed himself two spoons of chowder and nodded.

"Six hundred smacks, a coupla diamonds and a watch. Nothing touched."

"What was he doing on Pine Street at that time in the morning?"

"Damned if I know, brother. Chances are he was going home, but we can't find out where he'd been. Don't even know what direction he was walking in when he was knocked over. He was lying across the sidewalk with his feet to the curb; but that don't mean nothing—he could of turned around three or four times after he was hit."

"All apartment buildings in that block, aren't there?"

"Uh-huh. There's an alley or two running off from the south side; but Kelly says he could see the mouths of both alleys when the shot was fired—before he turned the corner—and nobody got away through them."

"Reckon somebody who lives in that block did the shooting?" I asked.

O'Gar tilted his bowl, scooped up the last drops of the chowder, put them in his mouth, and grunted.

"Maybe. But we got nothing to show that Gilmore knew anybody in that block."

"Many people gather around afterward?"

"A few. There's always people on the street to come running if anything happens. But Kelly says there wasn't anybody that looked wrong—just the ordinary night crowd. The boys gave the neighborhood a combing, but didn't turn up anything."

"Any cars around?"

"Kelly says there wasn't, that he didn't see any, and couldn't of missed seeing it if there'd been one."

"What do you think?" I asked.

He got to his feet, glaring at me.

"I don't think," he said disagreeably; "I'm a police detective."

I knew by that that somebody had been panning him for not finding the murderer.

"I have a line on a woman," I told him. "Want to come along and talk to her with me?"

"I want to," he growled, "but I can't. I got to be in court this afternoon—in half an hour."

3

IN THE VESTIBULE of the Garford Apartments, I pressed the button tagged Miss Cara Kenbrook several times before the door clicked open. Then I mounted a flight of stairs and walked down a hall to her door. It was opened presently by a tall girl of twenty-three or -four in a black and white crepe dress.

"Miss Cara Kenbrook?"

"Yes."

I gave her a card—one of those that tell the truth about me. "I'd like to ask you a few questions; may I come in?"

"Do."

Languidly she stepped aside for me to enter, closed the door behind me, and led me back into a living-room that was littered with newspapers, cigarettes in all stages of consumption from unlighted freshness to cold ash, and miscellaneous articles of feminine clothing. She made room for me on a chair by dumping off a pair of pink silk stockings and a hat, and herself sat on some magazines that occupied another chair.

"I'm interested in Bernard Gilmore's death," I said, watching her face.

It wasn't a beautiful face, although it should have been. Everything was there—perfect features; smooth, white skin; big, almost enormous, brown eyes—but the eyes were dead-dull, and the face was as empty of expression as a china doorknob, and what I said didn't change it.

"Bernard Gilmore," she said without interest. "Oh, yes."

"You and he were pretty close friends, weren't you?" I asked, puzzled by her blankness.

"We had been—yes."

"What do you mean by *had been?*"

She pushed back a lock of her short-cut brown hair with a lazy hand.

"I gave him the air last week," she said casually, as if speaking of something that had happened years ago.

"When was the last time you saw him?"

"Last week—Monday, I think—a week before he was killed."

"Was that the time when you broke off with him?"

"Yes."

"Have a row, or part friends?"

"Not exactly either. I just told him that I was through with him."

"How did he take it?"

"It didn't break his heart. I guess he'd heard the same thing before."

"Where were you the night he was killed?"

"At the Coffee Cup, eating and dancing with friends until about one o'clock. Then I came home and went to bed."

"Why did you split with Gilmore?"

"Couldn't stand his wife."

"Huh?"

"She was a nuisance." This without the faintest glint of either annoyance or humor. "She came here one night and raised a racket; so I told Bernie that if he couldn't keep her away from me he'd have to find another playmate."

"Have you any idea who might have killed him?" I asked.

"Not unless it was his wife—these excitable women are always doing silly things."

"If you had given her husband up, what reason would she have for killing him, do you think?"

"I'm sure I don't know," she replied with complete indifference. "But I'm not the only girl that Bernie ever looked at."

"Think there were others, do you? Know anything, or are you just guessing?"

"I don't know any names," she said, "but I'm not just guessing."

I let that go at that and switched back to Mrs. Gilmore, wondering if this girl could be full of dope.

"What happened the night his wife came here?"

"Nothing but that. She followed Bernie here, rang the bell, rushed past me when I opened the door, and began to cry and call Bernie names. Then she started on me, and I told him that if he didn't take her away I'd hurt her, so he took her home."

Admitting I was licked for the time, I got up and moved to the door. I couldn't do anything with this baby just now. I didn't think she was telling the whole truth, but on the other hand it wasn't reasonable to believe that anybody would lie so woodenly—with so little effort to be plausible.

"I may be back later," I said as she let me out.

"All right."

Her manner didn't even suggest that she hoped I wouldn't.

4

FROM THIS UNSATISFACTORY interview I went to the scene of the killing, only a few blocks away, to get a look at the neighborhood. I found the block just as I had remembered it and as O'Gar had described it: lined on both sides by apartment buildings, with two blind alleys—one of which was dignified with a name, Touchard Street—running from the south side.

The murder was four days old; I didn't waste any time snooping around the vicinity; but, after strolling the length of the block, boarded a Hyde Street car, transferred at California Street, and went up to see Mrs. Gilmore again. I was curious to know why she hadn't told me about her call on Cara Kenbrook.

The same plump maid who had admitted me earlier in the afternoon opened the door.

"Mrs. Gilmore is not at home," she said. "But I think she'll be back in half an hour or so."

"I'll wait," I decided.

The maid took me into the library, an immense room on the second floor, with barely enough books in it to give it that name. She switched on a light—the windows were too heavily curtained to let in much daylight—crossed to the door, stopped, moved over to straighten some books on a shelf, looked at me with a half-questioning, half-inviting look in her green eyes, started for the door again, and halted.

By that time I knew she wanted to say something, and needed encouragement. I leaned back in my chair and grinned at her, and decided I had made a mistake—the smile into which her slack lips curved held more coquetry than anything else. She came over to me, walking with an exaggerated swing of the hips, and stood close in front of me.

"What's on your mind?" I asked.

"Suppose—suppose a person knew something that nobody else knew; what would it be worth to them?"

"That," I stalled, "would depend on how valuable it was."

"Suppose I knew who killed the boss?" She bent her face close down to mine, and spoke in a husky whisper. "What would that be worth?"

"The newspapers say that one of Gilmore's clubs has offered a thousand-dollar reward. You'd get that."

Her green eyes went greedy, and then suspicious.

"If *you* didn't."

I shrugged. I knew she'd go through with it—whatever it was—now; so I didn't even explain to her that the Continental doesn't touch rewards, and doesn't let its hired men touch them.

"I'll give you my word," I said; "but you'll have to use your own judgment about trusting me."

She licked her lips.

"You're a good fellow, I guess. I wouldn't tell the police, because I know they'd beat me out of the money. But you look like I can trust you." She leered into my face. "I used to have a gentleman friend who was the very image of you, and he was the grandest—"

"Better speak your piece before somebody comes in," I suggested.

She shot a look at the door, cleared her throat, licked her loose mouth again, and dropped on one knee beside my chair.

"I was coming home late Monday night—the night the boss was killed—and was standing in the shadows saying good night to my friend, when the boss came out of the house and walked down the street. And he had hardly got to the corner, when she—Mrs. Gilmore—came out, and went down the street after him. Not trying to catch up with him, you understand; but following him. What do you think of that?"

"What do *you* think of it?"

"*I* think that she finally woke up to the fact that all of her Bernie's dates didn't have anything to do with the building business."

"Do you know that they didn't?"

"Do I know it? I knew that man! He liked 'em—liked 'em all." She smiled into my face, a smile that suggested all evil. "I found *that* out soon after I first came here."

"Do you know when Mrs. Gilmore came back that night—what time?"

"Yes," she said; "at half-past three."

"Sure?"

"Absolutely! After I got undressed I got a blanket and sat at the head of the front stairs. My room's in the rear of the top floor. I wanted to see if they came home together, and if there was a fight. After she came in alone I went back to my room, and it was just twenty-five minutes to four then. I looked at my alarm clock."

"Did you see her when she came in?"

"Just the top of her head and shoulders when she turned toward her room at the landing."

"What's your name?" I asked.

"Lina Best."

"All right, Lina," I told her. "If this is the goods I'll see that you collect on it. Keep your eyes open, and if anything else turns up you can get in touch with me at the Continental office. Now you'd better beat it, so nobody will know we've had our heads together."

Alone in the library, I cocked an eye at the ceiling and considered the information Lina Best had given me. But I soon gave that up—no use trying to guess at things that will work out for themselves in a while. I found a book, and spent the next half-hour reading about a sweet young she-chump and a big strong he-chump and all their troubles.

Then Mrs. Gilmore came in, apparently straight from the street.

I got up and closed the doors behind her, while she watched me with wide eyes.

"Mrs. Gilmore," I said, when I faced her again, "why didn't you tell me that you followed your husband the night he was killed?"

"That's a lie!" she cried; but there was no truth in her voice. "That's a lie!"

"Don't you think you're making a mistake?" I urged. "Don't you think you'd better tell me the whole thing?"

She opened her mouth, but only a dry sobbing sound came out; and she began to sway with a hysterical rocking motion, the fingers of one black-gloved hand plucking at her lower lip, twisting and pulling it.

I stepped to her side and set her down in the chair I had been sitting in, making foolish clucking sounds—meant to soothe her—with my tongue. A disagreeable ten minutes—and gradually she pulled herself together; her eyes lost their glassiness, and she stopped clawing at her mouth.

"I did follow him." It was a hoarse whisper, barely audible.

Then she was out of the chair, kneeling, with arms held up to me, and her voice was a thin scream.

"But I didn't kill him! I didn't! Please believe that I didn't!"

I picked her up and put her back in the chair.

"I didn't say you did. Just tell me what did happen."

"I didn't believe him when he said he had a business engagement," she moaned. "I didn't trust him. He had lied to me before. I followed him to see if he went to that woman's rooms."

"Did he?"

"No. He went into an apartment house on Pine Street, in the block where he was killed. I don't know exactly which house it was—I was too far behind him to make sure. But I saw him go up the steps and into one—near the middle of the block."

"And then what did you do?"

"I waited, hiding in a dark doorway across the street. I knew the woman's apartment was on Bush Street, but I thought she might have moved, or be meeting him here. I waited a long time, shivering and trembling. It was chilly and I was frightened—afraid somebody would come into the vestibule where I was. But I made myself stay. I wanted to see if he came out alone, or if that woman came out. I had a right to do it—he had deceived me before.

"It was terrible, horrible—crouching there in the dark—cold and scared. Then—it must have been about half-past two—I couldn't stand it any longer. I decided to telephone the woman's apartment and find out if she were home. I went down to an all-night lunchroom on Ellis Street and called her up."

"Was she home?"

"No! I tried for fifteen minutes, or maybe longer, but nobody answered the phone. So I knew she was in that Pine Street building."

"And what did you do then?"

"I went back there, determined to wait until he came out. I walked up Jones Street. When I was between Bush and Pine I heard a shot. I thought it was a noise made by an automobile then, but now I know that it was the shot that killed Bernie.

"When I reached the corner of Pine and Jones, I could see a policeman bending over Bernie on the sidewalk, and I saw people gathering around. I didn't know then that it was Bernie lying on the sidewalk. In the dark and at that distance I couldn't even see whether it was a man or a woman.

"I was afraid that Bernard would come out to see what was going on, or look out of a window, and discover me; so I didn't go down that way. I was afraid to stay in the neighborhood now, for fear the police would ask me what I was doing loitering in the street at three in the morning—and have it come out that I had been following my husband. So I kept on walking up Jones Street, to California, and then straight home."

"And then what?" I led her on.

"Then I went to bed. I didn't go to sleep—lay there worrying over Bernie; but still not thinking it was he I had seen lying in the street. At nine o'clock that morning two police detectives came and told me Bernie had been killed. They questioned me so sharply that I was afraid to tell them the whole truth. If they had known I had reason for being jealous, and had followed my husband that night, they would have accused me of shooting him. And what could I have done? Everybody would have thought me guilty.

"So I didn't say anything about the woman. I thought they'd find the murderer, and then everything would be all right. I didn't think she had done it then, or I would have told you the whole thing the first time you were here. But four days went by without the police finding the murderer, and I began to think they suspected me! It was terrible! I couldn't go to them and confess that I had lied to them, and I was sure that the woman had killed him and that the police had failed to suspect her because I hadn't told them about her.

"So I employed you. But I was afraid to tell even you the whole truth. I thought that if I just told you there had been another woman and who she was, you could do the rest without having to know that I had followed Bernie that night. I was afraid *you* would think I had killed him, and would turn me over to the police if I told you everything. And now you *do* believe it! And you'll have me arrested! And they'll hang me! I know it! I know it!"

She began to rock crazily from side to side in her chair.

"Sh-h-h," I soothed her. "You're not arrested yet. Sh-h-h."

I didn't know what to make of her story. The trouble with these nervous, hysterical women is that you can't possibly tell when they're lying and when telling the truth unless you have outside evidence—half of the time they themselves don't know.

"When you heard the shot," I went on when she had quieted down a bit, "you were walking north on Jones, between Bush and Pine? You could see the corner of Pine and Jones?"

"Yes—clearly."

"See anybody?"

"No—not until I reached the corner and looked down Pine Street. Then I saw a policeman bending over Bernie, and two men walking toward them."

"Where were the two men?"

"On Pine Street east of Jones. They didn't have hats on—as if they had come out of a house when they heard the shot."

"Any automobiles in sight either before or after you heard the shot?"

"I didn't see or hear any."

"I have some more questions, Mrs. Gilmore," I said; "but I'm in a hurry now. Please don't go out until you hear from me again."

"I won't," she promised; "but—"

I didn't have any answers for anybody's questions, so I ducked my head and left the library.

Near the street door Lina Best appeared out of a shadow, her eyes bright and inquisitive.

"Stick around," I said without any meaning at all, stepped around her, and went on out into the street.

5

I RETURNED THEN to the Garford Apartments, walking, because I had a lot of things to arrange in my mind before I faced Cara Kenbrook again. And, even though I walked slowly, they weren't all exactly filed in alphabetical order when I got there. She had changed the black and white dress for a plush-like gown of bright green, but her empty doll's face hadn't changed.

"Some more questions," I explained when she opened her door.

She admitted me without word or gesture, and led me back into the room where we had talked before.

"Miss Kenbrook," I asked, standing beside the chair she had offered me, "why did you tell me you were home in bed when Gilmore was killed?"

"Because it's so." Without the flicker of a lash.

"And you wouldn't answer the doorbell?"

I had to twist the facts to make my point. Mrs. Gilmore had phoned, but I couldn't afford to give this girl a chance to shunt the blame for her failure to answer off on central.

She hesitated for a split second.

"No—because I didn't hear it."

One cool article, this baby! I couldn't figure her. I didn't know then, and I don't know now, whether she was the owner of the world's best poker face or was just naturally stupid. But whichever she was, she was thoroughly and completely it!

I stopped trying to guess, and got on with my probing.

"And you wouldn't answer the phone either?"

"It didn't ring—or not enough to awaken me."

I chuckled—an artificial chuckle—because central could have been ringing the wrong number. However….

"Miss Kenbrook," I lied, "your phone rang at 2:30 and at 2:40 that morning. And your doorbell rang almost continually from about 2:50 until after 3:00."

"Perhaps," she said; "but I wonder who'd be trying to get me at that hour."

"You didn't hear either?"

"No."

"But you were here?"

"Yes—who was it?" carelessly.

"Get your hat," I bluffed, "and I'll show them to you down at headquarters."

She glanced down at the green gown and walked toward an open bedroom door.

"I suppose I'd better get a cloak, too," she said.

"Yes," I advised her; "and bring your toothbrush."

She turned around then and looked at me, and for a moment it seemed that some sort of expression—surprise maybe—was about to come into her big brown eyes; but none actually came. The eyes stayed dull and empty.

"You mean you're arresting me?"

"Not exactly. But if you stick to your story about being home in bed at 3:00 last Tuesday morning I can promise you you *will* be arrested. If I were you I'd think up another story while we're riding down to the Hall of Justice."

She left the doorway slowly and came back into the room, as far as a chair that stood between us, put her hands on its back, and leaned over it to look at me. For perhaps a minute neither of us spoke—just stood there staring at each other, while I tried to keep my face as expressionless as hers.

"Do you really think," she asked at last, "that I wasn't here when Bernie was killed?"

"I'm a busy man, Miss Kenbrook." I put all the certainty I could fake into my voice. "If you want to stick to your funny story, it's all right with me. But please don't expect me to stand here and argue about it. Get your hat and cloak."

She shrugged, and came around the chair on which she had been leaning.

"I suppose you *do* know something," she said, sitting down. "Well, it's tough on Stan, but women and children first."

My ears twitched at the name *Stan*, but I didn't interrupt her.

"I *was* in the Coffee Cup until one o'clock," she was saying, her voice still flat and emotionless. "And I *did* come home afterward. I'd been drinking *vino* all evening, and it always makes me blue. So after I came home I got to worrying over things. Since Bernie and I split, finances haven't been so good. I took stock that night—or morning—and found only four dollars in my purse. The rent was due, and the world looked pretty damned blue.

"Half-lit on Dago wine as I was, I decided to run over and see Stan, tell him all my troubles, and make a touch. Stan is a good egg and he's always willing to go the limit for me. Sober, I wouldn't have gone to see him at three in the morning; but it seemed a perfectly sensible thing to do at the time.

"It's only a few minutes' walk from here to Stan's. I went down Bush Street to Leavenworth, and up Leavenworth to Pine. I was in the middle of that last block when Bernie was shot—I heard it. And when I turned the corner into Pine Street I saw a copper bending over a man on the pavement right in front of Stan's. I hesitated for a couple of minutes, standing in the shadow of a pole, until three or four men had gathered around the man on the sidewalk. Then I went over.

"It was Bernie. And just as I got there I heard the copper tell one of the men that he had been shot. It was an awful shock to me. You know how things like that will hit you!"

I nodded; though God knows there was nothing in this girl's face, manner, or voice to suggest shock. She might have been talking about the weather.

"Dumfounded, not knowing what to do," she went on, "I didn't even stop. I went on, passing as close to Bernie as I am to you now, and rang Stan's bell. He let me in. He had been half-undressed when I rang. His rooms are in the rear of the building, and he hadn't heard the shot, he said. He didn't know Bernie had been killed until I told him. It sort of knocked the wind out of him. He said Bernie had been there—in Stan's rooms—since midnight, and had just left.

"Stan asked me what I was doing there, and I told him my tale of woe. That was the first time Stan knew that Bernie and I were so thick. I met Bernie through Stan, but Stan didn't know we had got so chummy.

"Stan was worried for fear it would come out that Bernie had been to see him that night, because it would make a lot of trouble for him—some sort of shady deal they had on, I guess. So he didn't go out to see Bernie. That's about all there is to it. I got some money from Stan, and stayed in his rooms until the police had cleared out of the neighborhood; because neither of us wanted to get mixed up in anything. Then I came home.

That's straight—on the level."

"Why didn't you get this off your chest before?" I demanded, knowing the answer.

It came.

"I was afraid. Suppose I told about Bernie throwing me down, and said I was close to him—a block or so away—when he was killed, and was half-full of vino? The first thing everybody would have said was that I had shot him! I'd lie about it still if I thought you'd believe me."

"So Bernie was the one who broke off, and not you?"

"Oh, yes," she said lightly.

6

I LIT A Fatima and breathed smoke in silence for a while, and the girl sat placidly watching me.

Here I had two women—neither normal. Mrs. Gilmore was hysterical, abnormally nervous. This girl was dull, subnormal. One was the dead man's wife; the other his mistress; and each with reason for believing she had been thrown down for the other. Liars, both; and both finally confessing that they had been near the scene of the crime at the time of the crime, though neither admitted seeing the other. Both, by their own accounts, had been at that time even further from normal than usual—Mrs. Gilmore filled with jealousy; Cara Kenbrook half-drunk.

What was the answer? Either could have killed Gilmore; but hardly both—unless they had formed some sort of crazy partnership, and in that event—

Suddenly all the facts I had gathered—true and false—clicked together in my head. I had the answer—the one simple, satisfying answer!

I grinned at the girl, and set about filling in the gaps in my solution.

"Who is Stan?" I asked.

"Stanley Tennant—he has something to do with the city."

Stanley Tennant. I knew him by reputation, a—

A key rattled in the hall door.

The hall door opened and closed, and a man's footsteps came toward the open doorway of the room in which we were. A tall, broad-shouldered man in tweeds filled the doorway—a ruddy-faced man of thirty-five or so, whose appearance of athletic blond wholesomeness was marred by close-set eyes of an indistinct blue.

Seeing me, he stopped—a step inside the room.

"Hello, Stan!" the girl said lightly. "This gentleman is from the Continental Detective Agency. I've just emptied myself to him about Bernie. Tried to stall him at first, but it was no good."

The man's vague eyes switched back and forth between the girl and me. Around the pale irises his eyeballs were pink.

He straightened his shoulders and smiled too jovially.

"And what conclusion have you come to?" he inquired.

The girl answered for me.

"I've already had *my* invitation to take a ride."

Tennant bent forward. With an unbroken swing of his arms, he swept a chair up from the floor into my face. Not much force behind it, but quick.

I went back against the wall, fending off the chair with both arms—threw it aside—and looked into the muzzle of a nick-eled revolver.

A table drawer stood open—the drawer from which he had grabbed the gun while I was busy with the chair. The revolver, I noticed, was of .38 caliber.

"Now," his voice was thick, like a drunk's, "turn around."

I turned my back to him, felt a hand moving over my body, and my gun was taken away.

"All right," he said, and I faced him again.

He stepped back to the girl's side, still holding the nick-el-plated revolver on me. My own gun wasn't in sight—in his pocket perhaps. He was breathing noisily, and his eyeballs had gone from pink to red. His face, too, was red, with veins bulging in the forehead.

"You know me?" he snapped.

"Yes, I know you. You're Stanley Tennant, assistant city engineer, and your record is none too lovely." I chattered away on the theory that conversation is always somehow to the advantage of the man who is looking into the gun. "You're supposed to be the lad who supplied the regiment of well-trained witnesses who turned last year's investigation of graft charges against the engineer's office into a comedy. Yes, Mr. Tennant, I know you. You're the answer to why Gilmore was so lucky in landing city contracts with bids only a few dollars beneath his competitors.' Yes, Mr. Tennant, I know you. You're the bright boy who—"

I had a lot more to tell him, but he cut me off.

"That will do out of you!" he yelled. "Unless you want me to knock a corner off your head with this gun."

Then he addressed the girl, not taking his eyes from me.

"Get up, Cara."

She got out of her chair and stood beside him. His gun was in his right hand, and that side was toward her. He moved around to the other side.

The fingers of his left hand hooked themselves inside of the girl's green gown where it was cut low over the swell of her breasts. His gun never wavered from me. He jerked his left hand, ripping her gown down to the waistline.

"*He* did that, Cara," Tennant said.

She nodded.

His fingers slid inside of the flesh-colored undergarment that was now exposed, and he tore that as he had torn the gown.

"*He* did that."

She nodded again.

His bloodshot eyes darted little measuring glances at her face—swift glances that never kept his eyes from me for the flash of time I would have needed to tie into him.

Then—eyes and gun on me—he smashed his left fist into the girl's blank white face.

One whimper—low and not drawn out—came from her as she went down in a huddle against the wall. Her face— well, there wasn't *much* change in it. She looked dumbly up at Tennant from where she had fallen.

"*He* did that," Tennant was saying.

She nodded, got up from the floor, and returned to her chair.

"Here's our story." The man talked rapidly, his eyes alert on me. "Gilmore was never in my rooms in his life, Cara, and neither were you. The night he was killed you were home shortly after one o'clock, and stayed there. You were sick— probably from the wine you had been drinking—and called a doctor. His name is Howard. I'll see that he's fixed. He got here at 2:30 and stayed until 3:30.

"Today, this gumshoe, learning that you had been intimate with Gilmore, came here to question you. He knew you hadn't killed Gilmore, but he made certain suggestions to you—you can play them up as strong as you like; maybe say that he's been annoying you for months—and when you turned him down he threatened to frame you.

"You refused to have anything to do with him, and he grabbed you, tearing your clothes, and bruising your face when you resisted. I happened to come along then, having an engage- ment with you, and heard you scream. Your front door was unlocked, so I rushed in, pulled this fellow away, and disarmed him. Then we held him until the police—whom we will phone for—came. Got that?"

"Yes, Stan."

"Good! Now listen: When the police get here this fellow will spill all he knows, of course, and the chances are that all three of us will be taken in. That's why I want you to know what's what right now. I ought to have enough pull to get you and me out on bail tonight, or, if worst comes to worst, to see that my lawyer gets to me tonight—so I can arrange for the witnesses we'll need. Also I ought to be able to fix it so our little fat friend will be held for a day or two, and not allowed to see anybody until late tomorrow—which will give us a good start on him. I don't know how much he knows, but between your story and the stories of a couple of other smart little ladies I have in mind, I'll fix him up with a rep that will keep any jury in the world from ever believing him about anything."

"How do you like that?" he asked me, triumphantly.

"You big clown," I laughed at him, "I think it's funny!"

But I didn't really think so. In spite of what I thought I knew about Gilmore's murder—in spite of my simple, satisfactory solution—something was crawling up my back, my knees felt jerky, and my hands were wet with sweat. I had had people try to frame me before—no detective stays in the business long without having it happen—but I had never got used to it. There's a peculiar deadliness about the thing—especially if you know how erratic juries can be—that makes your flesh crawl, no matter how safe your judgment tells you you are.

"Phone the police," Tennant told the girl; "and for God's sake keep your story straight!"

As he tried to impress that necessity on the girl his eyes left me.

I was perhaps five feet from him and his level gun.

A jump—not straight at him—off to one side—put me close.

The gun roared under my arm. I was surprised not to feel the bullet. It seemed that he *must* have hit me.

There wasn't a second shot.

I looped my right fist over as I jumped. It landed when I landed. It took him too high—up on the cheekbone—but it rocked him back a couple of steps.

I didn't know what had happened to his gun. It wasn't in his hand any more. I didn't stop to look for it. I was busy, crowding him back—not letting him set himself—staying close to him—driving at him with both hands.

He was a head taller than I, and had longer arms, but he wasn't any heavier or stronger. I suppose he hit me now and then as I hammered him across the room. He must have. But I didn't feel anything.

I worked him into a corner. Jammed him back in a corner with his legs cramped under him—which didn't give him much leverage to hit from. I got my left arm around his body, holding him where I wanted him. And I began to throw my right fist into him.

I liked that. His belly was flabby, and it got softer every time I hit it. I hit it often.

He was chopping at my face, but by digging my nose into his chest and holding it there I kept my beauty from being altogether ruined. Meanwhile I threw my right fist into him.

Then I became aware that Cara Kenbrook was moving around behind me; and I remembered the revolver that had fallen somewhere when I had charged Tennant. I didn't like that; but there was nothing I could do about it—except put more weight in my punches. My own gun, I thought, was in one of his pockets. But neither of us had time to hunt for it now.

Tennant's knees sagged the next time I hit him.

Once more, I said to myself, and then I'll step back, let him have one on the button, and watch him fall.

But I didn't get that far.

Something that I knew was the missing revolver struck me on the top of the head. An ineffectual blow—not clean enough to stun me—but it took the steam out of my punches.

Another.

They weren't hard, these taps, but to hurt a skull with a hunk of metal you don't have to hit it hard.

I tried to twist away from the next bump, and failed. Not only failed, but let Tennant wiggle away from me.

That was the end.

I wheeled on the girl just in time to take another rap on the head, and then one of Tennant's fists took me over the ear.

I went down in one of those falls that get pugs called quitters—my eyes were open, my mind was alive, but my legs and arms wouldn't lift me up from the floor.

Tennant took my own gun out of a pocket, and with it held on me, sat down in a Morris chair, to gasp for the air I had pounded out of him. The girl sat in another chair; and I, finding I could manage it, sat up in the middle of the floor and looked at them.

Tennant spoke, still panting.

"This is fine—all the signs of a struggle we need to make our story good!"

"If they don't believe you were in a fight," I suggested sourly, pressing my aching head with both hands, "you can strip and show them your little tummy."

"And you can show them this!"

He leaned down and split my lip with a punch that spread me on my back.

Anger brought my legs to life. I got up on them. Tennant moved around behind the Morris chair. My black gun was steady in his hand.

"Go easy," he warned me. "My story will work if I have to kill you—maybe work better." That was sense. I stood still.

"Phone the police, Cara," he ordered.

She went out of the room, closing the door behind her; and all I could hear of her talk was a broken murmur.

7

TEN MINUTES LATER three uniformed policemen arrived. All three knew Tennant, and they treated him with respect. Tennant reeled off the story he and the girl had cooked up, with a few changes to take care of the shot that had been fired from the nickeled gun and our rough-house. She nodded her head vigorously whenever a policeman looked at her. Tennant turned both guns over to the white-haired sergeant in charge.

I didn't argue, didn't deny anything, but told the sergeant:

"I'm working with Detective-Sergeant O'Gar on a job. I want to talk to him over the phone and then I want you to take all three of us down to the detective bureau."

Tennant objected to that, of course; not because he expected to gain anything, but on the off-chance that he might. The white-haired sergeant looked from one of us to the other in puzzlement. Me, with my skinned face and split lip; Tennant, with a red lump under one eye where my first wallop had landed; and the girl, with most of the clothes above the waistline ripped off and a bruised cheek.

"It has a queer look, this thing," the sergeant decided aloud; "and I shouldn't wonder but what the detective bureau was the place for the lot of you."

One of the patrolmen went into the hall with me, and I got O'Gar on the phone at his home. It was nearly ten o'clock by now, and he was preparing for bed.

"Cleaning up the Gilmore murder," I told him. "Meet me at

the Hall. Will you get hold of Kelly, the patrolman who found Gilmore, and bring him down there? I want him to look at some people."

"I will that," O'Gar promised, and I hung up.

The "wagon" in which the three policemen had answered Cara Kenbrook's call carried us down to the Hall of Justice, where we all went into the captain of detectives' office. McTighe, a lieutenant, was on duty.

I knew McTighe, and we were on pretty good terms; but I wasn't an influence in local politics, and Tennant was. I don't mean that McTighe would have knowingly helped Tennant frame me; but with me stacked up against the assistant city engineer, I knew who would get the benefit of any doubt there might be.

My head was thumping and roaring just now, with knots all over it where the girl had beaned me. I sat down, kept quiet, and nursed my head while Tennant and Cara Kenbrook, with a lot of details that they had not wasted on the uniformed men, told their tale and showed their injuries.

Tennant was talking—describing the terrible scene that had met his eyes when, drawn by the girl's screams, he had rushed into her apartment—when O'Gar came into the office. He recognized Tennant with a lifted eyebrow, and came over to sit beside me.

"What the hell is all this?" he muttered.

"A lovely mess," I whispered back. "Listen—in that nickel gun on the desk there's an empty shell. Get it for me."

He scratched his head doubtfully, listened to the next few words of Tennant's yarn, glanced at me out of the corner of his eye, and then went over to the desk and picked up the revolver.

McTighe looked at him—a sharp, questioning look.

"Something on the Gilmore killing," the detective-sergeant said, breaking the gun.

The lieutenant started to speak, changed his mind, and O'Gar brought the shell over and handed it to me.

"Thanks," I said, putting it in my pocket. "Now listen to my friend there. It's a good act, if you like it."

Tennant was winding up his history.

"… Naturally a man who tried a thing like that on an unprotected woman would be yellow; so it wasn't very hard to handle him after I got his gun away from him. I hit him a couple of times, and he quit—begging me to stop, getting down on his knees. Then we called the police."

McTighe looked at me with eyes that were cold and hard. Tennant had made a believer of him, and not only of him—the police-sergeant and his two men were glowering at me. I suspected that even O'Gar—with whom I had been through a dozen storms—would have been half-convinced if the engineer hadn't added the neat touches about my kneeling.

"Well, what have *you* got to say?" McTighe challenged me in a tone which suggested that it didn't make much difference what I said.

"I've got nothing to say about this dream," I said shortly. "I'm interested in the Gilmore murder—not in this stuff." I turned to O'Gar. "Is the patrolman here?"

The detective-sergeant went to the door, and called: "Oh, Kelly!"

Kelly came in—a big, straight-standing man, with iron-gray hair and an intelligent fat face.

"You found Gilmore's body?" I asked.

"I did."

I pointed at Cara Kenbrook.

"Ever see her before?"

His gray eyes studied her carefully.

"Not that I remember," he answered.

"Did she come up the street while you were looking at Gilmore, and go into the house he was lying in front of?"

"She did not."

I took out the empty shell O'Gar had got for me, and chucked it down on the desk in front of the patrolman.

"Kelly," I asked, *"why did you kill Gilmore?"*

Kelly's right hand went under his coat-tail at his hip.

I jumped for him.

Somebody grabbed me by the neck. Somebody else piled on my back. McTighe aimed a big fist at my face, but it missed. My legs had been suddenly kicked from under me, and I went down hard with men all over me.

When I was yanked to my feet again, big Kelly stood straight up by the desk, weighing his service revolver in his hand. His clear eyes met mine, and he laid the weapon on the desk. Then he unfastened his shield and put it with the gun.

"It was an accident," he said simply.

By this time the birds who had been manhandling me woke up to the fact that maybe they were missing part of the play— that maybe I wasn't a maniac. Hands dropped off me; and presently everybody was listening to Kelly.

He told his story with unhurried evenness, his eyes never wavering or clouding. A deliberate man, though unlucky.

"I was walkin' my beat that night, an' as I turned the corner of Jones into Pine I saw a man jump back from the steps of a buildin' into the vestibule. A burglar, I thought, an' cat-footed it down there. It was a dark vestibule, an' deep, an' I saw somethin' that looked like a man in it, but I wasn't sure.

" 'Come out o' there!' I called, but there was no answer. I took my gun in my hand an' started up the steps. I saw him move just then, comin' out. An' then my foot slipped. It was worn smooth, the bottom step, an' my foot slipped. I fell forward, the gun went off, an' the bullet hit him. He had come out a ways by then, an' when the bullet hit him he toppled over frontwise, tumblin' down the steps onto the sidewalk.

"When I looked at him I saw it was Gilmore. I knew him to say 'howdy' to, an' he knew me—which is why he must o' ducked out of sight when he saw me comin' around the corner. He didn't want me to see him comin' out of a buildin' where I knew Mr. Tennant lived, I suppose, thinkin' I'd put two an' two together, an' maybe talk.

"I don't say that I did the right thing by lyin', but it didn't hurt anybody. It was an accident; but he was a man with a lot of friends up in high places, an'—accident or no—I stood a good chance of bein' broke, an' maybe sent over for a while. So I told my story the way you people know it. I couldn't say I'd seen anything suspicious without maybe puttin' the blame on some innocent party, an' I didn't want that. I'd made up my mind that if anybody was arrested for the murder, an' things looked bad for them, I'd come out an' say I'd done it. Home, you'll find a confession all written out—written out in case somethin' happened to me—so nobody else'd ever be blamed.

"That's why I had to say I'd never seen the lady here. I did see her—saw her go into the buildin' that night—the buildin' Gilmore had come out of. But I couldn't say so without makin' it look bad for her; so I lied. I could have thought up a better story if I'd had more time, I don't doubt; but I had to think quick. Anyways, I'm glad it's all over."

8

KELLY AND THE other uniformed policeman had left the office, which now held McTighe, O'Gar, Cara Kenbrook, Tennant and me. Tennant had crossed to my side, and was apologizing.

"I hope you'll let me square myself for this evening's work. But you know how it is when somebody you care for is in a jam. I'd have killed you if I had thought it would help Cara—on the level. Why didn't you tell us that you didn't suspect her?"

"But I did suspect the pair of you," I said. "It looked as if Kelly had to be the guilty one; but you people carried on so much that I began to feel doubtful. For a while it was funny—you thinking she had done it, and she thinking you had, though I suppose each had sworn to his or her innocence. But after a time it stopped being funny. You carried it too far."

"How did you rap to Kelly?" O'Gar, at my shoulder, asked.

"Miss Kenbrook was walking north on Leavenworth—and was half-way between Bush and Pine—when the shot was fired. She saw nobody, no cars, until she rounded the corner. Mrs. Gilmore, walking north on Jones, was about the same distance away when she heard the shot, and she saw nobody until she reached Pine Street. If Kelly had been telling the truth, she would have seen him on Jones Street. He said he didn't turn the corner until after the shot was fired.

"Either of the women could have killed Gilmore, but hardly both; and I doubted that either could have shot him and got away without running into Kelly or the other. Suppose both of them were telling the truth—what then? Kelly must have been lying! He was the logical suspect anyway—the nearest known person to the murdered man when the shot was fired.

"To back all this up, he had let Miss Kenbrook go into the apartment building at 3:00 in the morning, in front of which a man had just been killed, without questioning her or mentioning her in his report. That looked as if he *knew* who had done the killing. So I took a chance with the empty shell trick, it being a good bet that he would have thrown his away, and would think that—"

McTighe's heavy voice interrupted my explanation.

"How about this assault charge?" he asked, and had the decency to avoid my eye when I turned toward him with the others.

Tennant cleared his throat.

"Er—ah—in view of the way things have turned out, and knowing that Miss Kenbrook doesn't want the disagreeable publicity that would accompany an affair of this sort, why, I'd suggest that we drop the whole thing." He smiled brightly from McTighe to me. "You know nothing has gone on the records yet."

"Make the big heap play his hand out," O'Gar growled in my ear. "Don't let him drop it."

"Of course if Miss Kenbrook doesn't want to press the charge," McTighe was saying, watching me out of the tail of his eye, "I suppose—"

"If everybody understands that the whole thing was a plant," I said, "and if the policemen who heard the story are brought in here now and told by Tennant and Miss Kenbrook that it was all a lie—then I'm willing to let it go at that. Otherwise, I won't stand for a hush-up."

"You're a damned fool!" O'Gar whispered. "Put the screws on them!"

But I shook my head. I didn't see any sense in making a lot of trouble for myself just to make some for somebody else—and suppose Tennant *proved* his story....

So the policemen were found, and brought into the office again, and told the truth.

And presently Tennant, the girl, and I were walking together like three old friends through the corridors toward the door, Tennant still asking me to let him make amends for the evening's work.

"You've *got* to let me do something!" he insisted. "It's only right!"

His hand dipped into his coat, and came out with a thick bill-fold.

"Here," he said; "let me—"

We were going, at that happy moment, down the stone vestibule steps that led to Kearny Street—six or seven steps there are.

"No," I said; "let me—"

He was on the next to the top step, when I reached up and let go.

He settled in a rather limp pile at the bottom.

Leaving his empty-faced lady love to watch over him, I strolled up through Portsmouth Square toward a restaurant where the steaks come thick.

The Golden Horseshoe

In our recent voting contest for favorite Black Mask authors, Dashiell Hammett received thousands of votes because of his series of stories of the adventures of his San Francisco detective. He has created one of the most convincing and realistic characters in all detective fiction. The story, herewith, is one of his best to date. We know you'll enjoy it to the last word.

1

"I HAVEN'T ANYTHING very exciting to offer you this time," Vance Richmond said as we shook hands. "I want you to find a man for me—a man who is not a criminal."

There was an apology in his voice. The last couple of jobs this lean, grey-faced attorney had thrown my way had run to gun-play and other forms of rioting, and I suppose he thought anything less than that would put me to sleep. Was a time when he might have been right—when I was a young sprout of twenty or so, newly attached to the Continental Detective Agency. But the fifteen years that had slid by since then had dulled my appetite for rough stuff. I don't mean that I shuddered whenever I considered the possibility of some bird taking a poke at me; but I didn't call that day a total loss in which nobody tried to puncture my short, fat carcass.

"The man I want found," the lawyer went on, as we sat down, "is an English architect named Norman Ashcraft. He is a man of about thirty-seven, five feet ten inches tall, well built, and fair-skinned, with light hair and blue eyes. Four years ago he was a typical specimen of the clean-cut blond Britisher. He may not be like that now—those four years have been rather hard ones for him, I imagine.

"I want to find him for Mrs. Ashcraft, his wife. I know your Agency's rule against meddling with family affairs, but I can assure you that no matter how things turn out there will be no divorce proceedings in which you will be involved.

"Here is the story. Four years ago the Ashcrafts were living together in England, in Bristol. It seems that Mrs. Ashcraft is of a very jealous disposition, and he was rather high-strung. Furthermore, he had only what money he earned at his profession, while she had inherited quite a bit from her parents. Ashcraft was rather foolishly sensitive about being the husband of a wealthy woman—was inclined to go out of his way to show that he was not dependent upon her money, that he wouldn't be influenced by it. Foolish, of course, but just the sort of attitude a man of his temperament would assume. One night she accused him of paying too much attention to another woman. They quarreled, and he packed up and left.

"She was repentant within a week—especially repentant since she had learned that her suspicion had had no foundation outside of her own jealousy—and she tried to find him. But he was gone. It became manifest that he had left England. She had him searched for in Europe, in Canada, in Australia, and in the United States. She succeeded in tracing him from Bristol to New York, and then to Detroit, where he had been arrested and fined for disturbing the peace in a drunken row of some sort. After that he dropped out of sight until he bobbed up in Seattle ten months later."

The attorney hunted through the papers on his desk and found a memorandum.

"On May 23, 1923, he shot and killed a burglar in his room in a hotel there. The Seattle police seem to have suspected that there was something funny about the shooting, but had nothing to hold Ashcraft on. The man he killed was undoubtedly a burglar. Then Ashcraft disappeared again, and nothing was heard of him until just about a year ago. Mrs. Ashcraft had advertisements inserted in the personal columns of papers in the principal American cities.

"One day she received a letter from him, from San Francisco. It was a very formal letter, and simply requested her to stop advertising. Although he was through with the name Norman Ashcraft, he wrote, he disliked seeing it published in every newspaper he read.

"She mailed a letter to him at the General Delivery window here, and used another advertisement to tell him about it. He answered it, rather caustically. She wrote him again, asking him to come home. He refused, though he seemed less bitter toward her. They exchanged several letters, and she learned that he had become a drug addict, and what was left of his pride would not let him return to her until he looked—and was at least somewhat like—his former self. She persuaded him to accept enough money from her to straighten himself out. She sent him this money each month, in care of General Delivery, here.

"Meanwhile she closed up her affairs in England—she had no close relatives to hold her there—and came to San Francisco, to be on hand when her husband was ready to return to her. A year has gone. She still sends him money each month. She still waits for him to come back to her. He has repeatedly refused to see her, and his letters are evasive—filled with accounts of the struggle he is having, making headway against the drug one month, slipping back the next.

"She suspects by now, of course, that he has no intention of ever coming back to her; that he does not intend giving up the drug; that he is simply using her as a source of income. I have urged her to discontinue the monthly allowance for a while. That would at least bring about an interview, I think, and she could learn definitely what to expect. But she will not do that. You see, she blames herself for his present condition. She thinks her foolish flare of jealousy is responsible for his plight, and she is afraid to do anything that might either hurt him or induce him to hurt himself further. Her mind is unchangeably made up in that respect. She wants him back, wants him straightened out; but if he will not come, then she is content to continue the payments for the rest of his life. But she wants to know what she is to expect. She wants to end this devilish uncertainty in which she has been living.

"What we want, then, is for you to find Ashcraft. We want to know whether there is any likelihood of his ever becoming a man again, or whether he is gone beyond redemption. There is your job. Find him, learn whatever you can about him, and then, after we know something, we will decide whether it is wiser to force an interview between them—in hopes that she will be able to influence him—or not."

"I'll try it," I said. "When does Mrs. Ashcraft send him his monthly allowance?"

"On the first of each month."

"Today is the twenty-eighth. That'll give me three days to wind up a job I have on hand. Got a photo of him?"

"Unfortunately, no. In her anger immediately after their row, Mrs. Ashcraft destroyed everything she had that would remind her of him. But I don't think a photograph would be of any great help at the post office. Without consulting me, Mrs. Ashcraft watched for her husband there on several occasions, and did not see him. It is more than likely that he has someone else call for his mail."

I got up and reached for my hat.

"See you around the second of the month," I said, as I left the office.

2

ON THE AFTERNOON of the first, I went down to the post office and got hold of Lusk, the inspector in charge of the division at the time.

"I've got a line on a scratcher from up north," I told Lusk, "who is supposed to be getting his mail at the window. Will you fix it up so I can get a spot on him?"

Post office inspectors are all tied up with rules and regulations that forbid their giving assistance to private detectives except on certain criminal matters. But a friendly inspector doesn't have to put you through the third degree. You lie to him—so that he will have an alibi in case there's a kick-back—and whether he thinks you're lying or not doesn't matter.

So presently I was downstairs again, loitering within sight of the A to D window, with the clerk at the window instructed to give me the office when Ashcraft's mail was called for. There was no mail for him there at the time. Mrs. Ashcraft's letter would hardly get to the clerks that afternoon, but I was taking no chances. I stayed on the job until the windows closed at eight o'clock, and then went home.

At a few minutes after ten the next morning I got my action. One of the clerks gave me the signal. A small man in a blue suit and a soft gray hat was walking away from the window with an envelope in his hand. A man of perhaps forty years, though he looked older. His face was pasty, his feet dragged, and, although his clothes were fairly new, they needed brushing and pressing.

He came straight to the desk in front of which I stood

fiddling with some papers. Out of the tail of my eye I saw that he had not opened the envelope in his hand—was not going to open it. He took a large envelope from his pocket, and I got just enough of a glimpse of its front to see that it was already stamped and addressed. I twisted my neck out of joint trying to read the address, but failed. He kept the addressed side against his body, put the letter he had got from the window in it, and licked the flap backward, so that there was no possible way for anybody to see the front of the envelope. Then he rubbed the flap down carefully and turned toward the mailing slots. I went after him. There was nothing to do but to pull the always reliable stumble.

I overtook him, stepped close and faked a fall on the marble floor, bumping into him, grabbing him as if to regain my balance. It went rotten. In the middle of my stunt my foot really did slip, and we went down on the floor like a pair of wrestlers, with him under me. To botch the trick thoroughly, he fell with the envelope pinned under him.

I scrambled up, yanked him to his feet, mumbled an apology and almost had to push him out of the way to beat him to the envelope that lay face down on the floor. I had to turn it over as I handed it to him in order to get the address:

Mr. Edward Bohannon,
    Golden Horseshoe Café,
    Tijuana, Baja California,
  Mexico.

I had the address, but I had tipped my mitt. There was no way in God's world for this little man in blue to miss knowing that I had been trying to get that address.

I dusted myself off while he put his envelope through a slot. He didn't come back past me, but went on down toward the Mission Street exit. I couldn't let him get away with what he knew. I didn't want Ashcraft tipped off before I got to him. I would have to try another trick as ancient as the one the slippery floor had bungled for me. I set out after the little man again.

Just as I reached his side he turned his head to see if he was being followed.

"Hello, Micky!" I hailed him. "How's everything in Chi?"

"You got me wrong." He spoke out of the side of his gray-lipped mouth, not stopping. "I don't know nothin' about Chi."

His eyes were pale blue, with needlepoint pupils—the eyes of a heroin or morphine user.

"Quit stalling." I walked along at his side. We had left the building by this time and were going down Mission Street. "You fell off the rattler only this morning."

He stopped on the sidewalk and faced me.

"Me? Who do you think I am?"

"You're Micky Parker. The Dutchman gave us the rap that you were headed here. They got him—if you don't already know it."

"You're cuckoo," he sneered. "I don't know what the hell you're talkin' about!"

That was nothing—neither did I. I raised my right hand in my overcoat pocket.

"Now I'll tell one," I growled at him. "And keep your hands away from your clothes or I'll let the guts out of you."

He flinched away from my bulging pocket.

"Hey, listen, brother!" he begged. "You got me wrong—on the level. My name ain't Micky Parker, an' I ain't been in Chi in six years. I been here in Frisco for a solid year, an' that's the truth."

"You got to show me."

"I can do it," he exclaimed, all eagerness. "You come down the drag with me, an' I'll show you. My name's Ryan, an' I been livin' aroun' the corner here on Sixth Street for six or eight months."

"Ryan?" I asked.

"Yes—John Ryan."

I chalked that up against him. Of course there have been Ryans christened John, but not enough of them to account for the number of times that name appears in criminal records. I don't suppose there are three old-time yeggs in the country who haven't used the name at least once; it's the John Smith of yeggdom.

This particular John Ryan led me around to a house on Sixth Street, where the landlady—a rough-hewn woman of fifty, with bare arms that were haired and muscled like the village smithy's—assured me that her tenant had to her positive knowledge been in San Francisco for months, and that she remembered seeing him at least once a day for a couple of weeks back. If I had been really suspicious that this Ryan was my mythical Micky Parker from Chicago, I wouldn't have taken the woman's word for it, but as it was I pretended to be satisfied.

That seemed to be all right then. Mr. Ryan had been led astray, had been convinced that I had mistaken him for another crook, and that I was not interested in the Ashcraft letter. I would be safe—reasonably safe—in letting the situation go as it stood. But loose ends worry me. And you can't always count on people doing and thinking what you want. This bird was a hop-head, and he had given me a phoney-sounding name, so....

"What do you do for a living?" I asked him.

"I ain't been doin' nothin' for a coupla months," he pattered, "but I expec' to open a lunch room with a fella nex' week."

"Let's go up to your room," I suggested. "I want to talk to you."

He wasn't enthusiastic, but he took me up. He had two rooms and a kitchen on the third floor. They were dirty, foul-smelling rooms. I dangled a leg from the corner of a table and waved him into a squeaky rocking chair in front of me. His pasty face and dopey eyes were uneasy.

"Where's Ashcraft?" I threw at him. He jerked, and then looked at the floor.

"I don't know what you're talkin' about," he mumbled.

"You'd better figure it out," I advised him, "or there's a nice cool cell down in the booby-hutch that will be wrapped around you."

"You ain't got nothin' on me."

"What of that? How'd you like to do a thirty or a sixty on a vag charge?"

"Vag, hell!" he snarled, looking up at me. "I got five hundred smacks in my kick. Does that look like you can vag me?"

I grinned down at him.

"You know better than that, Ryan. A pocketful of money'll get you nothing in California. You've got no job. You can't show where your money comes from. You're made to order for the vag law."

I had this bird figured as a dope peddler. If he was—or was anything else off color that might come to light when he was vagged—the chances were that he would be willing to sell Ashcraft out to save himself; especially since, so far as I knew, Ashcraft wasn't on the wrong side of the criminal law.

"If I were you," I went on while he stared at the floor and thought, "I'd be a nice, obliging fellow and do my talking now. You're—"

He twisted sidewise in his chair and one of his hands went behind him.

I kicked him out of his chair.

The table slipped under me or I would have stretched him. As it was, the foot that I aimed at his jaw took him on the chest and carried him over backward, with the rocking-chair piled on top of him. I pulled the chair off and took his gun—a cheap nickel-plated .32. Then I went back to my seat on the corner of the table.

He had only that one flash of fight in him. He got up sniveling.

"I'll tell you. I don't want no trouble, an' it ain't nothin' to me. I didn't know there was nothin' wrong. This Ashcraft told me he was jus' stringin' his wife along. He give me ten bucks a throw to get his letter ever' month an' send it to him in Tijuana. I knowed him here, an' when he went south six months ago—he's got a girl down there—I promised I'd do it for him. I knowed it was money—he said it was his 'alimony'—but I didn't know there was nothin' wrong."

"What sort of a hombre is this Ashcraft? What's his graft?"

"I don't know. He could be a con man—he's got a good front. He's a Englishman, an' mostly goes by the name of Ed Bohannon. He hits the hop. I don't use it myself"—that was a good one—"but you know how it is in a burg like this, a man runs into all kinds of people. I don't know nothin' about what he's up to. I jus' send the money ever' month an' get my ten."

That was all I could get out of him. He couldn't—or wouldn't—tell me where Ashcraft had lived in San Francisco or who he had mobbed up with. However, I had learned that Bohannon was Ashcraft, and not another go-between, and that was something.

Ryan squawked his head off when he found that I was going to vag him anyway. For a moment it looked like I would have to kick him loose from his backbone again.

"You said you'd spring me if I talked," he wailed.

"I did not. But if I had—when a gent flashes a rod on me I figure it cancels any agreement we might have had. Come on."

I couldn't afford to let him run around loose until I got in touch with Ashcraft. He would have been sending a telegram before I was three blocks away, and my quarry would be on his merry way to points north, east, south and west.

It was a good hunch I played in nabbing Ryan. When he was fingerprinted at the Hall of Justice he turned out to be one Fred Rooney, alias "Jamocha," a peddler and smuggler who had crushed out of the Federal Prison at Leavenworth, leaving eight years of a tenner still unserved.

"Will you sew him up for a couple of days?" I asked the captain of the city jail. "I've got work to do that will go smoother if he can't get any word out for a while."

"Sure," the captain promised. "The federal people won't take him off our hands for two or three days. I'll keep him air-tight till then."

3

FROM THE JAIL I went up to Vance Richmond's office and turned my news over to him.

"Ashcraft is getting his mail in Tijuana. He's living down there under the name of Ed Bohannon, and maybe has a woman there. I've just thrown one of his friends—the one who handled the mail and an escaped con—in the cooler."

"Was that necessary?" Richmond asked. "We don't want to work any hardships. We're really trying to help Ashcraft, you know."

"I could have spared this bird," I admitted. "But what for? He was all wrong. If Ashcraft can be brought back to his wife, he's better off with some of his shady friends out of the way. If he can't, what's the difference? Anyway, we've got one line on him safely stowed away where we can find it when we want it."

The attorney shrugged, and reached for the telephone.

He called a number. "Is Mrs. Ashcraft there?... This is Mr. Richmond.... No, we haven't exactly found him, but I think we know where he is.... Yes.... In about fifteen minutes."

He put down the telephone and stood up.

"We'll run up to Mrs. Ashcraft's house and see her."

Fifteen minutes later we were getting out of Richmond's car in Jackson Street near Gough. The house was a three-story white stone building, set behind a carefully sodded little lawn with an iron railing around it.

Mrs. Ashcraft received us in a drawing-room on the second floor. A tall woman of less than thirty, slimly beautiful in a gray dress. Clear was the word that best fits her; it described the blue of her eyes, the pink-white of her skin, and the light brown of her hair.

Richmond introduced me to her, and then I told her what I had learned, omitting the part about the woman in Tijuana. Nor did I tell her that the chances were her husband was a crook nowadays.

"Mr. Ashcraft is in Tijuana, I have been told. He left San Francisco about six months ago. His mail is being forwarded to him in care of a café there, under the name of Edward Bohannon."

Her eyes lighted up happily, but she didn't throw a fit. She wasn't that sort. She addressed the attorney.

"Shall I go down? Or will you?"

Richmond shook his head.

"Neither. You certainly shouldn't go, and I cannot—not at present. I must be in Eureka by the day after tomorrow, and shall have to spend several days there." He turned to me. "You'll have to go. You can no doubt handle it better than I could. You will know what to do and how to do it. There are no definite instructions I can give you. Your course will have to depend on Mr. Ashcraft's attitude and condition. Mrs. Ashcraft doesn't wish to force herself on him, but neither does she wish to leave anything undone that might help him."

Mrs. Ashcraft held a strong, slender hand out to me.

"You will do whatever you think wisest."

It was partly a question, partly an expression of confidence.

"I will," I promised.

I liked this Mrs. Ashcraft.

4

TIJUANA HADN'T CHANGED much in the two years I had been away. Still the same six or seven hundred feet of dusty and dingy street running between two almost solid rows of saloons,—perhaps thirty-five of them to a row,—with dirtier side streets taking care of the dives that couldn't find room on the main street.

The automobile that had brought me down from San Diego dumped me into the center of the town early in the afternoon, and the day's business was just getting under way. That is, there were only two or three drunks wandering around among the dogs and loafing Mexicans in the street, although there was already a bustle of potential drunks moving from one saloon to the next. But this was nothing like the crowd that would be here the following week, when the season's racing started.

In the middle of the next block I saw a big gilded horseshoe. I went down the street and into the saloon behind the sign. It was a fair sample of the local joint. A bar on your left as you came in, running half the length of the building, with three or four slot machines on one end. Across from the bar, against the right-hand wall, a dance floor that ran from the front wall to a raised platform, where a greasy orchestra was now preparing to go to work. Behind the orchestra was a row of low stalls or booths, with open fronts and a table and two benches apiece. Opposite them, in the space between the bar and the rear of the building, a man with a hair-lip was shaking pills out of a keno goose.

It was early in the day, and there were only a few buyers present, so the girls whose business it is to speed the sale of drinks charged down on me in a flock.

"Buy me a drink? Let's have a little drink? Buy a drink, honey?"

I shooed them away—no easy job—and caught a bartender's eye. He was a beefy, red-faced Irishman, with sorrel hair plastered down in two curls that hid what little forehead he had.

"I want to see Ed Bohannon," I told him confidentially.

He turned blank fish-green eyes on me.

"I don't know no Ed Bohannon."

Taking out a piece of paper and a pencil I scribbled, *Jamocha is copped*, and slid the paper over to the bartender.

"If a man who says he's Ed Bohannon asks for that, will you give it to him?"

"I guess so."

"Good," I said. "I'll hang around a while."

I walked down the room and sat at a table in one of the stalls. A lanky girl who had done something to her hair that made it purple was camped beside me before I had settled in my seat.

"Buy me a little drink?" she asked.

The face she made at me was probably meant for a smile. Whatever it was, it beat me. I was afraid she'd do it again, so I surrendered.

"Yes," I said, and ordered a bottle of beer for myself from the waiter who was already hanging over my shoulder.

The beer wasn't bad, for green beer; but at four bits a bottle it wasn't anything to write home about. This Tijuana happens to be in Mexico—by about a mile—but it's an American town, run by Americans, who sell American artificial booze at American prices. If you know your way around the United States you can find lots of places—especially near the Canadian line—where good booze can be bought for less than you are soaked for poison in Tijuana.

The purple-haired woman at my side downed her shot of whiskey, and was opening her mouth to suggest that we have another drink,—hustlers down there don't waste any time at all,—when a voice spoke from behind me.

"Cora, Frank wants you."

Cora scowled, looking over my shoulder.

Then she made that damned face at me again, said "All right, Kewpie. Will you take care of my friend here?" and left me.

Kewpie slid into the seat beside me. She was a little chunky girl of perhaps eighteen—not a day more than that. Just a kid. Her short hair was brown and curly over a round, boyish face with laughing, impudent eyes. Rather a cute little trick.

I bought her a drink and got another bottle of beer.

"What's on your mind?" I asked her.

"Hooch." She grinned at me—a grin that was as boyish as the straight look of her brown eyes. "Gallons of it."

"And besides that?"

I knew this switching of girls on me hadn't been purposeless.

"I hear you're looking for a friend of mine," Kewpie said.

"That might be. What friends have you got?"

"Well, there's Ed Bohannon for one. You know Ed?"

I shook my head.

"No—not yet."

"But you're looking for him?"

"Uh-huh."

"Maybe I could tell you how to find him, if I knew you were

all right."

"It doesn't make any difference to me," I said carelessly. "I've a few more minutes to waste, and if he doesn't show up by then it's all one to me."

She cuddled against my shoulder.

"What's the racket? Maybe I could get word to Ed."

I stuck a cigarette in her mouth, one in my own, and lit them.

"Let it go," I bluffed. "This Ed of yours seems to be as exclusive as all hell. Well, it's no skin off *my* face. I'll buy you another drink and then trot along."

She jumped up.

"Wait a minute. I'll see if I can get him. What's your name?"

"Parker will do as well as any other," I said, the name I had used on Ryan popping first into my mind.

"You wait," she called back as she moved toward the back door. "I think I can find him."

"I think so too," I agreed.

Ten minutes went by, and a man came to my table from the front of the establishment. He was a blond Englishman of less than forty, with all the marks of the gentleman gone to pot on him. Not altogether on the rocks yet, but you could see evidence of the downhill slide plainly in the dullness of his blue eyes, in the pouches under his eyes, in the blurred lines around his mouth and the mouth's looseness, and in the grayish tint of his skin. He was still fairly attractive in appearance—enough of his former wholesomeness remained for that.

He sat down facing me across the table.

"You're looking for me?"

There was only a hint of the Britisher in his accent.

"You're Ed Bohannon?"

He nodded.

"Jamocha was picked up a couple of days ago," I told him, "and ought to be riding back to the Kansas big house by now. He got word out for me to give you the rap. He knew I was heading this way."

"How did they come to get him?"

His blue eyes were suspicious on my face.

"Don't know," I said. "Maybe they picked him up on a circular."

He frowned at the table and traced a meaningless design with a finger in a puddle of beer. Then he looked sharply at me again.

"Did he tell you anything else?"

"*He* didn't tell me anything. He got word out to me by somebody's mouthpiece. I didn't see him."

"You're staying down here a while?"

"Yes, for two or three days," I said. "I've got something on the fire."

He stood up and smiled, and held out his hand.

"Thanks for the tip, Parker," he said. "If you'll take a walk with me I'll give you something real to drink."

I didn't have anything against that. He led me out of the Golden Horseshoe and down a side street to an adobe house set out where the town fringed off into the desert. In the front room he waved me to a chair and went into the next room.

"What do you fancy?" he called through the door. "Rye, gin, tequila, Scotch—"

"The last one wins," I interrupted his catalog.

He brought in a bottle of Black and White, a siphon and some glasses, and we settled down to drinking. When that bottle was empty there was another to take its place. We drank and talked, drank and talked, and each of us pretended to be drunker than he really was—though before long we were both as full as a pair of goats.

It was a drinking contest pure and simple. He was trying to drink me into a pulp—a pulp that would easily give up all of its secrets—and I was trying the same game on him. Neither of us made much progress. Neither he nor I was young enough in the world to blab much when we were drunk that wouldn't have come out if we had been sober. Few grown men do, unless they get to boasting, or are very skillfully handled. All that afternoon we faced each other over the table in the center of the room, drank and entertained each other.

"Y' know," he was saying somewhere along toward dark, "I've been a damn' ass. Got a wife—the nicesh woman in the worl'. Wantsh me t' come back to her, an' all tha' short of thing. Yet I hang around here, lappin' up this shtuff—hittin' the pipe— when I could be shomebody. Arc—architec', y' un'ershtand— good one, too. But I got in rut—got mixsh up with theshe people. C-can't sheem to break 'way. Goin' to, though—no spoofin'. Goin' back to li'l wife, nicesh woman in the worl'. Don't you shay anything t' Kewpie. She'd raishe hell 'f she knew I wash goin' t' shake her. Nishe girl, K-kewpie, but tough. S-shtick a bloomin' knife in me. Good job, too! But I'm goin' back to wife. Breakin' 'way from p-pipe an' ever'thing. Look at me. D' I look like a hop-head? Course not! Curin' m'self, tha's why. I'll show you—take a smoke now—show you I can take it or leave it alone."

Pulling himself dizzily up out of his chair, he wandered into the next room, bawling a song at the top of his voice:

"A dimber mort with a quarter-stone slum,

A-bubbin' of max with her cove—

A bingo fen in a crack-o'-dawn drum,

A-waitin' for—"

He came staggering into the room again carrying an elaborate opium layout—all silver and ebony—on a silver tray. He put it on the table and flourished a pipe at me.

"Have a li'l rear on me, Parker."

I told him I'd stick to the Scotch.

"Give y' shot of C. 'f y'd rather have it," he invited me.

I declined the cocaine, so he sprawled himself comfortably on the floor beside the table, rolled and cooked a pill, and our party went on—with him smoking his hop and me punishing the liquor—each of us still talking for the other's benefit, and trying to get the other to talk for our own.

I was holding down a lovely package by the time Kewpie came in, at midnight.

"Looks like you folks are enjoying yourselves," she laughed, leaning down to kiss the Englishman's rumpled hair as she stepped over him.

She perched herself on the table and reached for the Scotch.

"Everything's lovely," I assured her, though probably I didn't say it that clear.

I was fighting a battle with myself just about then. I had an idea that I wanted to dance. Down in Yucatan, four or five months before—hunting for a lad who had done wrong by the bank that employed him—I had seen some natives dance the *naual*. And that naual dance was the one thing in the world I wanted to do just then. (I was carrying a beautiful bun!) But

I knew that if I sat still—as I had been sitting all evening—I could keep my cargo in hand, while it wasn't going to take much moving around to knock me over.

I don't remember whether I finally conquered the desire to dance or not. I remember Kewpie sitting on the table, grinning her boy's grin at me, and saying:

"You ought to stay oiled all the time, Shorty; it improves you."

I don't know whether I made any answer to that or not. Shortly afterward, I know, I spread myself beside the Englishman on the floor and went to sleep.

5

THE NEXT TWO days were pretty much like the first one. Ashcraft and I were together twenty-four hours each of the days, and usually the girl was with us, and the only time we weren't drinking was when we were sleeping off what we had been drinking. We spent most of those three days in either the adobe house or the Golden Horseshoe, but we found time to take in most of the other joints in town now and then. I had only a hazy idea of some of the things that went on around me, though I don't think I missed anything entirely. On the second day someone added a first name to the alias I had given the girl—and thereafter I was "Painless" Parker to Tijuana, and still am to some of them. I don't know who christened me, or why.

Ashcraft and I were as thick as thieves, on the surface, but neither of us ever lost his distrust of the other, no matter how drunk we got—and we got plenty drunk. He went up against his mud-pipe regularly. I don't think the girl used the stuff, but she had a pretty capacity for hard liquor. I would go to sleep not knowing whether I was going to wake up or not; but I had nothing on me to give me away, so I figured that I was safe unless I talked myself into a jam. I didn't worry much,— bedtime usually caught me in a state that made worry impossible.

Three days of this, and then, sobering up, I was riding back to San Francisco, making a list of what I knew and guessed about Norman Ashcraft, alias Ed Bohannon.

The list went something like this:

(1) He suspected, if he didn't know, that I had come down to see him on his wife's account: he had been too smooth and had entertained me too well for me to doubt that; (2) he apparently had decided to return to his wife, though there was no guarantee that he would actually do so; (3) he was not incurably addicted to drugs; he merely smoked opium and, regardless of what the Sunday supplements say, an opium smoker is little, if any, worse off than a tobacco smoker; (4) he might pull himself together under his wife's influence, but it was doubtful: physically he hadn't gone to the dogs, but he had had his taste of the gutter and seemed to like it; (5) the girl Kewpie was crazily in love with him, while he liked her, but wasn't turning himself inside out over her.

A good night's sleep on the train between Los Angeles and San Francisco set me down in the Third and Townsend Street station with nearly normal head and stomach and not too many kinks in my nerves. I put away a breakfast that was composed of more food than I had eaten in three days, and went up to Vance Richmond's office.

"Mr. Richmond is still in Eureka," his stenographer told me. "I don't expect him back until the first of the week."

"Can you get him on the phone for me?"

She could, and did.

Without mentioning any names, I told the attorney what I knew and guessed.

"I see," he said. "Suppose you go out to Mrs. A's house and tell her. I will write her tonight, and I probably shall be back in the city by the day after tomorrow. I think we can safely delay action until then."

I caught a street car, transferred at Van Ness Avenue, and

went out to Mrs. Ashcraft's house. Nothing happened when I rang the bell. I rang it several times before I noticed that there were two morning newspapers in the vestibule. I looked at the dates—this morning's and yesterday morning's.

An old man in faded overalls was watering the lawn next door.

"Do you know if the people who live here have gone away?" I called to him.

"I don't guess so. The back door's open, I seen this mornin'."

He returned his attention to his hose, and then stopped to scratch his chin.

"They may of gone," he said slowly. "Come to think on it, I ain't seen any of 'em for—I don't remember seein' any of 'em yesterday."

I left the front steps and went around the house, climbed the low fence in back and went up the back steps. The kitchen door stood about a foot open. Nobody was visible in the kitchen, but there was a sound of running water.

I knocked on the door with my knuckles, loudly. There was no answering sound. I pushed the door open and went in. The sound of water came from the sink. I looked in the sink.

Under a thin stream of water running from one of the faucets lay a carving knife with nearly a foot of keen blade. The knife was clean, but the back of the porcelain sink—where water had splashed with only small, scattered drops—was freckled with red-brown spots. I scraped one of them with a finger-nail—dried blood.

Except for the sink, I could see nothing out of order in the kitchen. I opened a pantry door. Everything seemed all right there. Across the room another door led to the front of the house. I opened the door and went into a passageway. Not enough light came from the kitchen to illuminate the passageway. I fumbled in the dusk for the light-button that I knew should be there. I stepped on something soft.

Pulling my foot back, I felt in my pocket for matches, and struck one. In front of me, his head and shoulders on the floor, his hips and legs on the lower steps of a flight of stairs, lay a Filipino boy in his underclothes.

He was dead. One eye was cut, and his throat was gashed straight across, close up under his chin. I could see the killing without even shutting my eyes. At the top of the stairs—the killer's left hand dashing into the Filipino's face—thumb-nail gouging into eye—pushing the brown face back—tightening the brown throat for the knife's edge—the slash—and the shove down the steps.

The light from my second match showed me the button. I clicked on the lights, buttoned my coat, and went up the steps. Dried blood darkened them here and there, and at the second-floor landing the wall paper was stained with a big blot. At the head of the stairs I found another light-button, and pressed it.

I walked down the hall, poked my head into two rooms that seemed in order, and then turned a corner—and pulled up with a jerk, barely in time to miss stumbling over a woman who lay there.

She was huddled on the floor, face down, with knees drawn up under her and both hands clasped to her stomach. She wore a nightgown, and her hair was in a braid down her back.

I put a finger on the back of her neck. Stone-cold.

Kneeling on the floor—to avoid the necessity of turning her

over—I looked at her face. She was the maid who had admitted Richmond and me four days ago.

I stood up again and looked around. The maid's head was almost touching a closed door. I stepped around her and pushed the door open. A bedroom, and not the maid's. It was an expensively dainty bedroom in cream and gray, with French prints on the walls. Nothing in the room was disarranged except the bed. The bed clothes were rumpled and tangled, and piled high in the center of the bed—in a pile that was too large....

Leaning over the bed, I began to draw the covers off. The second piece came away stained with blood. I yanked the rest off.

Mrs. Ashcraft was dead there.

Her body was drawn up in a little heap, from which her head hung crookedly, dangling from a neck that had been cut clean through to the bone. Her face was marked with four deep scratches from temple to chin. One sleeve had been torn from the jacket of her blue silk pajamas. Bedding and pajamas were soggy with the blood that the clothing piled over her had kept from drying.

I put the blanket over her again, edged past the dead woman in the hall, and went down the front stairs, switching on more lights, hunting for the telephone. Near the foot of the stairs I found it. I called the police detective bureau first, and then Vance Richmond's office.

"Get word to Mr. Richmond that Mrs. Ashcraft has been murdered," I told his stenographer. "I'm at her house, and he can get in touch with me here any time during the next two or three hours."

Then I went out of the front door and sat on the top step, smoking a cigarette while I waited for the police.

I felt rotten. I've seen dead people in larger quantities than three in my time, and I've seen some that were hacked up pretty badly; but this thing had fallen on me while my nerves were ragged from three days of boozing.

The police automobile swung around the corner and began disgorging men before I had finished my first cigarette. O'Gar, the detective sergeant in charge of the Homicide Detail, was the first man up the steps.

"Hullo," he greeted me. "What have you got hold of this time?"

I was glad to see him. This squat, bullet-headed sergeant is as good a man as the department has, and he and I have always been lucky when we tied up together.

"I found three bodies in there before I quit looking," I told him as I led him indoors. "Maybe a regular detective like you— with a badge and everything—can find more."

"You didn't do bad—for a lad," he said.

My wooziness had passed. I was eager to get to work. These people lying dead around the house were merely counters in a game again—or almost. I remembered the feel of Mrs. Ashcraft's slim hand in mine, but I stuck that memory in the back of my mind. You hear now and then of detectives who have not become callous, who have not lost what you might call the human touch. I always feel sorry for them, and wonder why they don't chuck their jobs and find another line of work that wouldn't be so hard on their emotions. A sleuth who doesn't grow a tough shell is in for a gay life—day in and day out poking his nose into one kind of woe or another.

I showed the Filipino to O'Gar first, and then the two women. We didn't find any more. Detail work occupied all of us—O'Gar, the eight men under him, and me—for the next few hours. The house had to be gone over from roof to cellar. The neighbors had to be grilled. The employment agencies through which the servants had been hired had to be examined. Relatives and friends of the Filipino and the maid had to be traced and questioned. Newsboys, mail carriers, grocers' delivery men, laundrymen, had to be found, questioned and, when necessary, investigated.

When the bulk of the reports were in, O'Gar and I sneaked away from the others—especially away from the newspaper men, who were all over the place by now—and locked ourselves in the library.

"Night before last, huh? Wednesday night?" O'Gar grunted when we were comfortable in a couple of leather chairs, burning tobacco.

I nodded. The report of the doctor who had examined the bodies, the presence of the two newspapers in the vestibule, and the fact that neither neighbor, grocer nor butcher had seen any of them since Wednesday, combined to make Wednesday night—or early Thursday morning—the correct date.

"I'd say the killer cracked the back door," O'Gar went on, staring at the ceiling through smoke, "picked up the carving knife in the kitchen, and went upstairs. Maybe he went straight to Mrs. Ashcraft's room—maybe not. But after a bit he went in there. The torn sleeve and the scratches on her face mean that there was a tussle. The Filipino and the maid heard the noise—heard her scream maybe—and rushed to her room to find out what was the matter. The maid most likely got there just as the killer was coming out—and got hers. I guess the Filipino saw him then and ran. The killer caught him at the head of the back stairs—and finished him. Then he went down to the kitchen, washed his hands, dropped the knife, and blew."

"So far, so good," I agreed; "but I notice you skip lightly over the question of who he was and why he killed."

He pushed his hat back and scratched his bullet head.

"Don't crowd me," he rumbled; "I'll get around to that. There seem to be just three guesses to take your pick from. We know that nobody else lived in the house outside of the three that were killed. So the killer was either a maniac who did the job for the fun of it, a burglar who was discovered and ran wild, or somebody who had a reason for bumping off Mrs. Ashcraft, and then had to kill the two servants when they discovered him.

"Taking the knife from the kitchen would make the burglar guess look like a bum one. And, besides, we're pretty sure nothing was stolen. A good prowler would bring his own weapon with him if he wanted one. But the hell of it is that there are a lot of bum prowlers in the world—half-wits who would be likely to pick up a knife in the kitchen, go to pieces when the house woke up, slash everybody in sight, and then beat it without turning anything over.

"So it could have been a prowler; but my personal guess is that the job was done by somebody who wanted to wipe out Mrs. Ashcraft."

"Not so bad," I applauded. "Now listen to this: Mrs. Ashcraft has a husband in Tijuana, a mild sort of hop-head who is mixed up with a bunch of thugs. She was trying to persuade him to come back to her. He has a girl down there who is young, goofy over him, and a bad actor—one tough youngster. He was planning to run out on the girl and come back home."

"So-o-o?" O'Gar said softly.

"But," I continued, "I was with both him and the girl, in Tijuana, night before last—when this killing was done."

"So-o?"

A knock on the door interrupted our talk. It was a policeman to tell me that I was wanted on the phone. I went down to the first floor, and Vance Richmond's voice came over the wire.

"What is it? Miss Henry delivered your message, but she couldn't give me any details."

I told him the whole thing.

"I'll leave for the city tonight," he said when I had finished. "You go ahead and do whatever you want. You're to have a free hand."

"Right," I replied. "I'll probably be out of town when you get back. You can reach me through the Agency if you want to get in touch with me. I'm going to wire Ashcraft to come up—in your name."

After Richmond had hung up, I called the city jail and asked the captain if John Ryan, alias Fred Rooney, alias Jamocha, was still there.

"No. Federal officers left for Leavenworth with him and two other prisoners yesterday morning."

Up in the library again, I told O'Gar hurriedly:

"I'm catching the evening train south, betting my marbles that the job was made in Tijuana. I'm wiring Ashcraft to come up. I want to get him away from the Mexican town for a day or two, and if he's up here you can keep an eye on him. I'll give you a description of him, and you can pick him up at Vance

Richmond's office. He'll probably connect there first thing."

Half an hour of the little time I had left I spent writing and sending three telegrams. The first was to Ashcraft.

Edward Bohannon,

Golden Horseshoe Café,

Tijuana, Mexico.

> *Mrs. Ashcraft is dead. Can you come immediately?*
>
> *Vance Richmond.*

The other two were in code. One went to the Continental Detective Agency's Kansas City branch, asking that an operative be sent to Leavenworth to question Jamocha. The other requested the Los Angeles branch to have a man meet me in San Diego the next day.

Then I dashed out to my rooms for a bagful of clean clothes, and went to sleep riding south again.

6

SAN DIEGO WAS gay and packed when I got off the train early the next afternoon—filled with the crowd that the first Saturday of the racing season across the border had drawn. Movie folk from Los Angeles, farmers from the Imperial Valley, sailors from the Pacific Fleet, gamblers, tourists, grifters, and even regular people, from everywhere. I lunched, registered and left my bag at a hotel, and went up to the U.S. Grant Hotel to pick up the Los Angeles operative I had wired for.

I found him in the lobby—a freckle-faced youngster of twenty-two or so, whose bright gray eyes were busy just now with a racing program, which he held in a hand that had a finger bandaged with adhesive tape. I passed him and stopped at the cigar stand, where I bought a package of cigarettes and straightened out an imaginary dent in my hat. Then I went out to the street again. The bandaged finger and the business with the hat were our introductions. Somebody invented those tricks back before the Civil War, but they still worked smoothly, so their antiquity was no reason for discarding them.

I strolled up Fourth Street, getting away from Broadway—San Diego's main stem—and the operative caught up with me. His name was Gorman, and he turned out to be a pretty good lad. I gave him the lay.

"You're to go down to Tijuana and take a plant on the Golden Horseshoe Café. There's a little chunk of a girl hustling drinks in there—short curly brown hair; brown eyes; round face; rather large red mouth; square shoulders. You can't miss her;

she's a nice-looking kid of about eighteen, called Kewpie. She's the target for your eye. Keep away from her. Don't try to rope her. I'll give you an hour's start. Then I'm coming down to talk to her. I want to know what she does right after I leave, and what she does for the next few days. You can get in touch with me at the"—I gave him the name of my hotel and my room number—"each night. Don't give me a tumble anywhere else. I'll most likely be in and out of the Golden Horseshoe often."

We parted, and I went down to the plaza and sat on a bench under the palms for an hour. Then I went up to the corner and fought for a seat on a Tijuana stage.

Fifteen or more miles of dusty riding—packed five in a seat meant for three—a momentary halt at the Immigration Station on the line, and I was climbing out of the stage at the entrance to the race track. The ponies had been running for some time, but the turnstiles were still spinning a steady stream of customers into the track. I turned my back on the gate and went over to the row of jitneys in front of the Monte Carlo—the big wooden casino—got into one, and was driven over to the Old Town.

The Old Town had a deserted look. Nearly everybody was over watching the dogs do their stuff. Gorman's freckled face showed over a drink of mescal when I entered the Golden Horseshoe. I hoped he had a good constitution. He needed one if he was going to do his sleuthing on a distilled cactus diet.

The welcome I got from the Horseshoers was just like a homecoming. Even the bartender with the plastered-down curls gave me a grin.

"Where's Kewpie?" I asked.

"Brother-in-lawing, Ed?" a big Swede girl leered at me. "I'll see if I can find her for you."

Kewpie came through the back door just then.

"Hello, Painless!" She climbed all over me, hugging me, rubbing her face against mine, and the Lord knows what all. "Down for another swell souse?"

"No," I said, leading her back toward the stalls. "Business this time. Where's Ed?"

"Up north. His wife kicked off and he's gone to collect the remains."

"That makes you sorry?"

She showed her big white teeth in a boy's smile of pure happiness.

"You bet! It's tough on me that papa has come into a lot of sugar."

I looked at her out of the corner of my eyes—a glance that was supposed to be wise.

"And you think Ed's going to bring the jack back to you?"

Her eyes snapped darkly at me.

"What's eating you?" she demanded.

I smiled knowingly.

"One of two things is going to happen," I predicted. "Ed's going to ditch you—he was figuring on that, anyway—or he's going to need every brownie he can scrape up to keep his neck from being—"

"You God-damned liar!"

Her right shoulder was to me, touching my left. Her left hand flashed down under her short skirt. I pushed her shoulder forward, twisting her body sharply away from me. The knife her left hand had whipped up from her leg jabbed deep into the underside of the table. A thick-bladed knife, I noticed, balanced for accurate throwing.

She kicked backward, driving one of her sharp heels into my ankle. I slid my left arm around behind her and pinned her elbow to her side just as she freed the knife from the table.

"What th' hell's all 'is?"

I looked up.

Across the table a man stood glaring at me—legs apart, fists on hips. He was a big man, and ugly. A tall, raw-boned man with wide shoulders, out of which a long, skinny yellow neck rose to support a little round head. His eyes were black shoe-buttons stuck close together at the top of a little mashed nose. His mouth looked as if it had been torn in his face, and it was stretched in a snarl now, baring a double row of crooked brown teeth.

"Where d' yuh get 'at stuff?" this lovely person roared at me.

He was too tough to reason with.

"If you're a waiter," I told him, "bring me a bottle of beer and something for the kid. If you're not a waiter—sneak."

He leaned over the table and I gathered my feet in. It looked like I was going to need them to move around on.

"I'll bring yuh a—"

The girl wriggled out of my hands and shut him up.

"Mine's liquor," she said sharply.

He snarled, looked from one of us to the other, showed me his dirty teeth again, and wandered away.

"Who's your friend?"

"You'll do well to lay off him," she advised me, not answering my question.

Then she slid her knife back in its hiding place under her skirt and twisted around to face me.

"Now what's all this about Ed being in trouble?"

"You read about the killing in the papers?"

"Yes."

"You oughtn't need a map, then," I said. "Ed's only out is to put the job on you. But I doubt if he can get away with that. If he can't, he's nailed."

"You're crazy!" she exclaimed. "You weren't too drunk to know that both of us were here with you when the killing was done."

"I'm not crazy enough to think that proves anything," I corrected her. "But I am crazy enough to expect to go back to San Francisco wearing the killer on my wrist."

She laughed at me. I laughed back and stood up.

"See you some more," I said as I strolled toward the door.

I returned to San Diego and sent a wire to Los Angeles, asking for another operative. Then I got something to eat and spent the evening lying across the bed in my hotel room smoking and scheming and waiting for Gorman.

It was late when he arrived, and he smelled of mescal from San Diego to St. Louis and back, but his head seemed level enough.

"Looked like I was going to have to shoot you loose from the place for a moment," he grinned. "Between the twist flashing the pick and the big guy loosening a sap in his pocket, it looked like action was coming."

"You let me alone," I ordered. "Your job is to see what goes on, and that's all. If I get carved, you can mention it in your report, but that's your limit. What did you turn up?"

"After you blew, the girl and the big guy put their noodles together. They seemed kind of agitated—all agog, you might say. He slid out, so I dropped the girl and slid along behind him. He came to town and got a wire off. I couldn't crowd him close enough to see who it was to. Then he went back to the joint. Things were normal when I knocked off."

"Who is the big guy? Did you learn?"

"He's no sweet dream, from what I hear. 'Gooseneck' Flinn is the name on his calling cards. He's bouncer and general utility man for the joint. I saw him in action against a couple of gobs, and he's nobody's meat—as pretty a double throw-out as I've ever seen."

So this Gooseneck party was the Golden Horseshoe's clean-up man, and he hadn't been in sight during my three-day spree? I couldn't possibly have been so drunk that I'd forget his ugliness. And it had been on one of those three days that Mrs. Ashcraft and her servants had been killed.

"I wired your office for another op," I told Gorman. "He's to connect with you. Turn the girl over to him, and you camp on Gooseneck's trail. I think we're going to hang three killings on him, so watch your step. I'll be in to stir things up a little more tomorrow; but remember, no matter what happens, everybody plays his own game. Don't ball things up trying to help me."

"Aye, aye, Cap," and he went off to get some sleep.

The next afternoon I spent at the race track, fooling around with the bangtails while I waited for night. The track was jammed with the usual Sunday crowd. I ran into any number of old acquaintances, some of them on my side of the game, some on the other, and some neutral. One of the second lot was "Trick-hat" Schultz. At our last meeting—a copper was leading him out of a Philadelphia court room toward a fifteen-year bit—he had promised to open me up from my eyebrows to my ankles the next time he saw me. He greeted me this afternoon with an eight-inch smile, bought me a shot of what they sell for gin under the grandstand, and gave me a tip on a horse named Beeswax. I'm not foolish enough to play anybody's tips, so I didn't play this one. Beeswax ran so far ahead of the others that it looked like he and his competitors were in separate races, and he paid twenty-something to one. So Trick-hat had his revenge after all.

After the last race, I got something to eat at the Sunset Inn, and then drifted over to the big casino—the other end of the same building. A thousand or more people of all sorts were jostling one another there, fighting to go up against poker, craps, chuck-a-luck, wheels of fortune, roulette and twenty-one with whatever money the race track had left or given them. I didn't buck any of the games. My playtime was over. I walked around through the crowd looking for my men.

I spotted the first one—a sunburned man who was plainly a farm hand in his Sunday clothes. He was pushing toward the door, and his face held that peculiar emptiness which belongs to the gambler who has gone broke before the end of the game. It's a look of regret that is not so much for the loss of the money as for the necessity of quitting.

I got between the farm hand and the door.

"Clean you?" I asked sympathetically when he reached me.

A sheepish sort of nod.

"How'd you like to pick up five bucks for a few minutes' work?" I tempted him.

He would like it, but what was the work?

"I want you to go over to the Old Town with me and look at a man. Then you get your pay. There are no strings to it."

That didn't exactly satisfy him, but five bucks are five bucks;

and he could drop out any time he didn't like the looks of things. He decided to try it.

I put the farm hand over by a door, and went after another—a little, plump man with round, optimistic eyes and a weak mouth. He was willing to earn five dollars in the simple and easy manner I had outlined. The next man I braced was a little too timid to take a chance on a blind game. Then I got a Filipino—glorious in a fawn-colored suit, with a coat split to the neck and pants whose belled bottoms would have held a keg apiece—and a stocky young Greek who was probably either a waiter or a barber.

Four men were enough. My quartet pleased me immensely. They didn't look too intelligent for my purpose, and they didn't look like thugs or sharpers. I put them in a jitney and took them over to the Old Town.

"Now this is it," I coached them when we had arrived. "I'm going into the Golden Horseshoe Café, around the corner. Give me two or three minutes, and then come in and buy yourselves a drink." I gave the farm hand a five-dollar bill. "You pay for the drinks with that—it isn't part of your wages. There's a tall, broad-shouldered man with a long, yellow neck and a small ugly face in there. You can't miss him. I want you all to take a good look at him without letting him get wise. When you're sure you'd know him again anywhere, give me the nod, and come back here and you get your money. Be careful when you give me the nod. I don't want anybody in there to find out that you know me."

It sounded queer to them, but there was the promise of five dollars apiece, and there were the games back in the casino, where five dollars might buy a man into a streak of luck that—

write the rest of it yourself. They asked questions, which I refused to answer, but they stuck.

Gooseneck was behind the bar, helping out the bartenders, when I entered the place. They needed help. The joint bulged with customers. The dance floor looked like a mob scene. Thirsts were lined up four deep at the bar. A shotgun wouldn't have sounded above the din: men and women laughing, roaring and cursing; bottles and glasses rattling and banging; and louder and more disagreeable than any of those noises was the noise of the sweating orchestra. Turmoil, uproar, stink—a Tijuana joint on Sunday night.

I couldn't find Gorman's freckled face in the crowd, but I picked out the hatchet-sharp white face of Hooper, another Los Angeles operative, who, I knew then, had been sent down in response to my second telegram. Kewpie was farther down the bar, drinking with a little man whose meek face had the devil-may-care expression of a model husband on a tear. She nodded at me, but didn't leave her client.

Gooseneck gave me a scowl and the bottle of beer I had ordered. Presently my four hired men came in. They did their parts beautifully!

First they peered through the smoke, looking from face to face, and hastily avoiding eyes that met theirs. A little of this, and one of them, the Filipino, saw the man I had described, behind the bar. He jumped a foot in the excitement of his discovery, and then, finding Gooseneck glaring at him, turned his back and fidgeted. The three others spotted Gooseneck now, and sneaked looks at him that were as conspicuously furtive as a set of false whiskers. Gooseneck glowered at them.

The Filipino turned around, looked at me, ducked his head

sharply, and bolted for the street. The three who were left shot their drinks down their gullets and tried to catch my eye. I was reading a sign high on the wall behind the bar:

ONLY GENUINE PRE-WAR AMERICAN AND BRITISH WHISKEYS SERVED HERE

I was trying to count how many lies could be found in those nine words, and had reached four, with promise of more, when one of my confederates, the Greek, cleared his throat with the noise of a gasoline engine's backfire. Gooseneck was edging down the bar, a bungstarter in one hand, his face purple.

I looked at my assistants. Their nods wouldn't have been so terrible had they come one at a time; but they were taking no chances on my looking away again before they could get their reports in. The three heads bobbed together—a signal that nobody within twenty feet could, or did, miss—and they scooted out of the door, away from the long-necked man and his bung-starter.

I emptied my glass of beer, sauntered out of the saloon and around the corner. They were clustered where I had told them to wait.

"We'd know him! We'd know him!" they chorused.

"That's fine," I praised them. "You did great. I think you're all natural-born gumshoes. Here's your pay. Now if I were you boys, I think I'd sort of avoid that place after this; because, in spite of the clever way you covered yourselves up—and you did nobly!—he might possibly suspect something. There's no use taking chances, anyway."

They grabbed their wages and were gone before I had

finished my speech. I returned to the Golden Horseshoe—to be on hand in case one of them should decide to sell me out and come back there to spill the deal to Gooseneck.

Kewpie had left her model husband, and met me at the door. She stuck an arm through mine and led me toward the rear of the building. I noticed that Gooseneck was gone from behind the bar. I wondered if he was out gunning for my four ex-employees.

"Business looks good," I chattered as we pushed through the crowd. "You know, I had a tip on Beeswax this afternoon, and wouldn't play the pup." I made two or three more aimless cracks of that sort—just because I knew the girl's mind was full of something else. She paid no attention to anything I said.

But when we had dropped down in front of a vacant table, she asked:

"Who were your friends?"

"What friends?"

"The four jobbies who were at the bar when you were there a few minutes ago."

"Too hard for me, sister." I shook my head. "There were slews of men there. Oh, yes! I know who you mean! Those four gents who seemed kind of smitten with Gooseneck's looks. I wonder what attracted them to him—besides his beauty."

She grabbed my arm with both hands.

"So help me God, Painless," she swore, "if you tie anything on Ed, I'll kill you!"

Her brown eyes were big and damp. She was a hard and wise little baby—had rubbed the world's sharp corners with both shoulders—but she was only a kid, and she was worried sick over this man of hers. However, the business of a sleuth is to catch criminals, not to sympathize with their ladyloves.

I patted her hands.

"I could give you some good advice," I said as I stood up, "but you wouldn't listen to it, so I'll save my breath. It won't do any harm to tell you to keep an eye on Gooseneck, though—he's shifty."

There wasn't any special meaning to that speech, except that it might tangle things up a little more. One way of finding what's at the bottom of either a cup of coffee or a situation is to keep stirring it up until whatever is on the bottom comes to the surface. I had been playing that system thus far on this affair.

HOOPER CAME INTO my room in the San Diego hotel at a little before two the next morning.

"Gooseneck disappeared, with Gorman tailing him, immediately after your first visit," he said. "After your second visit, the girl went around to a 'dobe house on the edge of town, and she was still there when I knocked off. The place was dark."

Gorman didn't show up.

7

A BELL-HOP WITH a telegram roused me at ten o'clock in the morning. The telegram was from Mexicali:

> DROVE HERE LAST NIGHT HOLED UP WITH FRIENDS SENT TWO WIRES.
> GORMAN.

That was good news. The long-necked man had fallen for my play, had taken my four busted gamblers for four witnesses, had taken their nods for identifications. Gooseneck was the lad who had done the actual killing, and Gooseneck was in flight.

I had shed my pajamas and was reaching for my union suit when the boy came back with another wire. This one was from O'Gar, through the Agency:

> ASHCRAFT DISAPPEARED YESTERDAY

I used the telephone to get Hooper out of bed.

"Get down to Tijuana," I told him. "Stick up the house where you left the girl last night, unless you run across her at the Golden Horseshoe. Stay there until she shows. Stay with her until she connects with a big blond Englishman, and then switch to him. He's a man of less than forty, tall, with blue eyes and yellow hair. Don't let him shake you—he's the big boy in this party just now. I'll be down. If the Englishman and I stay together and the girl leaves us, take her, but otherwise stick to him."

I dressed, put down some breakfast and caught a stage for the Mexican town. The boy driving the stage made fair time, but you would have thought we were standing still to see a maroon roadster pass us near Palm City. Ashcraft was driving the roadster.

The roadster was empty, standing in front of the adobe house, when I saw it again. Up in the next block, Hooper was doing an imitation of a drunk, talking to two Indians in the uniforms of the Mexican Army.

I knocked on the door of the adobe house.

Kewpie's voice: "Who is it?"

"Me—Painless. Just heard that Ed is back."

"Oh!" she exclaimed. A pause. "Come in."

I pushed the door open and went in. The Englishman sat tilted back in a chair, his right elbow on the table, his right hand in his coat pocket—if there was a gun in that pocket it was pointing at me.

"Hello," he said. "I hear you've been making guesses about me."

"Call 'em anything you like." I pushed a chair over to within a couple of feet of him, and sat down. "But don't let's kid each other. You had Gooseneck knock your wife off so you could get what she had. The mistake you made was in picking a sap like Gooseneck to do the turn—a sap who went on a killing spree and then lost his nerve. Going to read and write just because three or four witnesses put the finger on him! And only going as far as Mexicali! That's a fine place to pick! I suppose he was so scared that the five- or six-hour ride over the hills seemed like a trip to the end of the world!"

The man's face told me nothing. He eased himself around in

his chair an inch or two, which would have brought the gun in his pocket—if a gun was there—in line with my thick middle. The girl was somewhere behind me, fidgeting around. I was afraid of her. She was crazily in love with this man in front of me, and I had seen the blade she wore on one leg. I imagined her fingers itching for it now. The man and his gun didn't worry me much. He was not rattle-brained, and he wasn't likely to bump me off either in panic or for the fun of it.

I kept my chin going.

"You aren't a sap, Ed, and neither am I. I want to take you riding north with bracelets on, but I'm in no hurry. What I mean is, I'm not going to stand up and trade lead with you. This is all in my daily grind. It isn't a matter of life or death with me. If I can't take you today, I'm willing to wait until tomorrow. I'll get you in the end, unless somebody beats me to you—and that won't break my heart. There's a rod between my vest and my belly. If you'll have Kewpie get it out, we'll be all set for the talk I want to make."

He nodded slowly, not taking his eyes from me. The girl came close to my back. One of her hands came over my shoulder, went under my vest, and my old black gun left me. Before she stepped away she laid the point of her knife against the nape of my neck for an instant—a gentle reminder. I managed not to squirm or jump.

"Good," I said when she gave my gun to the Englishman, who pocketed it with his left hand. "Now here's my proposition. You and Kewpie ride across the border with me—so we won't have to fool with extradition papers—and I'll have you locked up. We'll do our fighting in court. I'm not absolutely certain that I can tie the killings on either of you, and if I flop, you'll be free. If I make the grade—as I hope to—you'll swing, of course. But there's always a good chance of beating the courts—especially if you're guilty—and that's the only chance you have that's worth a damn.

"What's the sense of scooting? Spending the rest of your life dodging bulls? Only to be nabbed finally—or bumped off trying to get away? You'll maybe save your neck, but what of the money your wife left? That money is what you are in the game for—it's what you had your wife killed for. Stand trial and you've a chance to collect it. Run—and you kiss it good-by. Are you going to ditch it—throw it away just because your cat's-paw bungled the deal? Or are you going to stick to the finish—win everything or lose everything?"

A lot of these boys who make cracks about not being taken alive have been wooed into peaceful surrender with that kind of talk. But my game just now was to persuade Ed and his girl to bolt. If they let me throw them in the can I might be able to convict one of them, but my chances weren't any too large. It depended on how things turned out later. It depended on whether I could prove that Gooseneck had been in San Francisco on the night of the killings, and I imagined that he would be well supplied with all sorts of proof to the contrary. We had not been able to find a single finger-print of the killer's in Mrs. Ashcraft's house. And if I *could* convince a jury that he was in San Francisco at the time, then I would have to show that he had done the killing. And after that I would have the toughest part of the job still ahead of me—to prove that he had done the killing for one of these two, and not on his own account. I had an idea that when we picked Gooseneck up and put the screws to him he would talk. But that was only an idea.

What I was working for was to make this pair dust out. I didn't care where they went or what they did, so long as they scooted. I'd trust to luck and my own head to get profit out of their scrambling—I was still trying to stir things up.

The Englishman was thinking hard. I knew I had him worried, chiefly through what I had said about Gooseneck Flinn. If I had pulled the moth-eaten stuff—said that Gooseneck had been picked up and had squealed—this Englishman would have put me down as a liar; but the little I had said was bothering him.

He bit his lip and frowned. Then he shook himself and chuckled.

"You're balmy, Painless," he said. "But you—"

I don't know what he was going to say—whether I was going to win or lose.

The front door slammed open, and Gooseneck Flinn came into the room.

His clothes were white with dust. His face was thrust forward to the full length of his long, yellow neck.

His shoe-button eyes focused on me. His hands turned over. That's all you could see. They simply turned over—and there was a heavy revolver in each.

"Your paws on the table, Ed," he snarled.

Ed's gun—if that is what he had in his pocket—was blocked from a shot at the man in the doorway by a corner of the table. He took his hand out of his pocket, empty, and laid both palms down on the table-top.

"Stay where y'r at!" Gooseneck barked at the girl.

She was standing on the other side of the room. The knife with which she had pricked the back of my neck was not in sight.

Gooseneck glared at me for nearly a minute, but when he spoke it was to Ed and Kewpie.

"So this is what y' wired me to come back for, huh? A trap! Me the goat for yur! I'll be y'r goat! I'm goin' to speak my piece, an' then I'm goin' out o' here if I have to smoke my way through the whole damn' Mex army! I killed y'r wife all right—an' her help, too. Killed 'em for the thousand bucks—"

The girl took a step toward him, screaming:

"Shut up, damn you!"

Her mouth was twisting and working like a child's, and there was water in her eyes.

"Shut up, yourself!" Gooseneck roared back at her, and his thumb raised the hammer of the gun that threatened her. "I'm doin' the talkin'. I killed her for—"

Kewpie bent forward. Her left hand went under the hem of her skirt. The hand came up—empty. The flash from Gooseneck's gun lit on a flying steel blade.

The girl spun back across the room—hammered back by the bullets that tore through her chest. Her back hit the wall. She pitched forward to the floor.

Gooseneck stopped shooting and tried to speak. The brown haft of the girl's knife stuck out of his yellow throat. He couldn't get his words past the blade. He dropped one gun and tried to take hold of the protruding haft. Half-way up to it his hand came, and dropped. He went down slowly—to his knees—hands and knees—rolled over on his side—and lay still.

I jumped for the Englishman. The revolver Gooseneck had dropped turned under my foot, spilling me sidewise. My hand brushed the Englishman's coat, but he twisted away from me, and got his guns out.

His eyes were hard and cold and his mouth was shut until you could hardly see the slit of it. He backed slowly across the floor, while I lay still where I had tumbled. He didn't make a speech. A moment of hesitation in the doorway. The door jerked open and shut. He was gone.

I scooped up the gun that had thrown me, sprang to Gooseneck's side, tore the other gun out of his dead hand, and plunged into the street. The maroon roadster was trailing a cloud of dust into the desert behind it. Thirty feet from me stood a dirt-caked black touring car. That would be the one in which Gooseneck had driven back from Mexicali.

I jumped for it, climbed in, brought it to life, and pointed it at the dust-cloud ahead.

8

THE CAR UNDER me, I discovered, was surprisingly well engined for its battered looks—its motor was so good that I knew it was a border-runner's car. I nursed it along, not pushing it. There were still four or five hours of daylight left, and while there was any light at all I couldn't miss the cloud of dust from the fleeing roadster.

I didn't know whether we were following a road or not. Sometimes the ground under me looked like one, but mostly it didn't differ much from the rest of the desert. For half an hour or more the dust-cloud ahead and I held our respective positions, and then I found that I was gaining.

The going was roughening. Any road that we might originally have been using had petered out. I opened up a little, though the jars it cost me were vicious. But if I was going to avoid playing Indian among the rocks and cactus, I would have to get within striking distance of my man before he deserted his car and started a game of hide and seek on foot. I'm a city man. I have done my share of work in the open spaces, but I don't like it. My taste in playgrounds runs more to alleys, back-yards and cellars than to canyons, mesas and arroyos.

I missed a boulder that would have smashed me up—missed it by a hair—and looked ahead again to see that the maroon roadster was no longer stirring up the grit. It had stopped.

The roadster was empty. I kept on.

From behind the roadster a pistol snapped at me, three times. It would have taken good shooting to plug me at that instant.

I was bounding and bouncing around in my seat like a pellet of quicksilver in a nervous man's palm.

He fired again from the shelter of his car, and then dashed for a narrow arroyo—a sharp-edged, ten-foot crack in the earth—off to the left. On the brink, he wheeled to snap another cap at me—and jumped down out of sight.

I twisted the wheel in my hands, jammed on the brakes and slid the black touring car to the spot where I had seen him last. The edge of the arroyo was crumbling under my front wheels. I released the brake. Tumbled out. Shoved.

The car plunged down into the gully after him.

Sprawled on my belly, one of Gooseneck's guns in each hand, I wormed my head over the edge. On all fours, the Englishman was scrambling out of the way of the car. The car was mangled, but still sputtering. One of the man's fists was bunched around a gun—mine.

"Drop it and stand up, Ed!" I yelled.

Snake-quick, he flung himself around in a sitting position on the arroyo bottom, swung his gun up—and I smashed his forearm with my second shot.

He was holding the wounded arm with his left hand when I slid down beside him, picked up the gun he had dropped, and frisked him to see if he had any more.

He grinned at me.

"You know," he drawled, "I fancy your true name isn't Painless Parker at all. You don't act like it."

Twisting a handkerchief into a tourniquet of a sort, I knotted it around his wounded arm, which was bleeding.

"Let's go upstairs and talk," I suggested, and helped him up the steep side of the gully.

We climbed into his roadster.

"Out of gas," he said. "We've got a nice walk ahead of us."

"We'll get a lift. I had a man watching your house, and another one shadowing Gooseneck. They'll be coming out after me, I reckon. Meanwhile, we have time for a nice heart-to-heart talk."

"Go ahead, talk your head off," he invited; "but don't expect me to add much to the conversation. You've got nothing on me." (I'd like to have a dollar, or even a nickel, for every time I've heard that remark!) "You saw Kewpie bump Gooseneck off to keep him from peaching on her."

"So that's your play?" I inquired. "The girl hired Gooseneck to kill your wife—out of jealousy—when she learned that you were planning to shake her and return to your own world?"

"Exactly."

"Not bad, Ed, but there's one rough spot in it."

"Yes?"

"Yes," I repeated. "You are not Ashcraft!"

He jumped, and then laughed.

"Now your enthusiasm is getting the better of your judgment," he kidded me. "Could I have deceived another man's wife? Don't you think her lawyer, Richmond, made me prove my identity?"

"Well, I'll tell you, Ed, I think I'm a smarter baby than either of them. Suppose you had a lot of stuff that belonged to Ashcraft—papers, letters, things in his handwriting? If you were even a fair hand with a pen, you could have fooled his wife. She thought her husband had had four tough years and had become a hop-head. That would account for irregularities in his writing. And I don't imagine you ever got very familiar in your letters—not enough so to risk any missteps. As for the lawyer—his making you identify yourself was only a matter of form. It never occurred to him that you weren't Ashcraft. Identification is easy, anyway. Give me a week and I'll prove that I'm the Sultan of Turkey."

He shook his head sadly.

"That comes from riding around in the sun."

I went on.

"At first your game was to bleed Mrs. Ashcraft for an allowance—to take the cure. But after she closed out her affairs in England and came here, you decided to wipe her out and take everything. You knew she was an orphan and had no close relatives to come butting in. You knew it wasn't likely that there were many people in America who could say you were not Ashcraft. Now if you want to you can do your stalling for just as long as it takes us to send a photograph of you to England—to be shown to the people that knew him there. But you understand that you will do your stalling in the can, so I don't see what it will get you."

"Where do you think Ashcraft would be while I was spending his money?"

There were only two possible guesses. I took the more reasonable one.

"Dead."

I imagined his mouth tightened a little, so I took another shot, and added:

"Up north."

That got to him, though he didn't get excited. But his eyes became thoughtful behind his smile. The United States is all "up north" from Tijuana, but it was even betting that he thought I meant Seattle, where the last record of Ashcraft had come from.

"You may be right, of course," he drawled. "But even at that, I don't see just how you expect to hang me. Can you prove that Kewpie didn't think I was Ashcraft? Can you prove that she knew why Mrs. Ashcraft was sending me money? Can you prove that she knew anything about my game? I rather think not. There are still any number of reasons for her to have been jealous of this other woman.

"I'll do my bit for fraud, Painless, but you're not going to swing me. The only two who could possibly tie anything on me are dead behind us. Maybe one of them told you something. What of it? You know damned well that you won't be allowed to testify to it in court. What someone who is now dead may have told you—unless the person it affects was present—isn't evidence, and you know it."

"You may get away with it," I admitted. "Juries are funny, and I don't mind telling you that I'd be happier if I knew a few things about those murders that I don't know. Do you mind telling me about the ins and outs of your switch with Ashcraft—in Seattle?"

He squinted his blue eyes at me.

"You're a puzzling chap, Painless," he said. "I can't tell whether you know everything, or are just sharp-shooting." He puckered his lips and then shrugged. "I'll tell you. It won't matter greatly. I'm due to go over for this impersonation, so a confession to a little additional larceny won't matter."

9

"THE HOTEL-SNEAK USED to be my lay," the Englishman said after a pause. "I came to the States after England and the Continent got uncomfortable. I was rather good at it. I had the proper manner—the front. I could do the gentleman without sweating over it, you know. In fact there was a day, not so long ago, when I wasn't 'Liverpool Ed.' But you don't want to hear me brag about the select blood that flows through these veins.

"To get back to our knitting: I had rather a successful tour on my first American voyage. I visited most of the better hotels between New York and Seattle, and profited nicely. Then, one night in a Seattle hotel, I worked the barrel and put myself into a room on the fourth floor. I had hardly closed the door behind me before another key was rattling in it. The room was night-dark. I risked a flash from my light, picked out a closet door, and got behind it just in time.

"The clothes closet was empty; rather a stroke of luck, since there was nothing in it for the room's occupant to come for. He—it was a man—had switched on the lights by then.

"He began pacing the floor. He paced it for three solid hours—up and down, up and down, up and down—while I stood behind the closet door with my gun in my hand, in case he should pull it open. For three solid hours he paced that damned floor. Then he sat down and I heard a pen scratching on paper. Ten minutes of that and he was back at his pacing; but he kept it up for only a few minutes this time. I heard the latches of a valise click. And a shot!

"I bounded out of my retreat. He was stretched on the floor, with a hole in the side of his head. A bad break for me, and no mistake! I could hear excited voices in the corridor. I stepped over the dead chap, found the letter he had been writing on the writing-desk. It was addressed to Mrs. Norman Ashcraft, at a Wine Street number in Bristol, England. I tore it open. He had written that he was going to kill himself, and it was signed Norman. I felt better. A murder couldn't be made out of it.

"Nevertheless, I was here in this room with a flashlight, skeleton keys, and a gun—to say nothing of a handful of jewelry that I had picked up on the next floor. Somebody was knocking on the door.

" 'Get the police!' I called through the door, playing for time.

"Then I turned to the man who had let me in for all this. I would have pegged him for a fellow Britisher even if I hadn't seen the address on his letter. There are thousands of us on the same order—blond, fairly tall, well set up. I took the only chance there was. His hat and topcoat were on a chair where he had tossed them. I put them on and dropped my hat beside him. Kneeling, I emptied his pockets, and my own, gave him all my stuff, pouched all of his. Then I traded guns with him and opened the door.

"What I had in mind was that the first arrivals might not know him by sight, or not well enough to recognize him immediately. That would give me several seconds to arrange my disappearance in. But when I opened the door I found that my idea wouldn't work out as I had planned. The house detective was there, and a policeman, and I knew I was licked. There would be little chance of sneaking away from them. But I played my hand out. I told them I had come up to my room and found this chap on the floor going through my belongings. I had seized him, and in the struggle had shot him.

"Minutes went by like hours, and nobody denounced me. People were calling me Mr. Ashcraft. My impersonation was succeeding. It had me gasping then, but after I learned more about Ashcraft it wasn't so surprising. He had arrived at the hotel only that afternoon, and no one had seen him except in his hat and coat—the hat and coat I was wearing. We were of the same size and type—typical blond Englishmen.

"Then I got another surprise. When the detective examined the dead man's clothes he found that the maker's labels had been ripped out. When I got a look at his diary, later, I found the explanation of that. He had been tossing mental coins with himself, alternating between a determination to kill himself, and another to change his name and make a new place for himself in the world—putting his old life behind him. It was while he was considering the second plan that he had removed the markers from all of his clothing.

"But I didn't know that while I stood there among those people. All I knew was that miracles were happening. I met the miracles half-way, not turning a hair, accepting everything as a matter of course. I think the police smelled something wrong, but they couldn't put their hands on it. There was the dead man on the floor, with a prowler's outfit in his pockets, a pocketful of stolen jewelry, and the labels gone from his clothes—a burglar's trick. And there I was—a well-to-do Englishman whom the hotel people recognized as the room's rightful occupant.

"I had to talk small just then, but after I went through the dead man's stuff I knew him inside and outside, backward and forward. He had nearly a bushel of papers, and a diary that had everything he had ever done or thought in it. I put in the first night studying those things—memorizing them—and practicing his signature. Among the other things I had taken from his pockets were fifteen hundred dollars' worth of traveler's checks, and I wanted to be able to get them cashed in the morning.

"I stayed in Seattle for three days—as Norman Ashcraft. I had tumbled into something rich and I wasn't going to throw it away. The letter to his wife would keep me from being charged with murder if anything slipped, and I knew I was safer seeing the thing through than running. When the excitement had quieted down I packed up and came down to San Francisco, resuming my own name—Edward Bohannon. But I held onto all of Ashcraft's property, because I had learned from it that his wife had money, and I knew I could get some of it if I played my cards right.

"She saved me the trouble of figuring out a deal for myself. I ran across one of her advertisements in the *Examiner*, answered it, and—here we are."

I looked toward Tijuana. A cloud of yellow dust showed in a notch between two low hills. That would be the machine in which Gorman and Hooper were tracking me. Hooper would have seen me set out after the Englishman, would have waited for Gorman to arrive in the car in which he had followed Gooseneck from Mexicali—Gorman would have had to stay some distance in the rear—and then both of the operatives would have picked up my trail.

I turned to the Englishman.

"But you didn't have Mrs. Ashcraft killed?"

He shook his head.

"You'll never prove it."

"Maybe not," I admitted.

I took a package of cigarettes out of my pocket and put two of them on the seat between us.

"Suppose we play a game. This is just for my own satisfaction. It won't tie anybody to anything—won't prove anything. If you did a certain thing, pick up the cigarette that is nearer me. If you didn't do that thing, pick up the one nearer you. Will you play?"

"No, I won't," he said emphatically. "I don't like your game. But I do want a cigarette."

He reached out his uninjured arm and picked up the cigarette nearer *me*.

"Thanks, Ed," I said. "Now I hate to tell you this, but I'm going to swing you."

"You're balmy, my son."

"You're thinking of the San Francisco job, Ed," I explained. "I'm talking about Seattle. You, a hotel sneak-thief, were discovered in a room with a man who had just died with a bullet in his head. What do you think a jury will make out of that, Ed?"

He laughed at me. And then something went wrong with the laugh. It faded into a sickly grin.

"Of course you did," I said. "When you started to work out your plan to inherit all of Mrs. Ashcraft's wealth by having her killed, the first thing you did was to destroy that suicide letter of her husband's. No matter how carefully you guarded it, there was always a chance that somebody would stumble into it and knock your game on the head. It had served its purpose—you wouldn't need it. It would be foolish to take a chance on it turning up.

"I can't put you up for the murders you engineered in San Francisco; but I can sock you with the one you didn't do in Seattle—so justice won't be cheated. You're going to Seattle, Ed, to hang for Ashcraft's suicide."

And he did.

Who Killed Bob Teal?

Operative Teal went out to shadow a thief, who didn't even know he was suspected. Seven hours after Teal left his agency's office, he was found— shot to death. Whose hand cut him down?

1

"TEAL WAS KILLED last night."

The Old Man—the Continental Detective Agency's San Francisco manager—spoke without looking at me. His voice was as mild as his smile, and gave no indication of the turmoil that was seething in his mind.

If I kept quiet, waiting for the Old Man to go on, it wasn't because the news didn't mean anything to me. I had been fond of Bob Teal—we all had. He had come to the agency fresh from college two years before; and if ever a man had the makings of a crack detective in him, this slender, broad-shouldered lad had. Two years is little enough time in which to pick up the first principles of sleuthing, but Bob Teal, with his quick eye, cool nerve, balanced head, and whole-hearted interest in the work, was already well along the way to expertness. I had an almost fatherly interest in him, since I had given him most of his early training.

The Old Man didn't look at me as he went on. He was talking to the open window at his elbow.

"He was shot with a .32, twice, through the heart. He was shot behind a row of signboards on the vacant lot on the northwest corner of Hyde and Eddy Streets, at about ten last night. His body was found by a patrolman a little after eleven. The gun was found about fifteen feet away. I have seen him and I have gone over the ground myself. The rain last night wiped out any leads the ground may have held, but from the condition of Teal's clothing and the position in which he was found,

I would say that there was no struggle, and that he was shot where he was found, and not carried there afterward. He was lying behind the signboards, about thirty feet from the sidewalk, and his hands were empty. The gun was held close enough to him to singe the breast of his coat. Apparently no one either saw or heard the shooting. The rain and wind would have kept pedestrians off the street, and would have deadened the reports of a .32, which are not especially loud, anyway."

THE OLD MAN'S pencil began to tap the desk, its gentle clicking setting my nerves on edge. Presently it stopped, and the Old Man went on:

"Teal was shadowing a Herbert Whitacre—had been shadowing him for three days. Whitacre is one of the partners in the firm Ogburn & Whitacre, farm-development engineers. They have options on a large area of land in several of the new irrigation districts. Ogburn handles the sales end, while Whitacre looks after the rest of the business, including the bookkeeping.

"Last week Ogburn discovered that his partner had been making false entries. The books show certain payments made on the land, and Ogburn learned that these payments had not been made. He estimates that the amount of Whitacre's thefts may be anywhere from $150,000 to $250,000. He came in to see me three days ago and told me all this, and wanted to have Whitacre shadowed in an endeavor to learn what he has done with the stolen money. Their firm is still a partnership, and a partner cannot be prosecuted for stealing from the partnership, of course. Thus, Ogburn could not have his partner arrested, but he hoped to find the money, and then recover it through civil action. Also he was afraid that Whitacre might disappear.

"I sent Teal out to shadow Whitacre, who supposedly didn't know that his partner suspected him. Now I am sending you out to find Whitacre. I'm determined to find him and convict him if I have to let all regular business go and put every man I have on this job for a year. You can get Teal's reports from the clerks. Keep in touch with me."

All that, from the Old Man, was more than an ordinary man's oath written in blood.

IN THE CLERICAL office I got the two reports Bob had turned in. There was none for the last day, of course, as he would not have written that until after he had quit work for the night. The first of these two reports had already been copied and a copy sent to Ogburn; a typist was working on the other now.

In his reports Bob had described Whitacre as a man of about thirty-seven, with brown hair and eyes, a nervous manner, a smooth-shaven, medium-complexioned face, and rather small feet. He was about five feet eight inches tall, weighed about a hundred and fifty pounds, and dressed fashionably, though quietly. He lived with his wife in an apartment on Gough Street. They had no children. Ogburn had given Bob a description of Mrs. Whitacre: a short, plump, blond woman of something less than thirty.

Those who remember this affair will know that the city, the detective agency, and the people involved all had names different from the ones I have given them. But they will know also that I have kept the facts true. Names of some sort are essential to clearness, and when the use of the real names might cause embarrassment, or pain even, pseudonyms are the most satisfactory alternative.

In shadowing Whitacre, Bob had learned nothing that seemed to be of any value in finding the stolen money. Whitacre had gone about his usual business, apparently, and Bob had seen him do nothing downright suspicious. But Whitacre had seemed very nervous, had often stopped to look around, obviously suspecting that he was being shadowed without being sure of it. On several occasions Bob had had to drop him to avoid being recognized. On one of these occasions, while waiting in the vicinity of Whitacre's residence for him to return, Bob had seen Mrs. Whitacre—or a woman who fit the description Ogburn had given—leave in a taxicab. Bob had not tried to follow her, but he had made a memorandum of the taxi's license number.

THESE TWO REPORTS read and practically memorized, I left the agency and went down to Ogburn & Whitacre's suite in the Packard Building. A stenographer ushered me into a tastefully furnished office, where Ogburn sat at a desk signing mail. He offered me a chair. I introduced myself to him: a medium-sized man of perhaps thirty-five, with sleek brown hair and the cleft chin that is associated in my mind with orators, lawyers, and salesmen.

"Oh, yes!" he said, pushing aside the mail, his mobile, intelligent face lighting up. "Has Mr. Teal found anything?"

"Mr. Teal was shot and killed last night."

He looked at me blankly for a moment out of wide brown eyes, and then repeated: "Killed?"

"Yes," I replied, and told him what little I knew about it.

"You don't think—" he began when I had finished, and then stopped. "You don't think Herb would have done that?"

"What do you think?"

"I DON'T THINK Herb would commit murder! He's been jumpy the last few days, and I was beginning to think he suspected I had discovered his thefts, but I don't believe he would have gone that far, even if he knew Mr. Teal was following him. I honestly don't!"

"Suppose," I suggested, "that sometime yesterday Teal found where he had put the stolen money, and then Whitacre learned that Teal knew it. Don't you think that under those circumstances Whitacre might have killed him?"

"Perhaps," he said slowly, "but I'd hate to think so. In a moment of panic Herb might—but I really don't think he would."

"When did you see him last?"

"Yesterday. We were here in the office together most of the day. He left for home a few minutes before six. But I talked with him over the phone later. He called me up at home at a little after seven, and said he was coming down to see me, wanted to tell me something. I thought he was going to confess his dishonesty, and that maybe we would be able to straighten out this miserable affair. But he didn't show up; changed his mind, I suppose. His wife called up at about ten. She wanted him to bring something from downtown when he went home, but of course he was not there. I stayed in all evening waiting for him, but he didn't—"

He stuttered, stopped talking, and his face drained white.

"MY GOD. I'M wiped out!" he said faintly, as if the thought of his own position had just come to him. "Herb gone, money gone, three years' work gone for nothing! And I'm legally responsible for every cent he stole. God!"

He looked at me with eyes that pleaded for a contradiction, but I couldn't do anything except assure him that everything possible would be done to find both Whitacre and the money. I left him trying frantically to get his attorney on the telephone.

From Ogburn's office I went up to Whitacre's apartment. As I turned the corner below into Gough Street I saw a big, hulking man going up the apartment house steps, and recognized him as George Dean. Hurrying to join him, I regretted that he had been assigned to the job instead of some other member of the Police Detective Homicide Detail. Dean isn't a bad sort, but he isn't so satisfactory to work with as some of the others; that is, you can never be sure that he isn't holding out some important detail so that George Dean would shine as the clever sleuth in the end. Working with a man of that sort, you're bound to fall into the same habit—which doesn't make for teamwork.

I arrived in the vestibule as Dean pressed Whitacre's bell-button.

"Hello," I said. "You in on this?"

"Uh-huh. What d'you know?"

"Nothing. I just got it."

THE FRONT DOOR clicked open, and we went together up to the Whitacre's apartment on the third floor. A plump, blond woman in a light blue house-dress opened the apartment door. She was rather pretty in a thick-featured, stolid way.

"Mrs. Whitacre?" Dean inquired.

"Yes."

"Is Mr. Whitacre in?"

"No. He went to Los Angeles this morning," she said, and her face was truthful.

"Know where we can get in touch with him there?"

"Perhaps at the Ambassador, but I think he'll be back by to-morrow or the next day."

Dean showed her his badge.

"We want to ask you a few questions," he told her, and with no appearance of astonishment she opened the door wide for us to enter. She led us into a blue and cream living-room, where we found a chair apiece. She sat facing us on a big blue settle.

"Where was your husband last night?" Dean asked.

"Home. Why?" Her round blue eyes were faintly curious.

"Home all night?"

"Yes, it was a rotten rainy night. Why?" She looked from Dean to me.

Dean's glance met mine, and I nodded an answer to the question that I read there.

"Mrs. Whitacre," he said bluntly, "I have a warrant for your husband's arrest."

"A warrant? For what?"

"Murder."

"Murder?" It was a stifled scream.

"Exactly, an' last night."

"But—but I told you he was—"

"AND OGBURN TOLD me," I interrupted leaning forward, "that you called up his apartment last night, asking if your husband was there."

She looked at me blankly for a dozen seconds; and then she

laughed, the clear laugh of one who has been the victim of some slight joke.

"You win," she said, and there was neither shame nor humiliation in either face or voice. "Now listen"—the amusement had left her—"I don't know what Herb has done, or how I stand, and I oughtn't to talk until I see a lawyer. But I like to dodge all the trouble I can. If you folks will tell me what's what, on your word of honor, I'll maybe tell you what I know, if anything. What I mean is, if talking will make things any easier for me, if you can show me it will, maybe I'll talk—provided I know anything."

THAT SEEMED FAIR enough, if a little surprising. Apparently this plump woman who could lie with every semblance of candor, and laugh when she was tripped up, wasn't interested in anything much beyond her own comfort.

"You tell it," Dean said to me.

I shot it out all in a lump.

"Your husband had been cooking the books for some time, and got into his partner for something like $200,000 before Ogburn got wise to it. Then he had your husband shadowed, trying to find the money. Last night your husband took the man who was shadowing him over on a lot and shot him."

Her face puckered thoughtfully. Mechanically she reached for a package of a popular brand of cigarettes that lay on a table behind the settle, and proffered them to Dean and me. We shook our heads. She put a cigarette in her mouth, scratched a match on the sole of her slipper, lit the cigarette, and stared at the burning end. Finally she shrugged, her face cleared, and she looked up at us.

"I'M GOING TO talk," she said. "I never got any of the money, and I'd be a chump to make a goat of myself for Herb. He was all right, but if he's run out and left me flat, there's no use of me making a lot of trouble for myself over it. Here goes: I'm not Mrs. Whitacre, except on the register. My name is Mae Landis. Maybe there is a real Mrs. Whitacre, and maybe not. I don't know. Herb and I have been living together here for over a year.

"About a month ago he began to get jumpy, nervous, even worse than usual. He said he had business worries. Then a couple of days ago I discovered that his pistol was gone from the drawer where it had been kept ever since we came here, and that he was carrying it. I asked him: 'What's the idea?' He said he thought he was being followed, and asked me if I'd seen anybody hanging around the neighborhood as if watching our place. I told him no; I thought he was nutty.

"Night before last he told me that he was in trouble, and might have to go away, and that he couldn't take me with him, but would give me enough money to take care of me for a while. He seemed excited, packed his bags so they'd be ready if he needed them in a hurry, and burned up all his photos and a lot of letters and papers. His bags are still in the bedroom, if you want to go through them. When he didn't come home last night I had a hunch that he had beat it without his bags and without saying a word to me, much less giving me any money—leaving me with only twenty dollars to my name and not even much that I could hock, and with the rent due in four days."

"When did you see him last?"

"About eight o'clock last night. He told me he was going

down to Mr. Ogburn's apartment to talk some business over with him, but he didn't go there. I know that. I ran out of cigarettes—I like Elixir Russians, and I can't get them uptown here—so I called up Mr. Ogburn's to ask Herb to bring some home with him when he came, and Mr. Ogburn said he hadn't been there."

"How long have you known Whitacre?" I asked.

"Couple of years. I guess. I think I met him first at one of the Beach resorts."

"Has he got any people?"

"NOT THAT I know of. I don't know a whole lot about him. Oh, yes! I do know that he served three years in prison in Oregon for forgery. He told me that one night when he was lushed up. He served them under the name of Barber, or Barbee, or something like that. He said he was walking the straight and narrow now."

Dean produced a small automatic pistol, fairly new-looking in spite of the mud that clung to it, and handed it to the woman.

"Ever see that?"

She nodded her blond head.

"Yep! That's Herb's, or its twin."

Dean pocketed the gun again, and we stood up.

"Where do I stand now?" she asked. "You're not going to lock me up as a witness or anything, are you?"

"NOT JUST NOW." Dean assured her. "Stick around where we can find you if we want you, and you won't be bothered. Got any idea which direction Whitacre'd be likely to go in?"

"No."

"We'd like to give the place the once-over. Mind?"

"Go ahead," she invited. "Take it apart if you want to. I'm coming all the way with you people."

We very nearly did take the place apart, but we found not a thing of value. Whitacre, when he had burned the things that might have given him away, had made a clean job of it.

"Did he ever have any pictures taken by a professional photographer?" I asked just before we left.

"Not that I know of."

"Will you let us know if you hear anything or remember anything else that might help?"

"Sure," she said heartily; "sure."

Dean and I rode down in the elevator in silence, and walked out into Gough Street.

"What do you think of all that?" I asked when we were outside.

"She's a lil, huh?" He grinned. "I wonder how much she knows. She identified the gun an gave us that dope about the forgery sentence up north, but we'd of found out them things anyway. If she was wise she'd tell us everything she knew we'd find out, an' that would make her other stuff go over stronger. Think she's dumb or wise?"

"We won't guess," I said. "We'll slap a shadow on her and cover her mail. I have the number of a taxi she used a couple days ago. We'll look that up too."

At a corner drug store I telephoned the Old Man, asking him to detail a couple of the boys to keep Mae Landis and her apartment under surveillance night and day; also to have the Post Office Department let us know if she got any mail that might have been addressed by Whitacre. I told the Old Man I would see Ogburn and get some specimens of the fugitive's writing for comparison with the woman's mail.

Then Dean and I set about tracing the taxi in which Bob Teal had seen the woman ride away. Half an hour in the taxi company's office gave us the information that she had been driven to a number on Greenwich Street. We went to the Greenwich Street address.

IT WAS A ramshackle building, divided into apartments or flats of a dismal and dingy sort. We found the landlady in the basement: a gaunt woman in soiled gray, with a hard, thin-lipped mouth and pale, suspicious eyes. She was rocking vigorously in a creaking chair and sewing on a pair of overalls, while three dirty kids tussled with a mongrel puppy up and down the room.

Dean showed his badge, and told her that we wanted to speak to her in privacy. She got up to chase the kids and their dog out, and then stood with hands on hips facing us.

"Well, what do you want?" she demanded sourly.

"Want to get a line on your tenants," Dean said. "Tell us about them."

"Tell you about them?" She had a voice that would have been harsh enough even if she hadn't been in such a peevish mood. "What do you think I got to say about 'em? What do you think I am? I'm a woman that minds her own business! Nobody can't say that I don't run a respectable—"

This was getting us nowhere.

"Who lives in number one?" I asked.

"The Auds—two old folks and their grandchildren. If you

know anything against them, it's more'n them that has lived with 'em for ten years does!"

"Who lives in number two?"

"Mrs. Codman and her boys, Frank and Fred. They been here three years, and—"

I carried her from apartment to apartment, until finally we reached a second-floor one that didn't bring quite so harsh an indictment of my stupidity for suspecting its occupants of whatever it was that I suspected them of.

"THE QUIRKS LIVE there." She merely glowered now, whereas she had had a snippy manner before. "And they're decent people, if you ask me!"

"How long have they been here?"

"Six months or more."

"What does he do for a living?"

"I don't know." Sullenly: "Travels maybe."

"How many in the family?"

"Just him and her, and they're nice quiet people, too."

"What does he look like?"

"Like an ordinary man. I ain't a detective. I don't go 'round snoopin' into folks' faces to see what they look like, and prying into their business. I ain't—"

"How old a man is he?"

"Maybe between thirty-five and forty, if he ain't younger or older."

"Large or small?"

"He ain't as short as you, and he ain't as tall as this feller with you," glaring scornfully from my short stoutness to Dean's big bulk, "and he ain't as fat as neither of you."

"Mustache?"

"No."

"Light hair?"

"No." Triumphantly: "Dark."

"Dark eyes, too?"

"I guess so."

DEAN, STANDING OFF to one side, looked over the woman's shoulder at me. His lips framed the name: "Whitacre."

"Now how about Mrs. Quirk—what does she look like?" I went on.

"She's got light hair, is short and chunky, and maybe under thirty."

Dean and I nodded our satisfaction at each other; that sounded like Mae Landis, right enough.

"Are they home much?" I continued.

"I don't know," the gaunt woman snarled sullenly, and I knew she did know, so I waited, looking at her, and presently she added grudgingly: I think they're away a lot, but I ain't sure."

"I know," I ventured, "they are home very seldom, and then only in the daytime—and you know it."

She didn't deny it, so I asked: "Are they in now?"

"I don't think so, but they might be."

"Let's take a look at the joint, I suggested to Dean.

HE NODDED AND told the woman: "Take us up to their apartment an' unlock the door for us."

"I won't!" she said with sharp emphasis. "You got no right goin' into folks' homes unless you got a search-warrant. You got one?"

"We got nothin'," Dean grinned at her, "but we can get plenty if you want to put us to the trouble. You run this house; you can go into any of the flats any time you want, an' you can take us in. Take us up, an' we'll lay off you: but if you're going to put us to a lot of trouble, then you'll take your chances of bein' tied up with the Quirks, an' maybe sharin' a cell with 'em. Think that over."

She thought it over, and then, grumbling and growling with each step, took us up to the Quirks' apartment. She made sure they weren't at home, then admitted us.

The apartment consisted of three rooms, a bath, and a kitchen, furnished in the shabby fashion that the ramshackle exterior of the building had prepared us for. In these rooms we found a few articles of masculine and feminine clothing, toilet accessories, and so on. But the place had none of the marks of a permanent abode; there were no pictures, no cushions, none of the dozens of odds and ends of personal belongings that are usually found in homes. The kitchen had the appearance of long disuse; the interiors of the coffee, tea, spice, and flour containers were clean.

Two things we found that meant something: A handful of Elixer Russian cigarettes on a table; and a new box of .32 cartridges—ten of which were missing—in a dresser drawer.

ALL THROUGH OUR searching the landlady hovered over us, her pale eyes sharp and curious; but now we chased her out, telling her that, law or no law, we were taking charge of the apartment.

"This was or is a hide-out for Whitacre and his woman all right," Dean said when we were alone. "The only question is whether he intended to lay low here or whether it was just a place where he made preparations for his get-away. I reckon the best thing is to have the Captain put a man in here night and day until we turn up Brother Whitacre."

"That's safest," I agreed, and he went to the telephone in the front room to arrange it.

After Dean was through phoning, I called up the Old Man to see if anything new had developed.

"Nothing new," he told me. "How are you coming along?"

"Nicely. Maybe I'll have news for you this evening."

"Did you get those specimens of Whitacre's writing from Ogburn? Or shall I have someone else take care of it?"

"I'll get them this evening," I promised.

I wasted ten minutes trying to reach Ogburn at his office before I looked at my watch and saw that it was after six o'clock. I found his residence listed in the telephone directory, and called him there.

"Have you anything in Whitacre's writing at home?" I asked. "I want to get a couple of samples—would like to get them this evening, though if necessary I can wait until to-morrow."

"I THINK I have some of his letters here. If you come over now I'll give them to you."

"Be with you in fifteen minutes," I told him.

"I'm going down to Ogburn's," I told Dean, "to get some of Whitacre's scribbling while you're waiting for your man to come from Headquarters to take charge of this place. I'll meet you at the States as soon as you can get away. We'll eat there, and make our plans for the night."

"Uh-huh," he grunted, making himself comfortable in one chair, with his feet on another, as I let myself out.

Ogburn was dressing when I reached his apartment, and had his collar and tie in his hand when he came to the door to let me in.

"I found quite a few of Herb's letters," he said as we walked back to his bedroom.

I looked through the fifteen or more letters that lay on a table, selecting the ones I wanted, while Ogburn went on with his dressing.

"How are you progressing?" he asked presently.

"So-so. Heard anything that might help?"

"No, but just a few minutes ago I happened to remember that Herb used to go over to the Mills Building quite frequently. I've seen him going in and out often, but never thought anything of it. I don't know whether it is of any importance or—"

I jumped out of my chair.

"That does it!" I cried. "Can I use your phone?"

"Certainly. It's in the hallway, near the door." He looked at me in surprise. "It's a slot phone; have you a nickel in change?"

"Yes." I was going through the bedroom door.

"The switch is near the door," he called after me, "if you want a light. Do you think—"

BUT I DIDN'T stop to listen to his questions. I was making for the telephone, searching my pockets for a nickel. And, fumbling hurriedly with the nickel, I muffed it—not entirely by accident, for I had a hunch that I wanted to work out. The nickel rolled away down the carpeted hallway. I switched on the light, recovered the nickel, and called the "Quirks'" number. I'm glad I played that hunch.

Dean was still there.

"That joint's dead," I sang. "Take the landlady down to Headquarters, and grab the Landis woman, too. I'll meet you there—at Headquarters."

"You mean it?" he rumbled.

"Almost," I said, and hung up the receiver.

I switched off the hall light and, whistling a little tune to myself, walked back to the room where I had left Ogburn. The door was not quite closed. I walked straight up to it, kicked it open with one foot, and jumped back, hugging the wall.

Two shots—so close together that they were almost one—crashed.

Flat against the wall, I pounded my feet against the floor and wainscot, and let out a medley of shrieks and groans that would have done credit to a carnival wild-man.

A moment later Ogburn appeared in the doorway, a revolver in his hand, his face wolfish. He was determined to kill me. It was my life or his, so—

I slammed my gun down on the sleek, brown top of his head.

When he opened his eyes, two policemen were lifting him into the back of a patrol-wagon.

I FOUND DEAN in the detectives' assembly-room in the Hall of Justice.

"The landlady identifies Mae Landis as Mrs. Quirk," he said. "Now what?"

"Where is she now?"

"One of the policewomen is holding both of them in the Captain's office."

"Ogburn is over in the Pawnshop Detail office," I told him. "Let's take the landlady in for a look at him."

Ogburn sat leaning forward, holding his head in his hands and staring sullenly at the feet of the uniformed man who guarded him, when we took the gaunt landlady in to see him.

"Ever see him before?" I asked her.

"Yes"—reluctantly—"that's Mr. Quirk."

Ogburn didn't look up, and he paid not the least attention to any of us.

After we had told the landlady that she could go home, Dean led me back to a far corner of the assembly-room, where we could talk without disturbance.

"Now spill it!" he burst out. "How come all the startling developments, as the newspaper boys call 'em?"

"Well, first-off, I knew that the question *Who killed Bob Teal?* could have only one answer. Bob wasn't a boob! He might possibly have let a man he was trailing lure him behind a row of billboards on a dark night, but he would have gone prepared for trouble. He wouldn't have died with empty hands, from a gun that was close enough to scorch his coat. The murderer had to be somebody Bob trusted, so it couldn't be Whitacre. Now Bob was a conscientious sort of lad, and he wouldn't have stopped shadowing Whitacre to go over and talk with some friend. There was only one man who could have persuaded him to drop Whitacre for a while, and that one man was the one he was working for—Ogburn.

"IF I HADN'T known Bob, I might have thought he had hidden behind the billboards to watch Whitacre; but Bob wasn't an amateur. He knew better than to pull any of that spectacular gumshoe stuff. So there was nothing to it but Ogburn!

"With that to go on, the rest was duck soup. All the stuff Mae Landis gave us—identifying the gun as Whitacre's, and giving Ogburn an alibi by saying she had talked to him on the phone at ten o'clock—only convinced me that she and Ogburn were working together. When the landlady described 'Quirk' for us, I was fairly certain of it. Her description would fit either Whitacre or Ogburn, but there was no sense to Whitacre's having the apartment on Greenwich Street, while if Ogburn and the Landis woman were thick, they'd need a meeting-place of some sort. The rest of the box of cartridges there helped some too.

"Then to-night I put on a little act in Ogburn's apartment, chasing a nickel along the floor and finding traces of dried mud that had escaped the cleaning-up he no doubt gave the carpet and clothes after he came home from walking through the lot in the rain. We'll let the experts decide whether it *could* be mud from the lot on which Bob was killed, and the jury can decide whether it *is*.

"There are a few more odds and ends—like the gun. The Landis woman said Whitacre had had it for more than a year, but in spite of being muddy it looks fairly new to me. We'll send the serial number to the factory, and find when it was turned out.

"FOR MOTIVE, JUST now all I'm sure of is the woman, which should be enough. But I think that when Ogburn & Whitacre's books are audited, and their finances sifted, we'll find something there. What I'm banking on strong is that Whitacre will come in, now that he is cleared of the murder charge."

And that is exactly what happened.

Next day Herbert Whitacre walked into Police Headquarters at Sacramento and surrendered.

Neither Ogburn nor Mae Landis ever told what they knew, but with Whitacre's testimony, supported by what we were able to pick up here and there, we went into court when the time came and convinced the jury that the facts were these:

Ogburn and Whitacre had opened their farm development business as a plain swindle. They had options on a lot of land, and they planned to sell as many shares in their enterprise as possible before the time came to exercise their options. Then they intended packing up their bags and disappearing. Whitacre hadn't much nerve, and he had a clear remembrance of the three years he had served in prison for forgery; so, to bolster his courage, Ogburn had told his partner that he had a friend in the Post Office Department in Washington, D.C., who would tip him off the instant any official suspicion was aroused.

The two partners made a neat little pile out of their venture, Ogburn taking charge of the money until the time came for the split-up. Meanwhile Ogburn and Mae Landis—Whitacre's supposed wife—had become intimate, and had rented the apartment on Greenwich Street, meeting there afternoons when Whitacre was busy at the office, and when Ogburn was supposed to be out hunting fresh victims. In this apartment Ogburn and the woman had hatched their little scheme, whereby they were to get rid of Whitacre, keep all the loot, and clear Ogburn of criminal complicity in the affairs of Ogburn & Whitacre.

OGBURN HAD COME into the Continental Office and told his little tale of his partner's dishonesty, engaging Bob Teal to shadow him. Then he had told Whitacre that he had received a tip from his friend in Washington that an investigation was about to be made. The two partners planned to leave town on their separate ways the following week. The next night Mae Landis told Whitacre she had seen a man loitering in the neighborhood, apparently watching the building in which they lived. Whitacre—thinking Bob a Post Office Inspector—had gone completely to pieces, and it had taken the combined efforts of the woman and his partner—apparently working separately—to keep him from bolting immediately. They had persuaded him to stick it out another few days.

On the night of the murder, Ogburn, pretending skepticism of Whitacre's story about being followed, had met Whitacre for the purpose of learning if he really was being shadowed. They had walked the streets in the rain for an hour. Then Ogburn, convinced, had announced his intention of going back and talking to the supposed Post Office Inspector, to see if he could be bribed. Whitacre had refused to accompany his partner, but had agreed to wait for him in a dark doorway.

Ogburn had taken Bob Teal over behind the billboards on some pretext, and had murdered him. Then he had hurried back to his partner, crying: "My God! He grabbed me and I shot him. We'll have to leave!"

Whitacre, in blind panic, had left San Francisco without stopping for his bags or even notifying Mae Landis. Ogburn was supposed to leave by another route. They were to meet in Oklahoma City ten days later, where Ogburn—after getting the loot out of the Los Angeles banks, where he had deposited it under various names—was to give Whitacre his share, and then they were to part for good.

In Sacramento next day Whitacre had read the newspapers, and had understood what had been done to him. He had done all the bookkeeping; all the false entries in Ogburn & Whitacre's books were in his writing. Mae Landis had revealed his former criminal record, and had fastened the ownership of the gun—really Ogburn's—upon him. He was framed completely! He hadn't a chance of clearing himself.

He had known that his story would sound like a far-fetched and flimsy lie; he had a criminal record. For him to have surrendered and told the truth would have been merely to get himself laughed at.

As it turned out, Ogburn went to the gallows, Mae Landis is now serving a fifteen-year sentence, and Whitacre, in return for his testimony and restitution of the loot, was not prosecuted for his share in the land swindle.

Mike or Alec or Rufus

Mr. Hammett and his hard-boiled sleuth are too well known to black mask readers to need much of an introduction. That the following story is as interesting and surprising as any which Mr. Hammett has yet written, is all we need to say to arouse your interest.

I DON'T KNOW whether Jacob Coplin was tall or short. All of him I ever got a look at was his round head—naked scalp and wrinkled face, both of them the color and texture of Manila paper—propped up on white pillows in a big four-poster bed. The rest of him was buried under a thick pile of bedding.

Besides he and I in the room that first time, there were his wife, a roly-poly woman with lines in a plump white face like scratches in ivory; his daughter Phyllis, a smart little Jewess of the popular-member-of-the-younger-set type; and the maid who had opened the door for me, a bigboned blonde girl in apron and cap.

I had introduced myself as a representative of the North American Casualty Company's San Francisco office, which I was in a way. There was no immediate profit in admitting I was a Continental Detective Agency sleuth, just now in the casualty company's hire, so I held back that part.

"I want a list of the stuff you lost," I told Coplin; "but first—"

"Stuff?" Coplin's yellow sphere of a skull bobbed off the pillows, and he wailed to the ceiling: "A hundred thousand dollars if a nickel, and he calls it *stuff!*"

Mrs. Coplin pushed her husband's head down on the pillows again with a short-fingered fat hand.

"Now, Jakie, don'd ged excited," she soothed him.

Phyllis Coplin's dark eyes twinkled, and she winked one of them at me.

"Well, if you people want to call your seventy-five-thousand-dollar loss *stuff*, I guess I can stand it for twenty-five thousand."

"So it adds up to a hundred thousand?" I asked.

"Yes. None of them were insured to their full value, and some weren't insured at all."

That was very usual. I don't remember ever having anybody admit that anything stolen from them was insured to the hilt—always it was half, or, at most, three-quarters covered by the policy.

"Suppose you tell me exactly what happened," I suggested, and added, to head off another speech that usually comes: "I know you've already told the police the whole thing, but I'll have to have it from you."

"Well, we were getting dressed to go to the Lauers' last night. I brought my wife's and daughter's jewelry—the valuable pieces—home with me from the safe-deposit box. I had just got my coat on, and had called to them to hurry up with their dressing when the door-bell rang."

"What time was this?"

"Just about half past eight. I went out of this room into the sitting-room across the passageway, and was putting some cigars in my case when Hilda"—nodding at the blonde maid—"came walking into the room, backwards. I started to ask her if she had gone crazy, walking around backwards, when I saw the robber. He—"

"Just a moment." I turned to the maid. "What happened when you answered the bell?"

"Why, I opened the door, of course, and this man was standing there, and he had a revolver in his hand, and he stuck it against my—my stomach, and pushed me back into the room where Mr. Coplin was, and he shot Mr. Coplin, and—"

"When I saw him and the revolver in his hand," Coplin took the story away from his servant; "it gave me a fright, sort of, and I let my cigar case slip out of my hand. Trying to catch it again—no sense in ruining good cigars even if you are being robbed—he must have thought I was trying to get a gun or something. Anyway he shot me in the leg. My wife and Phyllis came running in when they heard the shot, and he pointed the revolver at them, took all their jewels, and had them empty my pockets. Then he made them drag me back into Phyllis's room, into the closet, and he locked us all in there. And, mind you, he don't say a word all this time, not a word—just makes motions with his gun and his left hand."

"How bad did he bang your leg?"

"Depends on whether you want to believe me or the doctor. He says it's nothing much. Just a scratch, he says, but it's my leg that's shot, not his!"

"Did he say anything when you opened the door?" I asked the maid.

"No, sir."

"Did any of you hear him say anything while he was here?" None of them had.

"What happened after he locked you in the closet?"

"Nothing that we knew about," Coplin said; "until McBirney and a policeman came and let us out."

"Who's McBirney?"

"The janitor."

"How'd he happen along with a policeman?"

"He heard the shot, and came upstairs just as the robber was

Mike or Alec or Rufus
by Dashiell Hammett

starting down after leaving here. The robber turned around and ran upstairs, then, into an apartment on the seventh floor, and stayed there—keeping the woman who lives there, a Miss Eveleth, quiet with his revolver—until he got a chance to sneak out and get away. He knocked her unconscious before he left, and—and that's all. McBirney called the police right after he saw the robber, but they got here too late to be any good."

"How long were you in the closet?"

"Ten minutes—maybe fifteen."

"What sort of looking man was the robber?"

"Short and thin and—"

"How short?"

"About your height, or maybe shorter."

"About five feet five or six, say? What would he weigh?"

"Oh, I don't know—maybe a hundred and fifteen or twenty. He was kind of puny."

"How old?"

"Not more than twenty-two or three."

"Oh, Papa," Phyllis objected; "he was thirty, or near it!"

"What do you think?" I asked Mrs. Coplin.

"Twendy-five, I'll say."

"And you?" to the maid.

"I don't know exactly, sir; but he wasn't very old."

"Light or dark?"

"He was light," Coplin said. "He needed a shave, and his beard was yellowish."

"More of a light brown," Phyllis amended.

"Maybe, but it was light."

"What color eyes?"

"I don't know. He had a cap pulled down over them. They looked dark, but that might have been because they were in the shadow."

"How would you describe the part of his face you could see?"

"Pale, and kind of weak looking—small chin. But you couldn't see much of his face: he had his coat collar turned up and his cap pulled down."

"How was he dressed?"

"A blue cap pulled down over his eyes, a blue suit, black shoes, and black gloves—silk ones."

"Shabby or neat?"

"Kind of cheap looking clothes, needing pressing, awfully wrinkled."

"What sort of gun?"

Phyllis Coplin put in her word ahead of her father.

"Papa and Hilda keep calling it a revolver, but it was an automatic—a .38."

"Would you folks know him if you saw him again?"

"Yes," they agreed.

I cleared a space on the bedside table and got out a pencil and sheet of paper.

"I want a list of what he got, with as thorough a description of each piece as possible, and the price you paid for it, where you bought it, and when."

I got the list half an hour later.

"Do you know the number of Miss Eveleth's apartment?" I asked as I reached for my hat.

"702, two floors above."

I WENT UP there and rang the bell. The door was opened by a girl of twenty-something, whose nose was hidden under adhesive tape. She had nice clear hazel eyes, dark hair, and outdoor athletics written all over her.

"Miss Eveleth?"

"Yes."

"I'm from the insurance company that insured the Coplin's jewelry, and I'm looking for information about the robbery."

She touched her bandaged nose and smiled ruefully.

"This is some of my information."

"How did it happen?"

"A penalty of femininity—I forgot to mind my own business. But what you want, I suppose, is what I know about the scoundrel. The doorbell rang a few minutes before nine last night, and when I opened the door he was here. As soon as I got the door open he jabbed a pistol at me, and said:

" 'Inside, kid!'

"I let him in with no hesitancy at all: I was quite instantaneous about it, and he kicked the door to behind him.

" 'Where's the fire-escape?' he asked.

"The fire-escape doesn't come to any of my windows, and I told him so, but he wouldn't take my word for it. He drove me ahead of him to each of the windows; but of course he didn't find his fire-escape, and he got peevish about it, as if it were my fault. I didn't like some of the things he called me, and he was such a little half-portion of a man, so I tried to take him in hand. But— well, man is still the dominant male so far as I'm concerned. In plain American, he busted me in the nose and left me where I fell. I was dazed, though not quite all the way out, and when I got up he had gone. I ran out into the corridor then, and found some policemen on the stairs. I sobbed out my pathetic little tale to them, and they told me of the Coplin robbery. Two of them came back here with me and searched the apartment. I hadn't seen him actually leave, and they thought he might be foxy enough or desperate enough to jump into a closet and stay there until the coast was clear. But they didn't find him here."

"How long do you think it was after he knocked you down that you ran out into the corridor?"

"Oh, it couldn't have been five minutes. Perhaps only half that time."

"What did Mr. Robber look like?"

"Small, not quite so large as I; with a couple of days' growth of light hair on his face; dressed in shabby blue clothes, with black cloth gloves."

"How old?"

"Not very. His beard was thin, patchy, and he had a boyish face."

"Notice his eyes?"

"Blue. His hair, where it showed under the edge of his cap was a very light yellow, almost white."

"What sort of voice?"

"Very deep bass, though he may have been putting that on."

"Know him if you'd see him again?"

"Yes, indeed!" She put a gentle finger on her bandaged nose. "My nose would know, as the ads say, anyway!"

FROM MISS EVELETH'S apartment I went down to the office on the first floor, where I found McBirney, the janitor, and his wife, who managed the apartment building. She was a scrawny little woman with the angular mouth and nose of a nagger; he was big, broad-shouldered; with sandy hair and mustache; good-humored, shiftless red face; and genial eyes of a pale and watery blue.

He drawled out what he knew of the looting.

"I was a-fixin' a spigot on the fourth floor when I heard the shot. I went up to see what was the matter, an' just as I got far enough up the front stairs to see the Coplins' door, the fella came out. We seen each other at the same time, an' he aims his gun at me. There's a lot o' things I might of done, but what I did do was to duck down an' get my head out o' range. I heard him run upstairs, an' I got up just in time to see him make the turn between the fifth and sixth floors.

"I didn't go after him. I didn't have a gun or nothin', an' I figured we had him cooped. A man could get out o' this buildin' to the roof of the next from the fourth floor, an' maybe from the fifth, but not from any above that; an' the Coplins' apartment is on the fifth. I figured we had this fella. I could stand in front of the elevator an' watch both the front an' back stairs; an' I rang for the elevator, an' told Ambrose, the elevatorboy, to give the alarm an' run outside an' keep his eye on the fire-escape until the police came.

"The missus came up with my gun in a minute or two, an' told me that Martinez—Ambrose's brother, who takes care of the switchboard an' the front door—was callin' the police. I could see both stairs plain, an' the fella didn't come down them; an' it wasn't more'n a few minutes before the police—a whole pack of 'em—came from the Richmond Station. Then we let the Coplins out of the closet where they were, an' started to search the buildin'. An' then Miss Eveleth came runnin' down the stairs, her face an' dress all bloody an' told about him bein' in her apartment; so we were pretty sure we'd land him. But we didn't. We searched every apartment in the buildin', but didn't find hide nor hair of him."

"Of course you didn't!" Mrs. McBirney said unpleasantly. "But if you had—"

"I know," the janitor said with the indulgent air of one who has learned to take his pannings as an ordinary part of married life; "if I'd been a hero an' grabbed him, an' got myself all mussed up. Well, I ain't foolish like old man Coplin, gettin' himself plugged in the foot, or Blanche Eveleth, gettin' her nose busted. I'm a sensible man that knows when he's licked; an' I ain't jumpin' at no guns!"

"No! You're not doing anything that—"

This Mr. and Mrs. stuff wasn't getting me anywhere, so I cut in with a question to the woman.

"Who is the newest tenant you have?"

"Mr. and Mrs. Jerald; they came the day before yesterday."

"What apartment?"

"704—next door to Miss Eveleth."

"Who are these Jeralds?"

"They come from Boston. He told me he came out here to open a branch of a manufacturing company. He's a man of at least fifty, thin and dyspeptic looking."

"Just him and his wife?"

"Yes. She's poorly too—been in a sanatorium for a year or two."

"Who's the next newest tenant?"

"Mr. Heaton, in 535. He's been here a couple of weeks; but he's down in Los Angeles right now. He went away three days ago, and said he would be gone for ten or twelve days."

"What does he look like, and what does he do?"

"He's with a theatrical agency, and he's kind of fat and red-faced."

"Who's the next newest?"

"Miss Eveleth. She's been here about a month."

"And the next?"

"The Wageners, in 923. They've been here going on two months."

"What are they?"

"He's a retired real estate agent. The others are his wife and son Jack—a boy of maybe nineteen. I see him with Phyllis Coplin a lot."

"How long have the Coplins been here?"

"It'll be two years next month."

I turned from Mrs. McBirney to her husband.

"Did the police search all these people's apartments?"

"Yeah," he said. "We went into every room, every alcove an' every closet from cellar to roof."

"Did you get a good look at the robber?"

"Yeah. There's a light in the hall outside of the Coplins' door, an' it was shinin' full on his face when I saw him."

"Could he have been one of your tenants?"

"No, he couldn't."

"Know him if you saw him again?"

"You bet."

"What did he look like?"

"A little runt; a light-complected youngster of twenty-three or four in an old blue suit."

"Can I get hold of Ambrose and Martinez—the elevator and door boys who were on duty last night—now?"

The janitor looked at his watch.

"Yeah. They ought to be on the job now. They come on at two."

I went out into the lobby and found them together, matching nickels. They were brothers: slim, bright-eyed Filipino boys. They didn't add much to my dope.

Ambrose had come down to the lobby and told his brother to call the police as soon as McBirney had given him his orders, and then he had beat it out the back door to take a plant on the fire-escapes. The fire-escapes ran down the back and one side wall. By standing a little off from the corner of those walls, the Filipino had been able to keep his eyes on both of them, as well as on the back door.

There was plenty of illumination, he said, and he could see both fire-escapes all the way to the roof, and he had seen nobody on them.

Martinez had given the police a rap on the phone, and had then watched the front door and the foot of the front stairs. He had seen nothing.

Neither of them had seen anyone in the building either

before or after the Coplins were turned for their jewels who fit the robber's description.

I had just finished questioning the Filipinos when the street door opened and two men came in. I knew one of them: Bill Garren, a police detective on the Pawn Shop Detail. The other was a small blond youth all flossy in pleated pants, short, square-shouldered coat, and patent-leather shoes with fawn spats to match his hat and gloves. His face wore a sullen pout. He didn't seem to like being with Garren.

"What are you up to around here?" the detective hailed me.

"The Coplin doings for the insurance company," I explained.

"Getting anywhere?" he wanted to know.

"About ready to make a pinch," I said, not altogether in earnest and not altogether joking.

"The more the merrier," he grinned. "I've already made mine." Nodding at the dressy youth. "Come on upstairs with us."

The three of us got into the elevator, and Ambrose carried us to the fifth floor. Before pressing the Coplins' bell, Garren gave me what he had.

"This lad tried to soak a ring in a Third Street shop a little while ago—an emerald and diamond ring that looks like one of the Coplin lot. He's doing the clam now; he hasn't said a word—yet. I'm going to show him to these people; then I'm going to take him down to the Hall of Justice and get words out of him—words that fit together in nice sentences and everything!"

The prisoner looked sullenly at the floor and paid no attention to this threat. Garren rang the bell, and the maid Hilda opened the door. Her eyes widened when she saw the dressy boy, but she didn't say anything as she led us into the sitting-room, where Mrs. Coplin and her daughter were. They looked up at us.

"Hello, Jack!" Phyllis greeted the prisoner.

" 'Lo, Phyl," he mumbled, not looking at her.

"Among friends, huh? Well, what's the answer?" Garren demanded of the girl.

She put her chin in the air, and although her face turned red, she looked haughtily at the police detective.

"Would you mind removing your hat?" she asked.

Bill isn't a bad bimbo, but he hasn't any meekness. He answered her by tilting his hat over one eye and turning to her mother.

"Ever see this lad before?"

"Why, cerdainly!" Mrs. Coplin exclaimed.

"Thad's Mr. Wagener who lives upsdairs."

"Well," said Bill; "Mr. Wagener was picked up in a hock-shop trying to get rid of this ring." He fished a gaudy green and white ring from his pocket. "Know it?"

"Cerdainly!" Mrs. Coplin said, looking at the ring. "Id belongs to my Phyllis, and the robber—" Her mouth dropped open as she began to understand. "How could Mr. Wagener—?"

"Yes, how?" Bill repeated.

The girl stepped between Garren and me, turning her back on him to face me.

"I can explain everything," she announced.

That sounded too much like a movie sub-title to be very promising, but—

"Go ahead," I encouraged her.

"I found that ring in the passageway near the front door after the excitement was over. The robber must have dropped it. I didn't say anything to Papa and Mama about it, because I thought nobody would ever know the difference, and it was insured, so I thought I might as well sell it and be that much money in. I asked Jack last night if he could sell it for me, and he said he knew just how to go about it. He didn't have anything to do with it outside of that; but I did think he'd have sense enough not to try to pawn it right away!"

She looked scornfully at her accomplice.

"See what you've done!" she accused him.

He fidgeted and pouted at his feet.

"Ha! Ha! Ha!" Bill Garren said sourly. "That's a nifty! Did you ever hear the one about the two Irishmen that got in the Y.W.C.A. by mistake?"

She didn't say whether she had heard it or not.

"Mrs. Coplin," I asked; "making allowances for the different clothes, and the unshaven face, could this lad have been the robber?"

She shook her head with emphasis.

"No! He could nod be id!"

"Set your prize down, Bill," I suggested; "and let's go over in a corner and whisper things at each other."

"Right."

He dragged a heavy chair to the center of the floor, sat Wagener on it, anchored him there with handcuffs,—not exactly necessary, but Bill was grouchy at not getting his prisoner identified as the robber,—and then he and I stepped out into the passageway. We could keep an eye on the sitting-room from there without having our low-voiced conversation overheard.

"This is simple!" I whispered into his big red ear. "There are only five ways to figure the lay. First: Wagener stole the stuff for the Coplins; Second: the Coplins framed the robbery themselves, and got Wagener to peddle it. Third: Wagener and the girl engineered the deal without the old folks being in on it. Fourth: Wagener pulled it on his own hook and the girl is covering him up. Fifth: she told us the truth. None of them explain why your little playmate should have been dumb enough to flash the ring downtown this morning; but that can't be explained by any system. Which of the five do you favor?"

"I like 'em all," he grumbled. "But what I like most is that I've got this baby right—got him trying to pass a hot ring. That suits me fine. You do the guessing. I don't ask for any more than I've got."

That wasn't so foolish.

"It doesn't irritate me any either," I agreed. "The way it stands the insurance company can welch on the policies; but I'd like to smoke it out a little further, far enough to put away anybody who has been trying to run a hooligan on the North American. We'll clean up all we can on this kid, stow him in the can, and then see what further damage we can do."

"All right," Garren said. "Suppose you get hold of the janitor and that Eveleth woman while I'm showing the boy to old man Coplin, and getting the maid's opinion."

I nodded and went out into the corridor, leaving the door unlocked behind me. I took the elevator to the seventh floor, and told Ambrose to get hold of McBirney and send him to the Coplins' apartment. Then I rang Blanche Eveleth's bell.

"Can you come downstairs for a minute or two?" I asked her. "We've a prize who might be your friend of last night."

"Will I?" She started toward the stairs with me. "And if he's the right one, can I pay him back for my battered beauty?"

"You can," I promised. "Go as far as you like, so you don't maul him too badly to stand trial."

I took her into the Coplins' apartment without ringing the bell, and found everybody in Jacob Coplin's bedroom. A look at Garren's glum face told me that neither the old man nor the maid had given him a nod on the prisoner.

I put the finger on Jack Wagener. Disappointment came into Blanche Eveleth's eyes.

"You're wrong," she said. "That's not he."

Garren scowled at her. It was a pipe that if the Coplins were tied up with young Wagener, they wouldn't identify him as the robber. Bill had been counting on that identification coming from the two outsiders,—Blanche Eveleth and the janitor,—and now one of them had flopped.

The other one rang the bell just then, and the maid brought him into the room.

I pointed at Jack Wagener, who stood beside Garren, staring sullenly at the floor.

"Know him, McBirney?"

"Yeah. Mr. Wagener's son Jack."

"Is he the man who shooed you away with a gun last night?"

McBirney's watery eyes popped in surprise.

"No," he said with decision, and began to look doubtful.

"In an old suit, cap pulled down, needing a shave—could it have been him?"

"No-o-o," the janitor drawled; "I don't think so, though it— You know, now that I come to think about it, there was something familiar about that fella, an' maybe—By cracky, I think maybe you're right—though I couldn't exactly say for sure."

"That'll do!" Garren grunted in disgust.

An identification of the sort the janitor was giving isn't worth a damn one way or the other. Even positive and immediate identifications aren't always the goods. A lot of people who don't know any better—and some who do, or should—have given circumstantial evidence a bad name. It is misleading sometimes. But for genuine, undiluted, pre-war untrustworthiness, it can't come within gunshot of human testimony. Take any man you like—unless he is the one in a hundred thousand with a mind trained to keep things straight, and not always even then—get him excited, show him something, give him a few hours to think it over and talk it over, and then ask him about it. It's dollars to marks that you'll have a hard time finding any connection between what he saw and what he says he saw. Like this McBirney—another hour, and he'd be ready to gamble his life on Jack Wagener's being the robber.

Garren wrapped his fingers around the boy's arm and started for the door.

"Where to, Bill?" I asked.

"Up to talk to his people. Coming along?"

"Stick around a while," I invited. "I'm going to put on a party. But first, tell me, did the coppers who came here when the alarm was turned in do a good job?"

"I didn't see it," the police detective said. "I didn't get here until the fireworks were pretty well over, but I understand the boys did all that could be expected of them."

I turned to Jacob Coplin. I did my talking to him chiefly because we—his wife and daughter, the maid, the janitor, Blanche Eveleth, Garren and his prisoner, and I—were grouped around the old man's bed, and by looking at him I could get at least a one-eyed view of everybody else.

"Somebody has been kidding me somewhere," I began my speech. "If all the things I've been told about this job are right, then so is Prohibition. Your stories don't fit together, not even almost. Take the bird who stuck you up. He seems to have been pretty well acquainted with your affairs. It might be luck that he hit your apartment at a time when all of your jewelry was on hand, instead of another apartment, or your apartment at another time. But I don't like luck. I'd rather figure that he knew what he was doing. He nicked you for your pretties, and then he galloped up to Miss Eveleth's apartment. He may have been about to go downstairs when he ran into McBirney, or he may not. Anyway, he went upstairs, into Miss Eveleth's apartment, looking for a fire-escape. Funny, huh? He knew enough about the place to make a push-over out of the stick-up, but he didn't know there were no fire-escapes on Miss Eveleth's side of the building.

"He didn't speak to you or to McBirney, but he talked to Miss Eveleth, in a bass voice. A very, very deep voice. Funny, huh? From Miss Eveleth's apartment he vanished with every exit watched. The police must have been here before he left her apartment, and they would have blocked the outlets first thing, whether McBirney and Ambrose had already done that or not. But he got away. Funny, huh? He wore a wrinkled suit, which might have been taken from a bundle just before he went to work, and he was a small man. Miss Eveleth isn't a small woman, but she would be a small man. A guy with a suspicious disposition would almost think Blanche Eveleth was the robber."

Jacob Coplin, his wife, young Wagener, the janitor and the maid were gaping at me. Garren was sizing up the Eveleth girl with narrowed eyes, while she glared white-hot at me. Phyllis Coplin was looking at me with a contemptuous sort of pity for my feeble-mindedness.

Bill Garren finished his inspection of the girl and nodded slowly.

"She could get away with it," he gave his opinion; "indoors and if she kept her mouth shut."

"Exactly," I said.

"Exactly my eye!" Phyllis Coplin exploded. "Do you two correspondence-school detectives think we wouldn't know the difference between a man and a woman dressed in man's clothes? He had a day or two's growth of hair on his face—real hair, if you know what I mean. Do you think he could have fooled us with false whiskers? This happened, you know; it's not in a play!"

The others stopped gaping, and heads bobbed up and down.

"Phyllis is right," Jacob Coplin backed up his offspring; "he was a man—no woman dressed like one."

His wife, the maid, and the janitor nodded vigorous endorsements.

But I'm a bullheaded sort of bird when it comes to going where the evidence leads. I spun to face Blanche Eveleth.

"Can you add anything to the occasion?" I asked her.

She smiled very sweetly at me and shook her head.

"All right, bum," I said. "You're pinched. Let's go."

Then it seemed she could add something to the occasion. She had something to say, quite a few things to say, and they were all about me. They weren't nice things. In anger her voice was shrill, and just now she was madder than you'd think anybody could get on short notice. I was sorry for that. This job had run along peacefully and gently so far, hadn't been marred by any rough stuff, had been almost ladylike in every particular; and I had hoped it would go that way to the end. But the more she screamed at me the nastier she got. She didn't have any words I hadn't heard before, but she fitted them together in combinations that were new to me. I stood as much of it as I could.

Then I knocked her over with a punch in the mouth.

"Here! Here!" Bill Garren yelled, grabbing my arm.

"Save your strength, Bill," I advised him, shaking his hand off and going over to yank the Eveleth person up from the floor. "Your gallantry does you credit, and all the like of that, but I think you'll find Blanche's real name is Mike or Alec or Rufus."

I hauled her or him—which ever you like—to his or her feet and asked it:

"Feel like telling us about it?"

For answer I got a snarl.

"All right," I said to the others; "in the absence of authoritative information I'll give you my dope. If Blanche Eveleth could have been the robber except for the beard and the difficulty of a woman passing for a man, why couldn't the robber have been Blanche Eveleth before and after the robbery by using a—what do you call it—strong depilatory on his face, and a wig? It's hard for a woman to masquerade as a man, but there are lots of men who can get away with the feminine role. Couldn't this bird, after renting his apartment as Blanche Eveleth and getting everything lined up, have stayed in his apartment for a couple of days letting his beard grow? Come down and knock the job over? Beat it upstairs, get the hair off his face, and get into his female rig in, say, fifteen minutes?

My guess is that he could. And he had fifteen minutes. I don't know about the smashed nose. Maybe he stumbled going up the stairs and had to twist his plans to account for it; or maybe he smacked himself intentionally."

My guesses weren't far off, though his name was Fred—Frederick Agnew Rudd. He was known in Toronto, having done a stretch in the Ontario Reformatory as a boy of nineteen, caught shop-lifting in his she-makeup. He wouldn't come through, and we never turned up his gun or the blue suit, cap, and black gloves, although we found a cavity in his mattress where he had stuffed them out of the police's sight until later that night, when he could get rid of them. The Coplin sparklers came to light piece by piece when we had plumbers take apart the drains and radiators in apartment 702.

The Whosis Kid

We have talked so many times of Mr. Hammett's "Shrewd, canny sleuth," his "hard-boiled detective," etc., that we're at the end of our rope for words to introduce him to new readers.... Well, he is a shrewd, canny, hard-boiled sleuth, and this is an exciting tale.

1

IT STARTED IN Boston, back in 1917. I ran into Lew Maher on the Tremont street sidewalk of the Touraine Hotel one afternoon, and we stopped to swap a few minutes' gossip in the snow.

I was telling him something or other when he cut in with:

"Sneak a look at this kid coming up the street. The one with the dark cap."

Looking, I saw a gangling youth of eighteen or so; pasty and pimply face, sullen mouth, dull hazel eyes, thick, shapeless nose. He passed the city sleuth and me without attention, and I noticed his ears. They weren't the battered ears of a pug, and they weren't conspicuously deformed, but their rims curved in and out in a peculiar crinkled fashion.

At the corner he went out of sight, turning down Boylston street toward Washington.

"There's a lad that will make a name for hisself if he ain't nabbed or rocked off too soon," Lew predicted. "Better put him on your list. The Whosis Kid. You'll be looking for him some one of these days."

"What's his racket?"

"Stick-up, gunman. He's got the makings of a good one. He can shoot, and he's plain crazy. He ain't hampered by nothing like imagination or fear of consequences. I wish he was. It's these careful, sensible birds that are easiest caught. I'd swear the Kid was in on a coupla jobs that were turned in Brookline last month. But I can't fit him to 'em. I'm going to clamp him some day, though—and that's a promise."

Lew never kept his promise. A prowler killed him in an Audubon Road residence a month later.

A week or two after this conversation I left the Boston branch of the Continental Detective Agency to try army life. When the war was over I returned to the Agency payroll in Chicago, stayed there for a couple of years, and got transferred to San Francisco.

So, all in all, it was nearly eight years later that I found myself sitting behind the Whosis Kid's crinkled ears at the Dreamland Rink.

Friday night is fight night at the Steiner Street house. This particular one was my first idle evening in several weeks. I had gone up to the rink, fitted myself to a hard wooden chair not too far from the ring, and settled down to watch the boys throw gloves at one another. The show was about a quarter done when I picked out this pair of odd and somehow familiar ears two rows ahead of me.

I didn't place them right away. I couldn't see their owner's face. He was watching Kid Cipriani and Bunny Keogh assault each other. I missed most of that fight. But during the brief wait before the next pair of boys went on, the Whosis Kid turned his head to say something to the man beside him. I saw his face and knew him.

He hadn't changed much, and he hadn't improved any. His eyes were duller and his mouth more wickedly sullen than I had remembered them. His face was as pasty as ever, if not so pimply.

He was directly between me and the ring. Now that I knew him, I didn't have to pass up the rest of the card. I could watch the boys over his head without being afraid he would get out on me.

So far as I knew, the Whosis Kid wasn't wanted anywhere—not by the Continental, anyway—and if he had been a pickpocket, or a con man, or a member of any of the criminal trades in which we are only occasionally interested, I would have let him alone. But stick-ups are always in demand. The Continental's most important clients are insurance companies of one sort or another, and robbery policies make up a good percentage of the insurance business these days.

When the Whosis Kid left in the middle of the main event—along with nearly half of the spectators, not caring what happened to either of the muscle-bound heavies who were putting on a room-mate act in the ring—I went with him.

He was alone. It was the simplest sort of shadowing. The streets were filled with departing fight fans. The Kid walked down to Fillmore street, took on a stack of wheats, bacon and coffee at a lunch room, and caught a No. 22 car.

He—and likewise I—transferred to a No. 5 car at McAllister street, dropped off at Polk, walked north one block, turned back west for a block and a fraction, and went up the front stairs of a dingy light-housekeeping room establishment that occupied the second and third floors over a repair shop on the south side of Golden Gate avenue, between Van Ness and Franklin.

That put a wrinkle in my forehead. If he had left the street car at either Van Ness or Franklin, he would have saved himself a block of walking. He had ridden down to Polk and walked back. For the exercise, maybe.

I loafed across the street for a short while, to see what—if anything—happened to the front windows. None that had been dark before the Kid went in lighted up now. Apparently he didn't have a front room—unless he was a very cautious young man. I knew he hadn't tumbled to my shadowing. There wasn't a chance of that. Conditions had been too favorable to me.

The front of the building giving me no information, I strolled down Van Ness avenue to look at the rear. The building ran through to Redwood street, a narrow back street that split the block in half. Four back windows were lighted, but they told me nothing. There was a back door. It seemed to belong to the repair shop. I doubted that the occupants of the upstairs rooms could use it.

On my way home to my bed and alarm clock, I dropped in at the office, to leave a note for the Old Man:

Tailing the Whosis Kid, stick-up, 25-27, 135, 5 foot 11 inches, sallow, br. hair, hzl. eyes, thick nose, crooked ears. Origin Boston. Anything on him? Will be vicinity Golden Gate and Van Ness.

2

EIGHT O'CLOCK THE next morning found me a block below the house in which the Kid had gone, waiting for him to appear. A steady, soaking rain was falling, but I didn't mind that. I was closed up inside a black coupé, a type of car whose tamely respectable appearance makes it the ideal one for city work. This part of Golden Gate avenue is lined with automobile repair shops, second-hand automobile dealers, and the like. There are always dozens of cars standing idle to the block. Although I stayed there all day, I didn't have to worry over my being too noticeable.

That was just as well. For nine solid, end-to-end hours I sat there and listened to the rain on the roof, and waited for the Whosis Kid, with not a glimpse of him, and nothing to eat except Fatimas. I wasn't any too sure he hadn't slipped me. I didn't know that he lived in this place I was watching. He could have gone to his home after I had gone to mine. However, in this detective business pessimistic guesses of that sort are always bothering you, if you let them. I stayed parked, with my eye on the dingy door into which my meat had gone the night before.

At a little after five that evening, Tommy Howd, our pug-nosed office boy, found me and gave me a memorandum from the Old Man:

Whosis Kid known to Boston branch as robbery-suspect, but have nothing definite on him. Real name believed to be Arthur Cory or

Carey. May have been implicated in Tunnicliffe jewelry robbery in
Boston last month. Employee killed, $60,000 unset stones taken. No
description of two bandits. Boston branch thinks this angle worth
running out. They authorize surveillance.

After I had read this memorandum, I gave it back to the
boy,—there's no wisdom in carrying around a pocketful of
stuff relating to your job,—and asked him:

"Will you call up the Old Man and ask him to send somebody up to relieve me while I get a bite of food? I haven't
chewed since breakfast."

"Swell chance!" Tommy said. "Everybody's busy. Hasn't been
an op in all day. I don't see why you fellas don't carry a hunk or
two of chocolate in your pockets to—"

"You've been reading about Arctic explorers," I accused him.
"If a man's starving he'll eat anything, but when he's just ordinarily hungry he doesn't want to clutter up his stomach with
a lot of candy. Scout around and see if you can pick me up a
couple of sandwiches and a bottle of milk."

He scowled at me, and then his fourteen-year-old face grew
cunning.

"I tell you what," he suggested. "You tell me what this fella
looks like, and which building he's in, and I'll watch while you
go get a decent meal. Huh? Steak, and French fried potatoes,
and pie, and coffee."

Tommy has dreams of being left on the job in some such
circumstance, of having everything break for him while he's
there, and of rounding up regiments of desperadoes all by
himself. I don't think he'd muff a good chance at that, and I'd
be willing to give him a whack at it. But the Old Man would

scalp me if he knew I turned a child loose among a lot of thugs.

So I shook my head.

"This guy wears four guns and carries an ax, Tommy. He'd eat you up."

"Aw, applesauce! You ops are all the time trying to make out nobody else could do your work. These crooks can't be such tough mugs—or they wouldn't let you catch 'em!"

There was some truth in that, so I put Tommy out of the coupé into the rain.

"One tongue sandwich, one ham, one bottle of milk. And make it sudden."

But I wasn't there when he came back with the food. He had barely gone out of sight when the Whosis Kid, his overcoat collar turned up against the rain that was driving down in close-packed earnest just now, came out of the rooming-house doorway.

He turned south on Van Ness.

When the coupé got me to the corner he was not in sight. He couldn't have reached McAllister street. Unless he had gone into a building, Redwood street—the narrow one that split the block—was my best bet. I drove up Golden Gate avenue another block, turned south, and reached the corner of Franklin and Redwood just in time to see my man ducking into the back door of an apartment building that fronted on McAllister street.

I drove on slowly, thinking.

The building in which the Kid had spent the night and this building into which he had just gone had their rears on the same back street, on opposite sides, a little more than half a block apart. If the Kid's room was in the rear of his building, and he had a pair of strong glasses, he could keep a pretty sharp eye on all the windows—and probably much of the interiors—of the rooms on that side of the McAllister street building.

Last night he had ridden a block out of his way. Having seen him sneak into the back door just now, my guess was that he had not wished to leave the street car where he could be seen from this building. Either of his more convenient points of departure from the car would have been in sight of this building. This would add up to the fact that the Kid was watching someone in this building, and did not want them to be watching him.

He had now gone calling through the back door. That wasn't difficult to explain. The front door was locked, but the back door—as in most large buildings—probably was open all day. Unless the Kid ran into a janitor or someone of the sort, he could get in with no trouble. The Kid's call was furtive, whether his host was at home or not.

I didn't know what it was all about, but that didn't bother me especially. My immediate problem was to get to the best place from which to pick up the Kid when he came out.

If he left by the back door, the next block of Redwood street—between Franklin and Gough—was the place for me and my coupé. But he hadn't promised me he would leave that way. It was more likely that he would use the front door. He would attract less attention walking boldly out the front of the building than sneaking out the back. My best bet was the corner of McAllister and Van Ness. From there I could watch the front door as well as one end of Redwood street.

I slid the coupé down to that corner and waited.

Half an hour passed. Three quarters.

The Whosis Kid came down the front steps and walked toward me, buttoning his overcoat and turning up the collar as he walked, his head bent against the slant of the rain.

A curtained black Cadillac touring car came from behind me, a car I thought had been parked down near the City Hall when I took my plant here.

It curved around my coupé, slid with chainless recklessness in to the curb, skidded out again, picking up speed somehow on the wet paving.

A curtain whipped loose in the rain.

Out of the opening came pale fire-streaks. The bitter voice of a small-caliber pistol. Seven times.

The Whosis Kid's wet hat floated off his head—a slow balloon-like rising.

There was nothing slow about the Kid's moving.

Plunging, in a twisting swirl of coat-skirts, he flung into a shop vestibule.

The Cadillac reached the next corner, made a dizzy sliding turn, and was gone up Franklin street. I pointed the coupé at it.

Passing the vestibule into which the Kid had plunged, I got a one-eyed view of him, on his knees, still trying to get a dark gun untangled from his overcoat. Excited faces were in the doorway behind him. There was no excitement in the street. People are too accustomed to automobile noises nowadays to pay much attention to the racket of anything less than a six-inch gun.

By the time I reached Franklin street, the Cadillac had gained another block on me. It was spinning to the left, up Eddy street.

I paralleled it on Turk street, and saw it again when I reached the two open blocks of Jefferson Square. Its speed was decreasing. Five or six blocks further, and it crossed ahead of me—on Steiner street—close enough for me to read the license plate. Its pace was moderate now. Confident that they had made a clean getaway, its occupants didn't want to get in trouble through speeding. I slid into their wake, three blocks behind.

Not having been in sight during the early blocks of the flight, I wasn't afraid that they would suspect my interest in them now.

Out on Haight street near the park panhandle, the Cadillac stopped to discharge a passenger. A small man—short and slender—with cream-white face around dark eyes and a tiny black mustache. There was something foreign in the cut of his dark coat and the shape of his gray hat. He carried a walking-stick.

The Cadillac went on out Haight street without giving me a look at the other occupants. Tossing a mental nickel, I stuck to the man afoot. The chances always are against you being able to trace a suspicious car by its license number, but there is a slim chance.

My man went into a drug store on the corner and used the telephone. I don't know what else he did in there, if anything. Presently a taxicab arrived. He got in and was driven to the Marquis Hotel. A clerk gave him the key to room 761. I dropped him when he stepped into an elevator.

3

AT THE MARQUIS I am among friends.

I found Duran, the house copper, on the mezzanine floor, and asked him:

"Who is 761?"

Duran is a white-haired old-timer who looks, talks, and acts like the president of an exceptionally strong bank. He used to be captain of detectives in one of the larger Middle Western cities. Once he tried too hard to get a confession out of a safe-ripper, and killed him. The newspapers didn't like Duran. They used that accident to howl him out of his job.

"761?" he repeated in his grandfatherly manner. "That is Mr. Maurois, I believe. Are you especially interested in him?"

"I have hopes," I admitted. "What do you know about him?"

"Not a great deal. He has been here perhaps two weeks. We shall go down and see what we can learn."

We went to the desk, the switchboard, the captain of bell-hops, and upstairs to question a couple of chambermaids. The occupant of 761 had arrived two weeks ago, had registered as *Edouard Maurois, Dijon, France*, had frequent telephone calls, no mail, no visitors, kept irregular hours and tipped freely. Whatever business he was in or had was not known to the hotel people.

"What is the occasion of your interest in him, if I may ask?" Duran inquired after we had accumulated these facts. He talks like that.

"I don't exactly know yet," I replied truthfully. "He just

connected with a bird who is wrong, but this Maurois may be all right himself. I'll give you a rap the minute I get anything solid on him."

I couldn't afford to tell Duran I had seen his guest snapping caps at a gunman under the eves of the City Hall in daylight. The Marquis Hotel goes in for respectability. They would have shoved the Frenchman out in the streets. It wouldn't help me to have him scared up.

"Please do," Duran said. "You owe us something for our help, you know, so please don't withhold any information that might save us unpleasant notoriety."

"I won't," I promised. "Now will you do me another favor? I haven't had my teeth in anything except my mouth since seven-thirty this morning. Will you keep an eye on the elevators, and let me know if Maurois goes out? I'll be in the grill, near the door."

"Certainly."

On my way to the grillroom I stopped at the telephone booths and called up the office. I gave the night office man the Cadillac's license number.

"Look it up on the list and see whom it belongs to."

The answer was: "H. J. Paterson, San Pablo, issued for a Buick roadster."

That about wound up that angle. We could look up Paterson, but it was safe betting it wouldn't get us anything. License plates, once they get started in crooked ways, are about as easy to trace as Liberty Bonds.

All day I had been building up hunger. I took it into the grillroom and turned it loose. Between bites I turned the day's events over in my mind. I didn't think hard enough to spoil my appetite. There wasn't that much to think about.

The Whosis Kid lived in a joint from which some of the McAllister street apartments could be watched. He visited the apartment building furtively. Leaving, he was shot at, from a car that must have been waiting somewhere in the vicinity. Had the Frenchman's companion in the Cadillac—or his companions, if more than one—been the occupant of the apartment the Kid had visited? Had they expected him to visit it? Had they tricked him into visiting it, planning to shoot him down as he was leaving? Or were they watching the front while the Kid watched the rear? If so, had either known that the other was watching? And who lived there?

I couldn't answer any of these riddles. All I knew was that the Frenchman and his companions didn't seem to like the Whosis Kid.

Even the sort of meal I put away doesn't take forever to eat. When I finished it, I went out to the lobby again.

Passing the switchboard, one of the girls—the one whose red hair looks as if it had been poured into its waves and hardened—gave me a nod.

I stopped to see what she wanted.

"Your friend just had a call," she told me.

"You get it?"

"Yes. A man is waiting for him at Kearny and Broadway. Told him to hurry."

"How long ago?"

"None. They're just through talking."

"Any names?"

"No."

"Thanks."

I went on to where Duran was stalling with an eye on the elevators.

"Shown yet?" I asked.

"No."

"Good. The red-head on the switchboard just told me he had a phone call to meet a man at Kearny and Broadway. I think I'll beat him to it."

Around the corner from the hotel, I climbed into my coupé and drove down to the Frenchman's corner.

The Cadillac he had used that afternoon was already there, with a new license plate. I passed it and took a look at its one occupant—a thick-set man of forty-something with a cap pulled low over his eyes. All I could see of his features was a wide mouth slanting over a heavy chin.

I put the coupé in a vacant space down the street a way. I didn't have to wait long for the Frenchman. He came around the corner afoot and got into the Cadillac. The man with the big chin drove. They went slowly up Broadway. I followed.

4

WE DIDN'T GO far, and when we came to rest again, the Cadillac was placed conveniently for its occupants to watch the Venetian Café, one of the gaudiest of the Italian restaurants that fill this part of town.

Two hours went by.

I had an idea that the Whosis Kid was eating at the Venetian. When he left, the fireworks would break out, continuing the celebration from where it had broken off that afternoon on McAllister street. I hoped the Kid's gun wouldn't get caught in his coat this time. But don't think I meant to give him a helping hand in his two-against-one fight.

This party had the shape of a war between gunmen. It would be a private one as far as I was concerned. My hope was that by hovering on the fringes until somebody won, I could pick up a little profit for the Continental, in the form of a wanted crook or two among the survivors.

My guess at the Frenchman's quarry was wrong. It wasn't the Whosis Kid. It was a man and a woman. I didn't see their faces. The light was behind them. They didn't waste any time between the Venetian's door and their taxicab.

The man was big—tall, wide, and thick. The woman looked small at his side. I couldn't go by that. Anything weighing less than a ton would have seemed tiny beside him.

As the taxicab pulled away from the café, the Cadillac went after it. I ran in the Cadillac's wake.

It was a short chase.

The taxicab turned into a dark block on the edge of China-town. The Cadillac jumped to its side, bearing it over to the curb.

A noise of brakes, shouting voices, broken glass. A woman's scream. Figures moving in the scant space between touring car and taxicab. Both cars rocking. Grunts. Thuds. Oaths.

A man's voice: "Hey! You can't do that! Nix! Nix!"

It was a stupid voice.

I had slowed down until the coupé was barely moving toward this tussle ahead. Peering through the rain and darkness, I tried to pick out a detail or so as I approached, but I could see little.

I was within twenty feet when the curbward door of the taxicab banged open. A woman bounced out. She landed on her knees on the sidewalk, jumped to her feet, and darted up the street.

Putting the coupé closer to the curb, I let the door swing open. My side windows were spattered with rain. I wanted to get a look at the woman when she passed. If she should take the open door for an invitation, I didn't mind talking to her.

She accepted the invitation, hurrying as directly to the car as if she had expected me to be waiting for her. Her face was a small oval above a fur collar.

"Help me!" she gasped. "Take me from here—quickly."

There was a suggestion of foreignness too slight to be called an accent.

"How about—?"

I shut my mouth. The thing she was jabbing me in the body with was a snub-nosed automatic.

"Sure! Get in," I urged her.

She bent her head to enter. I looped an arm over her neck,

throwing her down across my lap. She squirmed and twist-ed—a small-boned, hard-fleshed body with strength in it.

I wrenched the gun out of her hand and pushed her back on the seat beside me.

Her fingers dug into my arms.

"Quick! Quick! Ah, please, quickly! Take me—"

"What about your friend?" I asked.

"Not him! He is of the others! Please, quickly!"

A man filled the open coupé door—the big-chinned man who had driven the Cadillac.

His hand seized the fur at the woman's throat.

She tried to scream—made the gurgling sound of a man with a slit throat. I smacked his chin with the gun I had taken from her.

He tried to fall into the coupé. I pushed him out.

Before his head had hit the sidewalk, I had the door closed, and was twisting the coupé around in the street.

We rode away. Two shots sounded just as we turned the first corner. I don't know whether they were fired at us or not. I turned other corners. The Cadillac did not appear again.

So far, so good. I had started with the Whosis Kid, dropped him to take Maurois, and now let him go to see who this woman was. I didn't know what this confusion was all about, but I seemed to be learning *who* it was all about.

"Where to?" I asked presently.

"To home," she said, and gave me an address.

I pointed the coupé at it with no reluctance at all. It was the McAllister street apartments the Whosis Kid had visited earlier in the evening.

We didn't waste any time getting there. My companion

might know it or might not, but I knew that all the other players in this game knew that address. I wanted to get there before the Frenchman and Big Chin.

Neither of us said anything during the ride. She crouched close to me, shivering. I was looking ahead, planning how I was to land an invitation into her apartment. I was sorry I hadn't held on to her gun. I had let it fall when I pushed Big Chin out of the car. It would have been an excuse for a later call if she didn't invite me in.

I needn't have worried. She didn't invite me. She insisted that I go in with her. She was scared stiff.

"You will not leave me?" she pleaded as we drove up McAllister street. "I am in complete terror. You cannot go from me! If you will not come in, I will stay with you."

I was willing enough to go in, but I didn't want to leave the coupé where it would advertise me.

"We'll ride around the corner and park the car," I told her, "and then I'll go in with you."

I drove around the block, with an eye in each direction for the Cadillac. Neither eye found it. I left the coupé on Franklin street and we returned to the McAllister street building.

She had me almost running through the rain that had lightened now to a drizzle.

The hand with which she tried to fit a key to the front door was a shaky, inaccurate hand. I took the key and opened the door. We rode to the third floor in an automatic elevator, seeing no one. I unlocked the door to which she led me, near the rear of the building.

Holding my arm, with one hand, she reached inside and snapped on the lights in the passageway.

I didn't know what she was waiting for, until she cried:

"Frana! Frana! Ah, Frana!"

The muffled yapping of a small dog replied. The dog did not appear.

She grabbed me with both arms, trying to crawl up my damp coat-front.

"They are here!" she cried in the thin dry voice of utter terror. "They are here!"

5

"IS ANYBODY SUPPOSED to be here?" I asked, putting her around to one side, where she wouldn't be between me and the two doors across the passageway.

"No! Just my little dog Frana, but—"

I slid my gun half out of my pocket and back again, to make sure it wouldn't catch if I needed it, and used my other hand to get rid of the woman's arms.

"You stay here. I'll see if you've got company."

Moving to the nearest door, I heard a seven-year-old voice—Lew Maher's—saying: *"He can shoot and he's plain crazy. He ain't hampered by nothing like imagination or fear of consequences."*

With my left hand I turned the first door's knob. With my left foot I kicked it open.

Nothing happened.

I put a hand around the frame, found the button, switched on the lights.

A sitting-room, all orderly.

Through an open door on the far side of the room came the muffled yapping of Frana. It was louder now and more excited. I moved to the doorway. What I could see of the next room, in the light from this, seemed peaceful and unoccupied enough. I went into it and switched on the lights.

The dog's voice came through a closed door. I crossed to it, pulled it open. A dark fluffy dog jumped snapping at my leg. I grabbed it where its fur was thickest and lifted it squirming and snarling. The light hit it. It was purple—purple as a grape! Dyed purple!

Carrying this yapping, yelping artificial hound a little away from my body with my left hand, I moved on to the next room—a bedroom. It was vacant. Its closet hid nobody. I found the kitchen and bathroom. Empty. No one was in the apartment. The purple pup had been imprisoned by the Whosis Kid earlier in the day.

Passing through the second room on my way back to the woman with her dog and my report, I saw a slitted envelope lying face-down on a table. I turned it over. The stationery of a fashionable store, it was addressed to Mrs. Inés Almad, here.

The party seemed to be getting international. Maurois was French; the Whosis Kid was Boston American; the dog had a Bohemian name (at least I remember nabbing a Czech forger a few months before whose first name was Frana); and Inés, I imagine, was either Spanish or Portuguese. I didn't know what Almad was, but she was undoubtedly foreign, and not, I thought, French.

I returned to her. She hadn't moved an inch.

"Everything seems to be all right," I told her. "The dog got himself caught in a closet."

"There is no one here?"

"No one."

She took the dog in both hands, kissing its fluffy stained head, crooning affectionate words to it in a language that made no sense to me.

"Do your friends—the people you had your row with tonight—know where you live?" I asked.

I knew they did. I wanted to see what she knew.

She dropped the dog as if she had forgotten it, and her brows puckered.

"I do not know that," she said slowly. "Yet it may be. If they do—"

She shuddered, spun on her heel, and pushed the hall door violently shut.

"They may have been here this afternoon," she went on. "Frana has made himself prisoner in closets before, but I fear everything. I am coward-like. But there is none here now?"

"No one," I assured her again.

We went into the sitting-room. I got my first good look at her when she shed her hat and dark cape.

She was a trifle under medium height, a dark-skinned woman of thirty in a vivid orange gown. She was dark as an Indian, with bare brown shoulders round and sloping, tiny feet and hands, her fingers heavy with rings. Her nose was thin and curved, her mouth full-lipped and red, her eyes—long and thickly lashed—were of an extraordinary narrowness. They were dark eyes, but nothing of their color could be seen through the thin slits that separated the lids. Two dark gleams through veiling lashes. Her black hair was disarranged just now in fluffy silk puffs. A rope of pearls hung down on her dark chest. Earrings of black iron—in a peculiar club-like design—swung beside her cheeks.

Altogether, she was an odd trick. But I wouldn't want to be quoted as saying that she wasn't beautiful—in a wild way.

She was shaking and shivering as she got rid of her hat and cloak. White teeth held her lower lip as she crossed the room to turn on an electric heater. I took advantage of this opportunity to shift my gun from my overcoat pocket to my pants. Then I took off the coat.

Leaving the room for a second, she returned with a brown-filled quart bottle and two tumblers on a bronze tray, which she put on a little table near the heater.

The first tumbler she filled to within half an inch of its rim. I stopped her when she had the other nearly half full.

"That'll do fine for me," I said.

It was brandy, and not at all hard to get down. She shot her tumblerful into her throat as if she needed it, shook her bare shoulders, and sighed in a satisfied way.

"You will think, certainly, I am lunatic," she smiled at me. "Flinging myself on you, a stranger in the street, demanding of you time and troubles."

"No," I lied seriously. "I think you're pretty level-headed for a woman who, no doubt, isn't used to this sort of stuff."

She was pulling a little upholstered bench closer to the electric heater, within reach of the table that held the brandy. She sat down now, with an inviting nod at the bench's empty half.

The purple dog jumped into her lap. She pushed it out. It started to return. She kicked it sharply in the side with the pointed toe of her slipper. It yelped and crawled under a chair across the room.

I avoided the window by going the long way around the room. The window was curtained, but not thickly enough to hide all of the room from the Whosis Kid—if he happened to be sitting at his window just now with a pair of field-glasses to his eyes.

"But I am not level-headed, really," the woman was saying as I dropped beside her. "I am coward-like, terribly. And even becoming accustomed— It is my husband, or he who was my husband. I should tell you. Your gallantry deserves the explanation, and I do not wish you should think a thing that is not so."

I tried to look trusting and credulous. I expected to disbelieve everything she said.

"He is most crazily jealous," she went on in her low-pitched, soft voice, with a peculiar way of saying words that just missed being marked enough to be called a foreign accent. "He is an old man, and incredibly wicked. These men he has sent to me! A woman there was once—tonight's men are not first. I don't know what—what they mean. To kill me, perhaps—to maim, to disfigure—I do not know."

"And the man in the taxi with you was one of them?" I asked. "I was driving down the street behind you when you were attacked, and I could see there was a man with you. He was one of them?"

"Yes! I did not know it, but it must have been that he was. He does not defend me. A pretense, that is all."

"Ever try sicking the cops on this hubby of yours?"

"It is what?"

"Ever notify the police?"

"Yes, but"—she shrugged her brown shoulders—"I would as well have kept quiet, or better. In Buffalo it was, and they—they bound my husband to keep the peace, I think you call it. A thousand dollars! Poof! What is that to him in his jealousy? And I—I cannot stand the things the newspapers say—the jesting of them. I must leave Buffalo. Yes, once I do try sicking the cops on him. But not more."

"Buffalo?" I explored a little. "I lived there for a while—on Crescent avenue."

"Oh, yes. That is out by the Delaware Park."

That was right enough. But her knowing something about Buffalo didn't prove anything about the rest of her story.

6

SHE POURED MORE brandy. By speaking quick I held my drink down to a size suitable for a man who has work to do. Hers was as large as before. We drank, and she offered me cigarettes in a lacquered box—slender cigarettes, hand-rolled in black paper.

I didn't stay with mine long. It tasted, smelt and scorched like gunpowder.

"You don't like my cigarettes?"

"I'm an old-fashioned man," I apologized, rubbing its fire out in a bronze dish, fishing in my pocket for my own deck. "Tobacco's as far as I've got. What's in these fireworks?"

She laughed. She had a pleasant laugh, with a sort of coo in it.

"I am so very sorry. So many people do not like them. I have a Hindu incense mixed with the tobacco."

I didn't say anything to that. It was what you would expect of a woman who would dye her dog purple.

The dog moved under its chair just then, scratching the floor with its nails.

The brown woman was in my arms, in my lap, her arms wrapped around my neck. Close-up, opened by terror, her eyes weren't dark at all. They were gray-green. The blackness was in the shadow from her heavy lashes.

"It's only the dog," I assured her, sliding her back on her own part of the bench. "It's only the dog wriggling around under the chair."

"Ah!" she blew her breath out with enormous relief.

Then we had to have another shot of brandy.

"You see, I am most awfully the coward," she said when the third dose of liquor was in her. "But, ah, I have had so much trouble. It is a wonder that I am not insane."

I could have told her she wasn't far enough from it to do much bragging, but I nodded with what was meant for sympathy.

She lit another cigarette to replace the one she had dropped in her excitement. Her eyes became normal black slits again.

"I do not think it is nice"—there was a suggestion of a dimple in her brown cheek when she smiled like that—"that I throw myself into the arms of a man even whose name I do not know, or anything of him."

"That's easy to fix. My name is Young," I lied; "and I can let you have a case of Scotch at a price that will astonish you. I think maybe I could stand it if you call me Jerry. Most of the ladies I let sit in my lap do."

"Jerry Young," she repeated, as if to herself. "That is a nice name. And you are the bootlegger?"

"Not *the*," I corrected her; "just *a*. This is San Francisco."

The going got tough after that.

Everything else about this brown woman was all wrong, but her fright was real. She was scared stiff. And she didn't intend being left alone this night. She meant to keep me there—to massage any more chins that stuck themselves at her. Her idea—she being that sort—was that I would be most surely held with affection. So she must turn herself loose on me. She wasn't hampered by any pruderies or puritanisms at all.

I also have an idea. Mine is that when the last gong rings I'm going to be leading this baby and some of her playmates to the city prison. That is an excellent reason—among a dozen others I could think of—why I shouldn't get mushy with her.

I was willing enough to camp there with her until something happened. That apartment looked like the scene of the next action. But I had to cover up my own game. I couldn't let her know she was only a minor figure in it. I had to pretend there was nothing behind my willingness to stay but a desire to protect her. Another man might have got by with a chivalrous, knight-errant, protector-of-womanhood-without-personal-interest attitude. But I don't look, and can't easily act, like that kind of person. I had to hold her off without letting her guess that my interest wasn't personal. It was no cinch. She was too damned direct, and she had too much brandy in her.

I didn't kid myself that my beauty and personality were responsible for any of her warmth. I was a thick-armed male with big fists. She was in a jam. She spelled my name P-r-o-t-e-c-t-i-o-n. I was something to be put between her and trouble.

Another complication: I am neither young enough nor old enough to get feverish over every woman who doesn't make me think being blind isn't so bad. I'm at that middle point around forty where a man puts other feminine qualities—amiability, for one—above beauty on his list. This brown woman annoyed me. She was too sure of herself. Her work was rough. She was trying to handle me as if I were a farmer boy. But in spite of all this, I'm constructed mostly of human ingredients. This woman got more than a stand-off when faces and bodies were dealt. I didn't like her. I hoped to throw her in the can before I was through. But I'd be a liar if I didn't admit that she had me stirred up inside—between her cuddling against me, giving me the come-on, and the brandy I had drunk.

The going was tough—no fooling.

A couple of times I was tempted to bolt. Once I looked at my watch—2:06. She put a ring-heavy brown hand on the timepiece and pushed it down to my pocket.

"Please, Jerry!" the earnestness in her voice was real. "You cannot go. You cannot leave me here. I will not have it so. I will go also, through the streets following. You cannot leave me to be murdered here!"

I settled down again.

A few minutes later a bell rang sharply.

She went to pieces immediately. She piled over on me, strangling me with her bare arms. I pried them loose enough to let me talk.

"What bell is that?"

"The street door. Do not heed it."

I patted her shoulder.

"Be a good girl and answer it. Let's see who it is."

Her arms tightened.

"No! No! No! They have come!"

The bell rang again.

"Answer it," I insisted.

Her face was flat against my coat, her nose digging into my chest.

"No! No!"

"All right," I said. "I'll answer it myself."

I untangled myself from her, got up and went into the passageway. She followed me. I tried again to persuade her to do the talking. She would not, although she didn't object to my talking. I would have liked it better if whoever was downstairs didn't learn that the woman wasn't alone. But she was too stubborn in her refusal for me to do anything with her.

"Well?" I said into the speaking-tube.

"Who the hell are you?" a harsh, deep-chested voice asked.

"What do you want?"

"I want to talk to Inés."

"Speak your piece to me," I suggested, "and I'll tell her about it."

The woman, holding one of my arms, had an ear close to the tube.

"Billie, it is," she whispered. "Tell him that he goes away."

"You're to go away," I passed the message on.

"Yeah?" the voice grew harsher and deeper. "Will you open the door, or will I bust it in?"

There wasn't a bit of playfulness in the question. Without consulting the woman, I put a finger on the button that unlocks the street door.

"Welcome," I said into the tube.

"He's coming up," I explained to the woman. "Shall I stand behind the door and tap him on the skull when he comes in? Or do you want to talk to him first?"

"Do not strike him!" she exclaimed. "It is Billie."

That suited me. I hadn't intended putting the slug to him— not until I knew who and what he was, anyway. I had wanted to see what she would say.

7

BILLIE WASN'T LONG getting up to us. I opened the door when he rang, the woman standing beside me. He didn't wait for an invitation. He was through the doorway before I had the door half opened. He glared at me. There was plenty of him!

A big, red-faced, red-haired bale of a man—big in any direction you measured him—and none of him was fat. The skin was off his nose, one cheek was clawed, the other swollen. His hatless head was a tangled mass of red hair. One pocket had been ripped out of his coat, and a button dangled on the end of a six-inch ribbon of torn cloth.

This was the big heaver who had been in the taxicab with the woman.

"Who's this mutt?" he demanded, moving his big paws toward me.

I knew the woman was a goof. It wouldn't have surprised me if she had tried to feed me to the battered giant. But she didn't. She put a hand on one of his and soothed him.

"Do not be nasty, Billie. He is a friend. Without him I would not this night have escaped."

He scowled. Then his face straightened out and he caught her hand in both of his.

"So you got away, it's all right," he said huskily. "I'd a done better if we'd been outside. There wasn't no room in that taxi for me to turn around. And one of them guys crowned me."

That was funny. This big clown was apologizing for getting

mangled up protecting a woman who had scooted, leaving him to get out as well as he could.

The woman led him into the sitting-room, I tagging along behind. They sat on the bench. I picked out a chair that wasn't in line with the window the Whosis Kid ought to be watching.

"What did happen, Billie?" She touched his grooved cheek and skinned nose with her fingertips. "You are hurt."

He grinned with a sort of shamefaced delight. I saw that what I had taken for a swelling in one cheek was only a big hunk of chewing tobacco.

"I don't know all that happened," he said. "One of 'em crowned me, and I didn't wake up till a coupla hours afterwards. The taxi driver didn't give me no help in the fight, but he was a right guy and knowed where his money would come from. He didn't holler or nothing. He took me around to a doc that wouldn't squawk, and the doc straightened me out, and then I come up here."

"Did you see each one of those men?" she asked.

"Sure! I seen 'em, and felt 'em, and maybe tasted 'em."

"They were how many?"

"Just two of 'em. A little fella with a trick tickler, and a husky with a big chin on him."

"There was no other? There was not a younger man, tall and thin?"

That could be the Whosis Kid. She thought he and the Frenchman were working together?

Billie shook his shaggy, banged-up head.

"Nope. They was only two of 'em."

She frowned and chewed her lip.

Billie looked sidewise at me—a look that said "Beat it."

The woman caught the glance. She twisted around on the bench to put a hand on his head.

"Poor Billie," she cooed; "his head most cruelly hurt saving me, and now, when he should be at his home giving it rest, I keep him here talking. You go, Billie, and when it is morning and your poor head is better, you will telephone to me?"

His red face got dark. He glowered at me.

Laughing, she slapped him lightly on the cheek that bulged around his cud of tobacco.

"Do not become jealous of Jerry. Jerry is enamored of one yellow and white lady somewhere, and to her he is most faithful. Not even the smallest liking has he for dark women." She smiled a challenge at me. "Is it not so, Jerry?"

"No," I denied. "And, besides, all women are dark."

Billie shifted his chew to the scratched cheek and bunched his shoulders.

"What the hell kind of a crack is that to be making?" he rumbled.

"That means nothing it should not, Billie," she laughed at him. "It is only an epigram."

"Yeah?" Billie was sour and truculent. I was beginning to think he didn't like me. "Well, tell your little fat friend to keep his smart wheezes to himself. I don't like 'em."

That was plain enough. Billie wanted an argument. The woman, who held him securely enough to have steered him off, simply laughed again. There was no profit in trying to find the reason behind any of her actions. She was a nut. Maybe she thought that since we weren't sociable enough for her to keep both on hand, she'd let us tangle, and hold on to the one who rubbed the other out of the picture.

Anyway, a row was coming. Ordinarily I am inclined to peace. The day is past when I'll fight for the fun of it. But I've been in too many rumpuses to mind them much. Usually nothing very bad happens to you, even if you lose. I wasn't going to back down just because this big stiff was meatier than I. I've always been lucky against the large sizes. He had been banged up earlier in the evening. That would cut down his steam some. I wanted to hang around this apartment a little longer, if it could be managed. If Billie wanted to tussle—and it looked as if he did—he could.

It was easy to meet him half-way: anything I said would be used against me.

I grinned at his red face, and suggested to the woman, solemnly:

"I think if you'd dip him in blueing he'd come out the same color as the other pup."

As silly as that was, it served. Billie reared up on his feet and curled his paws into fists.

"Me and you'll take a walk," he decided; "out where there's space enough."

I got up, pushed my chair back with a foot, and quoted "Red" Burns to him: "If you're close enough, there's room enough."

He wasn't a man you had to talk to much. We went around and around.

It was fists at first. He started it by throwing his right at my head. I went in under it and gave him all I had in a right and left to the belly. He swallowed his chew of tobacco. But he didn't bend. Few big men are as strong as they look. Billie was.

He didn't know anything at all. His idea of a fight was to stand up and throw fists at your head—right, left, right, left.

His fists were as large as wastebaskets. They wheezed through the air. But always at the head—the easiest part to get out of the way.

There was room enough for me to go in and out. I did that. I hammered his belly. I thumped his heart. I mauled his belly again. Every time I hit him he grew an inch, gained a pound and picked up another horsepower. I don't fool when I hit, but nothing I did to this human mountain—not even making him swallow his hunk of tobacco—had any visible effect on him.

I've always had a reasonable amount of pride in my ability to sock. It was disappointing to have this big heaver take the best I could give him without a grunt. But I wasn't discouraged. He couldn't stand it forever. I settled down to make a steady job of it.

Twice he clipped me. Once on the shoulder. A big fist spun me half around. He didn't know what to do next. He came in on the wrong side. I made him miss, and got clear. The other time he caught me on the forehead. A chair kept me from going down. The smack hurt me. It must have hurt him more. A skull is tougher than a knuckle. I got out of his way when he closed in, and let him have something to remember on the back of his neck.

The woman's dusky face showed over Billie's shoulder as he straightened up. Her eyes were shiny behind their heavy lashes, and her mouth was open to let white teeth gleam through.

Billie got tired of the boxing after that, and turned the set-to into a wrestling match, with trimmings. I would rather have kept on with the fists. But I couldn't help myself. It was his party. He grabbed one of my wrists, yanked, and we thudded chest to chest.

He didn't know any more about this than he had about that. He didn't have to. He was big enough and strong enough to play with me.

I was underneath when we tumbled down on the floor and began rolling around. I did my best. It wasn't anything. Three times I put a scissors on him. His body was too big for my short legs to clamp around. He chucked me off as if he were amusing the baby. There was no use at all in trying to do things to his legs. No hold known to man could have held them. His arms were almost as strong. I quit trying.

Nothing I knew was any good against this monster. He was out of my range. I was satisfied to spend all that was left of my strength trying to keep him from crippling me—and waiting for a chance to out-smart him.

He threw me around a lot. Then my chance came.

I was flat on my back, with everything but one or two of my most centrally located intestines squeezed out. Kneeling astride me, he brought his big hands up to my throat and fastened them there.

That's how much he didn't know!

You can't choke a man that way—not if his hands are loose and he knows a hand is stronger than a finger.

I laughed in his purple face and brought my own hands up. Each of them picked one of his little fingers out of my flesh. It wasn't a dream at that. I was all in, and he wasn't. But no man's little finger is stronger than another's hand. I twisted them back. They broke together.

He yelped. I grabbed the next—the ring fingers.

One of them snapped. The other was ready to pop when he let go.

Jerking up, I butted him in the face. I twisted from between his knees. We came on our feet together.

The doorbell rang.

8

FIGHT INTEREST WENT out of the woman's face. Fear came in. Her fingers picked at her mouth.

"Ask who's there," I told her.

"Who—who is there?"

Her voice was flat and dry.

"Mrs. Keil," came from the corridor, the words sharp with indignation. "You will have to stop this noise immediately! The tenants are complaining—and no wonder! A pretty hour to be entertaining company and carrying on so!"

"The landlady," the dark woman whispered. Aloud: "I am sorry, Mrs. Keil. There will not be more noises."

Something like a sniff came through the door, and the sound of dimming footsteps.

Inés Almad frowned reproachfully at Billie.

"You should not have done this," she blamed him.

He looked humble, and at the floor, and at me. Looking at me, the purple began to flow back into his face.

"I'm sorry," he mumbled. "I told this fella we ought to take a walk. We'll do it now, and there won't be no more noise here."

"Billie!" her voice was sharp. She was reading the law to him. "You will go out and have attention for your hurts. If you have not won these fights, because of that am I to be left here alone to be murdered?"

The big man shuffled his feet, avoided her gaze and looked utterly miserable. But he shook his head stubbornly.

"I can't do it, Inés," he said. "Me and this guy has got to finish it. He busted my fingers, and I got to bust his jaw."

"Billie!"

She stamped one small foot and looked imperiously at him. He looked as if he'd like to roll over on his back and hold his paws in the air. But he stood his ground.

"I got to," he repeated. "There ain't no way out of it."

Anger left her face. She smiled very tenderly at him.

"Dear old Billie," she murmured, and crossed the room to a secretary in a corner.

When she turned, an automatic pistol was in her hand. Its one eye looked at Billie.

"Now, *lechón*," she purred, "go out!"

The red man wasn't a quick thinker. It took a full minute for him to realize that this woman he loved was driving him away with a gun. The big dummy might have known that his three broken fingers had disqualified him. It took another minute for him to get his legs in motion. He went toward the door in slow bewilderment, still only half believing this thing was really happening.

The woman followed him step by step. I went ahead to open the door.

I turned the knob. The door came in, pushing me back against the opposite wall.

In the doorway stood Edouard Maurois and the man I had swatted on the chin. Each had a gun.

I looked at Inés Almad, wondering what turn her craziness would take in the face of this situation. She wasn't so crazy as I had thought. Her scream and the thud of her gun on the floor sounded together.

"Ah!" the Frenchman was saying. "The gentlemen were leaving? May we detain them?"

The man with the big chin—it was larger than ever now with the marks of my tap—was less polite.

"Back up, you birds!" he ordered, stooping for the gun the woman had dropped.

I still was holding the doorknob. I rattled it a little as I took my hand away—enough to cover up the click of the lock as I pushed the button that left it unlatched. If I needed help, and it came, I wanted as few locks as possible between me and it.

Then—Billie, the woman and I walking backward—we all paraded into the sitting-room. Maurois and his companion both wore souvenirs of the row in the taxicab. One of the Frenchman's eyes was bruised and closed—a beautiful shiner. His clothes were rumpled and dirty. He wore them jauntily in spite of that, and he still had his walking stick, crooked under the arm that didn't hold his gun.

Big Chin held us with his own gun and the woman's while Maurois ran his hand over Billie's and my clothes, to see if we were armed. He found my gun and pocketed it. Billie had no weapons.

"Can I trouble you to step back against the wall?" Maurois asked when he was through.

We stepped back as if it was no trouble at all. I found my shoulder against one of the window curtains. I pressed it against the frame, and turned far enough to drag the curtain clear of a foot or more of pane.

If the Whosis Kid was watching, he should have had a clear view of the Frenchman—the man who had shot at him earlier in the evening. I was putting it up to the Kid. The corridor door was unlocked. If the Kid could get into the building—no great trick—he had a clear path. I didn't know where he fit in, but I wanted him to join us, and I hoped he wouldn't disappoint me. If everybody got together here, maybe whatever was going on would come out where I could see it and understand it.

Meanwhile, I kept as much of myself as possible out of the window. The Kid might decide to throw lead from across the alley.

Maurois was facing Inés. Big Chin's guns were on Billie and me.

"I do not comprends ze anglais ver' good," the Frenchman was mocking the woman. "So it is when you say you meet wit' me, I t'ink you say in New Orleans. I do not know you say San Francisc'. I am ver' sorry to make ze mistake. I am mos' sorry zat I keep you wait. But now I am here. You have ze share for me?"

"I have not." She held her hands out in an empty gesture. "The Kid took those—everything from me."

"What?" Maurois dropped his taunting smile and his vaude-ville accent. His one open eye flashed angrily. "How could he, unless—?"

"He suspected us, Edouard." Her mouth trembled with earnestness. Her eyes pleaded for belief. She was lying. "He had me followed. The day after I am there he comes. He takes all. I am afraid to wait for you. I fear your unbelief. You would not—"

"*C'est incroyable!*" Maurois was very excited over it. "I was on the first train south after our—our theatricals. Could the Kid have been on that train without my knowing it? *Non!* And how else could he have reached you before I? You are playing with me, *ma petite* Inés. That you did join the Kid, I do not doubt.

But not in New Orleans. You did not go there. You came here to San Francisco."

"Edouard!" she protested, fingering his sleeve with one brown hand, the other holding her throat as if she were having trouble getting the words out. "You cannot think that thing! Do not those weeks in Boston say it is not possible? For one like the Kid—or like any other—am I to betray you? You know me not more than to think I am like that?"

She was an actress. She was appealing, and pathetic, and anything else you like—including dangerous.

The Frenchman took his sleeve away from her and stepped back a step. White lines ringed his mouth below his tiny mustache, and his jaw muscles bulged. His one good eye was worried. She had got to him, though not quite enough to upset him altogether. But the game was young yet.

"I do not know what to think," he said slowly. "If I have been wrong—I must find the Kid first. Then I will learn the truth."

"You don't have to look no further, brother. I'm right among you!"

The Whosis Kid stood in the passageway door. A black revolver was in each of his hands. Their hammers were up.

9

IT WAS A pretty tableau.

There is the Whosis Kid in the door—a lean lad in his twenties, all the more wicked-looking because his face is weak and slack-jawed and dull-eyed. The cocked guns in his hands are pointing at everybody or at nobody, depending on how you look at them.

There is the brown woman, her cheeks pinched in her two fists, her eyes open until their green-grayishness shows. The fright I had seen in her face before was nothing to the fright that is there now.

There is the Frenchman—whirled doorward at the Kid's first word—his gun on the Kid, his cane still under his arm, his face a tense white blot.

There is Big Chin, his body twisted half around, his face over one shoulder to look at the door, with one of his guns following his face around.

There is Billie—a big, battered statue of a man who hasn't said a word since Inés Almad started to gun him out of the apartment.

And, last, here I am—not feeling so comfortable as I would home in bed, but not actually hysterical either. I wasn't altogether dissatisfied with the shape things were taking. Something was going to happen in these rooms. But I wasn't friendly enough to any present to care especially what happened to whom. For myself, I counted on coming through all in one piece. Few men get killed. Most of those who meet sudden ends get themselves killed. I've had twenty years of experience at dodging that. I can count on being one of the survivors of whatever blow-up there is. And I hope to take most of the other survivors for a ride.

But right now the situation belonged to the men with guns—the Whosis Kid, Maurois and Big Chin.

The Kid spoke first. He had a whining voice that came disagreeably through his thick nose.

"This don't look nothing like Chi to me, but, anyways, we're all here."

"Chicago!" Maurois exclaimed. "You did not go to Chicago!"

The Kid sneered at him.

"Did you? Did she? What would I be going there for? You think me and her run out on you, don't you? Well, we would of if she hadn't put the two X's to me the same as she done to you, and the same as the three of us done to the boob."

"That may be," the Frenchman replied; "but you do not expect me to believe that you and Inés are not friends? Didn't I see you leaving here this afternoon?"

"You seen me, all right," the Kid agreed; "but if my rod hadn't of got snagged in my flogger you wouldn't have seen nothing else. But I ain't got nothing against you now. I thought you and her had ditched me, just as you think me and her done you. I know different now, from what I heard while I was getting in here. She twisted the pair of us, Frenchy, just like we twisted the boob. Ain't you got it yet?"

Maurois shook his head slowly.

What put an edge to this conversation was that both men were talking over their guns.

"Listen," the Kid asked impatiently. "We was to meet up in Chi for a three-way split, wasn't we?"

The Frenchman nodded.

"But she tells me," the Kid went on, "she'll connect with me in St. Louis, counting you out; and she ribs you up to meet her in New Orleans, ducking me. And then she gyps the pair of us by running out here to Frisco with the stuff.

"We're a couple of suckers, Frenchy, and there ain't no use of us getting hot at each other. There's enough of it for a fat two-way cut. What I say is let's forget what's done, and me and you make it fifty-fifty. Understand, I ain't begging you. I'm making a proposition. If you don't like it, to hell with you! You know me. You never seen the day I wouldn't shoot it out with you or anybody else. Take your pick!"

The Frenchman didn't say anything for a while. He was converted, but he didn't want to weaken his hand by coming in too soon. I don't know whether he believed the Kid's words or not, but he believed the Kid's guns. You can get a bullet out of a cocked revolver a lot quicker than out of a hammerless automatic. The Kid had the bulge there. And the Kid had him licked because the Kid had the look of one who doesn't give a damn what happens next.

Finally Maurois looked a question at Big Chin. Big Chin moistened his lips, but said nothing.

Maurois looked at the Kid again, and nodded his head.

"You are right," he said. "We will do that."

"Good!" The Kid did not move from his door. "Now who are these plugs?"

"These two"—Maurois nodded at Billie and me—"are friends of our Inés. This"—indicating Big Chin—"is a confrere of mine."

"You mean he's in with you? That's all right with me." The

Kid spoke crisply. "But, you understand, his cut comes out of yours. I get half, and no trimming."

The Frenchman frowned, but he nodded in agreement.

"Half is yours, if we find it."

"Don't get no headache over that," the Kid advised him. "It's here and we'll get it."

He put one of his guns away and came into the room, the other gun hanging loosely at his side. When he walked across the room to face the woman, he managed it so that Big Chin and Maurois were never behind him.

"Where's the stuff?" he demanded.

Inés Almad wet her red mouth with her tongue and let her mouth droop a little and looked softly at the Kid, and made her play.

"One of us is as bad as are the others, Kid. We all—each of us tried to get for ourselves everything. You and Edouard have put aside what is past. Am I more wrong than you? I have them, true, but I have not them here. Until tomorrow will you wait? I will get them. We will divide them among us three, as it was to have been. Shall we not do that?"

"Not any!" The Kid's voice had finality in it.

"Is that just?" she pleaded, letting her chin quiver a bit. "Is there a treachery of which I am guilty that also you and Edouard are not? Do you—?"

"That ain't the idea at all," the Kid told her. "Me and Frenchy are in a fix where we got to work together to get anywhere. So we're together. With you it's different. We don't need you. We can take the stuff away from you. You're out! Where's the stuff?"

"Not here! Am I foolish sufficient to leave them here where

so easily you could find them? You *do* need my help to find them. Without me you cannot—"

"You're silly! I might flop for that if I didn't know you. But I know you're too damned greedy to let 'em get far away from you. And you're yellower than you're greedy. If you're smacked a couple of times, you'll kick in. And don't think I got any objections to smacking you over!"

She cowered back from his upraised hand.

The Frenchman spoke quickly.

"We should search the rooms first, Kid. If we don't find them there, then we can decide what to do next."

The Whosis Kid laughed sneeringly at Maurois.

"All right. But, get this, I'm not going out of here without that stuff—not if I have to take this rat apart. My way's quicker, but we'll hunt first if you want to. Your con-whatever-you-call-him can keep these plugs tucked in while me and you upset the joint."

They went to work. The Kid put away his gun and brought out a long-bladed spring-knife. The Frenchman unscrewed the lower two-thirds of his cane, baring a foot and a half of sword-blade.

No cursory search, theirs. They took the room we were in first. They gutted it thoroughly, carved it to the bone. Furniture and pictures were taken apart. Upholstering gave up its stuffing. Floor coverings were cut. Suspicious lengths of wallpaper were scraped loose. They worked slowly. Neither would let the other get behind him. The Kid would not turn his back on Big Chin.

The sitting-room wrecked, they went into the next room, leaving the woman, Billie and me standing among the litter.

Big Chin and his two guns watched over us.

As soon as the Frenchman and the Kid were out of sight, the woman tried her stuff out on our guardian. She had a lot of confidence in her power with men, I'll say that for her.

For a while she worked her eyes on Big Chin, and then, very softly:

"Can I—?"

"You can't!" Big Chin was loud and gruff. "Shut up!"

The Whosis Kid appeared at the door.

"If nobody don't say nothing maybe nobody won't get hurt," he snarled, and went back to his work.

The woman valued herself too highly to be easily discouraged. She didn't put anything in words again, but she looked things at Big Chin—things that had him sweating and blushing. He was a simple man. I didn't think she'd get anywhere. If there had been no one present but the two of them, she might have put Big Chin over the jumps; but he wouldn't be likely to let her get to him with a couple of birds standing there watching the show.

Once a sharp yelp told us that the purple Frana—who had fled rearward when Maurois and Big Chin arrived—had got in trouble with the searchers. There was only that one yelp, and it stopped with a suddenness that suggested trouble for the dog.

The two men spent nearly an hour in the other rooms. They didn't find anything. Their hands, when they joined us again, held nothing but the cutlery.

10

"I SAID TO you it was not here," Inés told them triumphantly. "Now will you—?"

"You can't tell me nothing I'll believe." The Kid snapped his knife shut and dropped it in his pocket. "I still think it's here."

He caught her wrist, and held his other hand, palm up, under her nose.

"You can put 'em in my hand, or I'll take 'em."

"They are not here! I swear it!"

His mouth lifted at the corner in a savage grimace.

"Liar!"

He twisted her arm roughly, forcing her to her knees. His free hand went to the shoulder-strap of her orange gown.

"I'll damn soon find out," he promised.

Billie came to life.

"Hey!" he protested, his chest heaving in and out. "You can't do that!"

"Wait, Kid!" Maurois—putting his sword-cane together again—called. "Let us see if there is not another way."

The Whosis Kid let go of the woman and took three slow steps back from her. His eyes were dead circles without any color you could name—the dull eyes of the man whose nerves quit functioning in the face of excitement. His bony hands pushed his coat aside a little and rested where his vest bulged over the sharp corners of his hip-bones.

"Let's me and you get this right, Frenchy," he said in his whining voice. "Are you with me or her?"

"You, most certainly, but—"

"All right. Then *be* with me! Don't be trying to gum every play I make. I'm going to frisk this dolly, and don't think I ain't. What are you going to do about it?"

The Frenchman pursed his mouth until his little black mustache snuggled against the tip of his nose. He puckered his eyebrows and looked thoughtfully out of his one good eye. But he wasn't going to do anything at all about it, and he knew he wasn't. Finally he shrugged.

"You are right," he surrendered. "She should be searched."

The Kid grunted contemptuous disgust at him and went toward the woman again.

She sprang away from him, to me. Her arms clamped around my neck in the habit they seemed to have.

"Jerry!" she screamed in my face. "You will not allow him! Jerry, please not!"

I didn't say anything.

I didn't think it was exactly genteel of the Kid to frisk her, but there were several reasons why I didn't try to stop him. First, I didn't want to do anything to delay the unearthing of this "stuff" there had been so much talk about. Second, I'm no Galahad. This woman had picked her playmates, and was largely responsible for this angle of their game. If they played rough, she'd have to make the best of it. And, a good strong third, Big Chin was prodding me in the side with a gun-muzzle to remind me that I couldn't do anything if I wanted to—except get myself slaughtered.

The Kid dragged Inés away. I let her go.

He pulled her over to what was left of the bench by the electric heater, and called the Frenchman there with a jerk of his head.

"You hold her while I go through her," he said.

She filled her lungs with air. Before she could turn it loose in a shriek, the Kid's long fingers had fit themselves to her throat.

"One chirp out of you and I'll tie a knot in your neck," he threatened.

She let the air wheeze out of her nose.

Billie shuffled his feet. I turned my head to look at him. He was puffing through his mouth. Sweat polished his forehead under his matted red hair. I hoped he wasn't going to turn his wolf loose until the "stuff" came to the surface. If he would wait a while I might join him.

He wouldn't wait. He went into action when—Maurois holding her—the Kid started to undress the woman.

He took a step toward them. Big Chin tried to wave him back with a gun. Billie didn't even see it. His eyes were red on the three by the bench.

"Hey, you can't do that!" he rumbled. "You can't do that!"

"No?" The Kid looked up from his work. "Watch me."

"Billie!" the woman urged the big man on in his foolishness.

Billie charged.

Big Chin let him go, playing safe by swinging both guns on me. The Whosis Kid slid out of the plunging giant's path. Maurois hurled the girl straight at Billie—and got his gun out.

Billie and Inés thumped together in a swaying tangle.

The Kid spun behind the big man. One of the Kid's hands came out of his pocket with the spring-knife. The knife clicked open as Billie regained his balance.

The Kid jumped close.

He knew knives. None of your clumsy downward strokes with the blade sticking out the bottom of his fist.

Thumb and crooked forefinger guided blade. He struck upward. Under Billie's shoulder. Once. Deep.

Billie pitched forward, smashing the woman to the floor under him. He rolled off her and was dead on his back among the furniture-stuffing. Dead, he seemed larger than ever, seemed to fill the room.

The Whosis Kid wiped his knife clean on a piece of carpet, snapped it shut, and dropped it back in his pocket. He did this with his left hand. His right was close to his hip. He did not look at the knife. His eyes were on Maurois.

But if he expected the Frenchman to squawk, he was disappointed. Maurois' little mustache twitched, and his face was white and strained, but:

"We'd better hurry with what we have to do, and get out of here," he suggested.

The woman sat up beside the dead man, whimpering. Her face was ashy under her dark skin. She was licked. A shaking hand fumbled beneath her clothes. It brought out a little flat silk bag.

Maurois—nearer than the Kid—took it. It was sewed too securely for his fingers to open. He held it while the Kid ripped it with his knife. The Frenchman poured part of the contents out in one cupped hand.

Diamonds. Pearls. A few colored stones among them.

11

BIG CHIN BLEW his breath out in a faint whistle. His eyes were bright on the sparkling stones. So were the eyes of Maurois, the woman, and the Kid.

Big Chin's inattention was a temptation. I could reach his jaw. I could knock him over. The strength Billie had mauled out of me had nearly all come back by now. I could knock Big Chin over and have at least one of his guns by the time the Kid and Maurois got set. It was time for me to do something. I had let these comedians run the show long enough. The stuff had come to light. If I let the party break up there was no telling when, if ever, I could round up these folks again.

But I put the temptation away and made myself wait a bit longer. No use going off half-cocked. With a gun in my hand, facing the Kid and Maurois, I still would have less than an even break. That's not enough. The idea in this detective business is to catch crooks, not to put on heroics.

Maurois was pouring the stones back in the bag when I looked at him again. He started to put the bag in his pocket. The Whosis Kid stopped him with a hand on his arm.

"I'll pack 'em."

Maurois' eyebrows went up.

"There's two of you and one of me," the Kid explained. "I trust you, and all the like of that, but just the same I'm carrying my own share."

"But—"

The doorbell interrupted Maurois' protest.

The Kid spun to the girl.

"You do the talking—and no wise breaks!"

She got up from the floor and went to the passageway.

"Who is there?" she called.

The landlady's voice, stern and wrathful:

"Another sound, Mrs. Almad, and I shall call the police. This is disgraceful!"

I wondered what she would have thought if she had opened the unlocked door and taken a look at her apartment—furniture whittled and gutted; a dead man—the noise of whose dying had brought her up here this second time—lying in the middle of the litter.

I wondered—I took a chance.

"Aw, go jump down the sewer!" I told her.

A gasp, and we heard no more from her. I hoped she was speeding her injured feelings to the telephone. I might need the police she had mentioned.

The Kid's gun was out. For a while it was a toss-up. I would lie down beside Billie, or I wouldn't. If I could have been knifed quietly, I would have gone. But nobody was behind me. The Kid knew I wouldn't stand still and quiet while he carved me. He didn't want any more racket than necessary, now that the jewels were on hand.

"Keep your clam shut or I'll shut it for you!" was the worst I got out of it.

The Kid turned to the Frenchman again. The Frenchman had used the time spent in this side-play to pocket the gems.

"Either we divvy here and now, or I carry the stuff," the Kid announced. "There's two of you to see I don't take a Micky Finn on you."

"But, Kid, we cannot stay here! Is not the landlady even now calling the police? We will go elsewhere to divide. Why cannot you trust me when you are with me?"

Two steps put the Kid between the door and both Maurois and Big Chin. One of the Kid's hands held the gun he had flashed on me. The other was conveniently placed to his other gun.

"Nothing stirring!" he said through his nose. "My cut of them stones don't go out of here in nobody else's kick. If you want to split 'em here, good enough. If you don't, I'll do the carrying. That's flat!"

"But the police!"

"You worry about them. I'm taking one thing at a time, and it's the stones right now."

A vein came out blue in the Frenchman's forehead. His small body was rigid. He was trying to collect enough courage to swap shots with the Kid. He knew, and the Kid knew, that one of them was going to have all the stuff when the curtain came down. They had started off by double-crossing each other. They weren't likely to change their habits. One would have the stones in the end. The other would have nothing—except maybe a burial.

Big Chin didn't count. He was too simple a thug to last long in his present company. If he had known anything, he would have used one of his guns on each of them right now. Instead, he continued to cover me, trying to watch them out of the tail of his eye.

The woman stood near the door, where she had gone to talk to the landlady. She was staring at the Frenchman and the Kid. I wasted precious minutes that seemed to run into hours trying to catch her eye. I finally got it.

I looked at the light-switch, only a foot from her. I looked at her. I looked at the switch again. At her. At the switch.

She got me. Her hand crept sidewise along the wall.

I looked at the two principal players in this button-button game.

The Kid's eyes were dead—and deadly—circles. Maurois' one open eye was watery. He couldn't make the grade. He put a hand in his pocket and brought out the silk bag.

The woman's brown finger topped the light-button. God knows she was nothing to gamble on, but I had no choice. I had to be in motion when the lights went. Big Chin would pump metal. I had to trust Inés not to balk. If she did, my name was Denis.

Her nail whitened.

I went for Maurois.

Darkness—streaked with orange and blue—filled with noise.

My arms had Maurois. We crashed down on dead Billie. I twisted around, kicking the Frenchman's face. Loosened one arm. Caught one of his. His other hand gouged at my face. That told me the bag was in the one I held. Clawing fingers tore my mouth. I put my teeth in them and kept them there. One of my knees was on his face. I put my weight on it. My teeth still held his hand. Both of my hands were free to get the bag.

Not nice, this work, but effective.

The room was the inside of a black drum on which a giant was beating the long roll. Four guns worked together in a prolonged throbbing roar.

Maurois' fingernails dug into my tongue. I had to open my mouth—let his hand escape. One of my hands found the bag. He wouldn't let go. I screwed his thumb. He cried out. I had the bag.

I tried to leave him then. He grabbed my legs. I kicked at him—missed. He shuddered twice—and stopped moving. A flying bullet had hit him, I took it. Rolling over to the floor, snuggling close to him, I ran a hand over him. A hard bulge came under my hand. I put my hand in his pocket and took back my gun.

On hands and knees—one fist around my gun, the other clutching the silk sack of jewels—I turned to where the door to the next room should have been. A foot wrong, I corrected my course. As I went through the door, the racket in the room behind me stopped.

12

HUDDLED CLOSE TO the wall inside the door, I stowed the silk bag away, and regretted that I hadn't stayed plastered to the floor behind the Frenchman. This room was dark. It hadn't been dark when the woman switched off the sitting-room lights. Every room in the apartment had been lighted then. All were dark now. Not knowing who had darkened them, I didn't like it.

No sounds came from the room I had quit.

The rustle of gently falling rain came from an open window that I couldn't see, off to one side.

Another sound came from behind me. The muffled tattoo of teeth on teeth.

That cheered me. Inés the scary, of course. She had left the sitting-room in the dark and put out the rest of the lights. Maybe nobody else was behind me.

Breathing quietly through wide-open mouth, I waited. I couldn't hunt for the woman in the dark without making noises. Maurois and the Kid had strewn furniture and parts of furniture everywhere. I wished I knew if she was holding a gun. I didn't want to have her spraying me.

Not knowing, I waited where I was.

Her teeth clicked on for minutes.

Something moved in the sitting-room. A gun thundered.

"Inés!" I hissed toward the chattering teeth.

No answer. Furniture scraped in the sitting-room. Two guns went off together. A groaning broke out.

"I've got the stuff," I whispered under cover of the groaning. That brought an answer.

"Jerry! Ah, come here to me!"

The groans went on, but fainter, in the other room. I crawled toward the woman's voice. I went on hands and knees, bumping as carefully as possible against things. I couldn't see anything. Midway, I put a hand down on a soggy bundle of fur—the late purple Frana. I went on.

Inés touched my shoulder with an eager hand.

"Give them to me," were her first words.

I grinned at her in the dark, patted her hand, found her head, and put my mouth to her ear.

"Let's get back in the bedroom," I breathed, paying no attention to her request for the loot. "The Kid will be coming." I didn't doubt that he had bested Big Chin. "We can handle him better in the bedroom."

I wanted to receive him in a room with only one door.

She led me—both of us on hands and knees—to the bedroom. I did what thinking seemed necessary as we crawled. The Kid couldn't know yet how the Frenchman and I had come out. If he guessed, he would guess that the Frenchman had survived. He would be likely to put me in the chump class with Billie, and think the Frenchman could handle me. The chances were that he had got Big Chin, and knew it by now. It was black as black in the sitting-room, but he must know by now that he was the only living thing there.

He blocked the only exit from the apartment. He would think, then, that Inés and Maurois were still alive in it, with the spoils. What would he do about it? There was no pretense of partnership now. That had gone with the lights. The Kid was after the stones. The Kid was after them alone.

I'm no wizard at guessing the other guy's next move. But my idea was that the Kid would be on his way after us, soon. He knew—he must know—that the police were coming; but I had him doped as crazy enough to disregard the police until they appeared. He'd figure that there would be only a couple of them—prepared for nothing more violent than a drinking-party. He could handle them—or he would think he could. Meanwhile, he would come after the stones.

The woman and I reached the bedroom, the room farthest back in the apartment, a room with only one door. I heard her fumbling with the door, trying to close it. I couldn't see, but I got my foot in the way.

"Leave it open," I whispered.

I didn't want to shut the Kid out. I wanted to take him in.

On my belly, I crawled back to the door, felt for my watch, and propped it on the sill, in the angle between door and frame. I wriggled back from it until I was six or eight feet away, looking diagonally across the open doorway at the watch's luminous dial.

The phosphorescent numbers could not be seen from the other side of the door. They faced me. Anybody who came through the door—unless he jumped—must, if only for a split-second, put some part of himself between me and the watch.

On my belly, my gun cocked, its butt steady on the floor, I waited for the faint light to be blotted out.

I waited a time. Pessimism: perhaps he wasn't coming; perhaps I would have to go after him; perhaps he would run out, and I would lose him after all my trouble.

Inés, beside me, breathed quaveringly in my ear, and shivered.

"Don't touch me," I growled at her as she tried to cuddle against me.

She was shaking my arm.

Glass broke in the next room.

Silence.

The luminous patches on the watch burnt my eyes. I couldn't afford to blink. A foot could pass the dial while I was blinking. I couldn't afford to blink, but I had to blink. I blinked. I couldn't tell whether something had passed the watch or not. I had to blink again. Tried to hold my eyes stiffly opened. Failed. I almost shot at the third blink. I could have sworn something had gone between me and the watch.

The Kid, whatever he was up to, made no sound.

The dark woman began to sob beside me. Throat noises that could guide bullets.

I lumped her with my eyes and cursed the lot—not aloud, but from the heart.

My eyes smarted. Moisture filmed them. I blinked it away, losing sight of the watch for precious instants. The butt of my gun was slimy with my hand's sweat. I was thoroughly uncomfortable, inside and out.

Gunpowder burned at my face.

A screaming maniac of a woman was crawling all over me.

My bullet hit nothing lower than the ceiling.

I flung, maybe kicked, the woman off, and snaked backward. She moaned somewhere to one side. I couldn't see the Kid—couldn't hear him. The watch was visible again, farther away. A rustling.

The watch vanished.

I fired at it.

Two points of light near the floor gave out fire and thunder.

My gun-barrel as close to the floor as I could hold it, I fired between those points. Twice.

Twin flames struck at me again.

My right hand went numb. My left took the gun. I sped two more bullets on their way. That left one in my gun.

I don't know what I did with it. My head filled up with funny notions. There wasn't any room. There wasn't any darkness. There wasn't anything....

I opened my eyes in dim light. I was on my back. Beside me the dark woman knelt, shivering and sniffling. Her hands were busy—in my clothes.

One of them came out of my vest with the jewel-bag.

Coming to life, I grabbed her arm. She squealed as if I were a stirring corpse. I got the bag again.

"Give them back, Jerry," she wailed, trying frantically to pull my fingers loose. "They are my things. Give them!"

Sitting up, I looked around.

Beside me lay a shattered bedside lamp, whose fall—caused by carelessness with my feet, or one of the Kid's bullets—had KO'd me. Across the room, face down, arms spread in a crucified posture, the Whosis Kid sprawled. He was dead.

From the front of the apartment—almost indistinguishable from the throbbing in my head—came the pounding of heavy blows. The police were kicking down the unlocked door.

The woman went quiet. I whipped my head around. The knife stung my cheek—put a slit in the lapel of my coat. I took it away from her.

There was no sense to this. The police were already here. I

humored her, pretending a sudden coming to full consciousness.

"Oh, it's you!" I said. "Here they are."

I handed her the silk bag of jewels just as the first policeman came into the room.

13

I DIDN'T SEE Inés again before she was taken back East to be hit with a life-sentence in the Massachusetts big house. Neither of the policemen who crashed into her apartment that night knew me. The woman and I were separated before I ran into anyone who did know me, which gave me an opportunity to arrange that she would not be tipped off to my identity. The most difficult part of the performance was to keep myself out of the newspapers, since I had to tell the coroner's jury about the deaths of Billie, Big Chin, Maurois and the Whosis Kid. But I managed it. So far as I know, the dark woman still thinks I am Jerry Young, the bootlegger.

The Old Man talked to her before she left San Francisco. Fitting together what he got from her and what the Boston branch got, the history runs like this:

A Boston jeweler named Tunnicliffe had a trusted employee named Binder. Binder fell in with a dark woman named Inés Almad. The dark woman, in turn, had a couple of shifty friends—a Frenchman named Maurois, and a native of Boston whose name was either Carey or Cory, but who was better known as the Whosis Kid. Out of that sort of combination almost anything was more than likely to come.

What came was a scheme. The faithful Binder—part of whose duties it was to open the shop in the morning and close it at night—was to pick out the richest of the unset stones bought for the holiday trade, carry them off with him one evening, and turn them over to Inés. She was to turn them into money.

To cover up Binder's theft, the Whosis Kid and the Frenchman were to rob the jeweler's shop immediately after the door was opened the following morning. Binder and the porter—who would not notice the absence of the most valuable pieces from the stock—would be the only ones in the shop. The robbers would take whatever they could get. In addition to their pickings, they were to be paid two hundred and fifty dollars apiece, and in case either was caught later, Binder could be counted on not to identify them.

That was the scheme as Binder knew it. There were angles he didn't suspect.

Between Inés, Maurois and the Kid there was another agreement. She was to leave for Chicago with the stones as soon as Binder gave them to her, and wait there for Maurois and the Kid. She and the Frenchman would have been satisfied to run off and let Binder hold the sack. The Whosis Kid insisted that the hold-up go through as planned, and that the foolish Binder be killed. Binder knew too much about them, the Kid said, and he would squawk his head off as soon as he learned he had been double-crossed.

The Kid had his way, and he had shot Binder.

Then had come the sweet mess of quadruple and sextuple crossing that had led all three into calamity: the woman's private agreements with the Kid and Maurois—to meet one in St. Louis and the other in New Orleans—and her flight alone with the loot to San Francisco.

Billie was an innocent bystander—or almost. A lumber-handler Inés had run into somewhere, and picked up as a sort of cushion against the rough spots along the rocky road she traveled.

www.ingramcontent.com/pod-product-compliance
Lightning Source LLC
Chambersburg PA
CBHW051140030726
47504CB00004B/963